THE HIGHROAD

For all the people who said everything was going to be all right.

I shall be telling this with a sigh
Somewhere ages and ages hence:
Two roads diverged in a wood, and I--
I took the one less traveled by,
And that has made all the difference.

— ROBERT FROST, *The Road Not Taken*

— A PASSAGE —
c h a p t e r | o n e

The world ended on a Monday. I wasn't surprised. Well, maybe I'm being a bit dramatic. Obviously, the world that contains life as we know it did not end. But my world did.

It's quite funny really. Well, not *really* funny, because I can assure you that the experience of watching my world crash down was not one I would like to relive just for some laughs. But it was one of those experiences where, when you tell it to people months later, you can't help but laugh – maybe because of the shock that it really happened or because of the afterthought of how overly ridiculous the whole thing was.

As I said, I wasn't surprised. Not because I saw it coming – because, believe me, I did not spot any sign of it approaching until it was already smacking me across the face – but because, when I thought about it later, I realized I had been putting myself into vulnerable situations for weeks beforehand.

I remember once being forced to watch an anti-bullying film on a grimy old television in fifth grade health class. The TV cart had scraped reluctantly as our teacher pushed it across the room, as if it knew what was coming. The video was ancient, at least twenty years old, and featured a stuffy British guy who droned on about the dangers of bullying. I found the video to be very boring, except for one quote which jumped out at me. "The bully has a Jekyll and Hyde nature," the man on the screen said. This caught my attention only because *The Strange Case of Dr. Jekyll and Mr. Hyde* had been one of my favorite childhood stories, but the narrator's next words were ones that struck my heart hard.

"They are vile, vicious and vindictive in private, but innocent and charming in front of witnesses; no-one can (or wants to) believe this individual has a vindictive nature – only the current target of the serial bully's aggression sees both sides; whilst the Jekyll side is described as 'charming' and convincing enough to deceive personnel, management and a tribunal, the Hyde side is frequently described as 'evil'; Hyde is the real person, Jekyll is an act."

I don't know how our teachers got the crazy idea of showing a video about bullying to a group of kids about to enter middle school. One thing I know is it certainly wasn't a good idea. The comparison of a bully to Jekyll and Hyde freaked me out. I had never before encountered the prospect of someone exploiting other people's weaknesses for the sole purpose of making them miserable. It had freaked me out so much that, when I reached home that day, I had flung my beat-up pink backpack on the floor and flown onto my dad's lap, complaining that I was scared and refusing to go on to middle school.

"Can't I just stay in fifth grade next year? Jacklyn will stay with me, and that way I'll still have my best friend and there will be nothing to worry about," I naively pleaded. I was shocked that my aforementioned best friend of five years and I would ever have to wander out of our comfort zone, into a world where people might – God forbid – be *mean*.

"No, unfortunately that's impossible, Audrey," my dad said, chuckling as he held me on his warm lap and fumbled with the gold pendant around my neck that had my name engraved on it: *Audrey Bass*.

I pouted my best ten-year-old pout and stared up into his blue eyes, cocking my head in wonder at the subtle streaks of yellow radiating from his irises, like the leftover paths of shooting stars. I saw his amusement shining between the streaks.

Let me just say that most people would look at your entire face when they talk to you. They do it without even thinking: concentrating on the lines of your face, absorbing your different facial expressions, getting a window into how the conversation is going. They watch your body language too, trying to find a passageway into your emotions.

I don't do any of that. I just look at people's eyes. Even before I was ten, I concentrated on people's pupils as they spoke to me, memorizing the subtle shades of their irises and looking for what lays within. Facial expressions might be a passageway to someone's emotions, but eyes are a passage into their soul.

My friends find this habit a bit weird. Some get uncomfortable with the way I stare right into their eyes while they talk to me.

"It's so weird," they've said to me many times. "Can't you just look at the big picture, like the rest of us?"

But that's the thing. I can't. It's like an addiction. I have to know if someone's eyes have twitched or if their pupils have dilated while I'm talking to them. And the habit does have its advantages. If you asked me what color, say, my grandma's eyes were, I'd be able to answer in a second, with no awkward pause.

My ten-year-old self continued to stare into my dad's eyes as he explained to me how bullying was something I was bound to encounter and nothing to spend my life fearing. Then my dad had the idea to tell me stories of how he was bullied when he was a kid. It was an awful idea really, but maybe at the time he had thought it would help us bond, or something ridiculous like that.

"When I was in middle school, the big kids liked to grab my backpack away from me," my dad told me in a voice usually reserved for telling scary stories at night with a flashlight beneath your chin. "If I protested, they would just pull harder and then knock me in the head with my own backpack. Eventually I learned not to complain, but they still stole it anyway because they had learned that things I cared about were in that backpack. They took that knowledge and *exploited* it. That's what bullies do."

I don't think my dad was completely serious as he told me this story. He spoke with a grin on his face, and the creepy voice was completely inappropriate for the situation. I partly knew this at the time, and rolled my eyes with a ten-year-old's sass. But deep down, the story terrified me and planted the seed of a fear that grew in my heart over the years. I didn't understand where bullying might happen, or how it could begin, but from that moment I was determined to make sure it would *never* happen to me. I didn't want to be like my dad in that story, with someone taking the things I cared about and hitting me over the head with them. I convinced myself at that early age that the only way to be safe was to never have any weaknesses.

The prospect of weaknesses scared me more than it probably should have, because of the whole eye thing. I'm so good at dissecting the meaning behind the tint and opacity of someone's eyes that I can often guess how a conversation is going to go, just by looking into the eyes of the person who's speaking to me. This accuracy came to frighten me. I came to believe that people could never keep their feelings secret when they approached me. I would always know.

So, what if they *wanted* to hide something from me? Everyone wants to be able to hide something every now and then. Everyone wants to have their own personal secrets. And they should be able to. But I have the power to invade their privacy and make it so they can't. I can exploit them without their even knowing.

Because of this, now I've started shying away from looking at eyes. I became cautious – as though I was scared of my own talent. Mostly because, ever since that day in fifth grade when I sat and watched a lecture about the psyche of a bully, I've been afraid that someday *I'd* be bullied.

I mean, I've never really studied my own eyes to look for psychological transparency. It's not the same if I just stare at myself in a mirror. That doesn't work, because then I *know* I'm trying to see whether my eyes are easy to read. That's cheating.

For all I know, I have eyes like glass and every time I talk, people like me can see exactly how I feel and what I'm thinking inside. If so, that's a serious weakness.

I'm fourteen now, and have learned that it is impossible for a human being *not* to have any weaknesses. I know that humans are always feeling emotions, and sometimes those emotions are going to cause us to care about people or things. Those cares are our weaknesses.

So, I learned how to hide those weaknesses. I also decided that my weaknesses could only be exploited if I was the weak person in a situation, like being the new girl at school or coming back from spring break with a super-awful haircut. I made a pact to avoid such situations.

It hasn't always been easy. I'm not exactly proud of some of the things my friends and I have done to stay on top. But I can't tell anyone that. I don't even tell *myself* that. Once or twice, I've thought about the shame I feel when I relive certain events, but most of the time I keep the thoughts buried deep inside my conscience, locked away where my parents, heck, not even my *friends* will be able to see it, no matter how hard they try to stare into my soul. Because, you see, it is those locked-away things that hold up the walls of my world.

— FENCES —
c h a p t e r | t w o

My parents didn't spend my childhood trying to teach me things that would help me survive later in life. I can't remember them ever telling me things about their own experiences in school, except for that lone time when my dad decided to recap his middle school bullying horrors. And that story had been pretty much the opposite of helpful.

So, as mentioned before, when I found out that after fifth grade I would have to continue on to an entirely new experience called middle school, it rocked my boat, to say the least. I had thought that I was going to be able to stay in my little elementary school world with my exact same circle of friends forever.

The idea of middle school terrified me. For the first time since I switched from preschool to kindergarten, I was terrified of school. New teachers, new homework load, new situations – it sounded like the perfect opportunity for someone to trick me into being weak. With my dad's comment about the danger of weaknesses forever engraved in my brain, I knew I had to do something to ensure otherwise.

That's when I found my perfect group of friends: my best friend Jacklyn Pearce, a girl named McKenna Marcum, and me. Jacklyn and I had been friends since first grade, and we were almost like twins. Not only did we look alike, but we also had very similar personalities and matching sarcastic attitudes. Jacklyn and I both had long straight white-blonde hair, though hers had a little more of a yellow shade to it. However, you only noticed the slight difference when we stood right next to each other.

McKenna came to our school at the beginning of fifth grade, but I never really talked to her until the end of that year. She was very tall and had a bob of hair the color of otter fur, which she prided herself on for its silkiness. McKenna had two sides to her. One second she could be doing something completely daring, like putting something sharp on a teacher's chair right before they sat down, that made you laugh so hard you were afraid your milk was going to come spurting out of your nose, and then the next moment she could be standing up straight and speaking in that perfect angel voice that makes adults smile.

McKenna, Jacklyn, and I made an invincible team, but disaster struck near the end of seventh grade. The economy was bad and lots of people were getting laid off from their jobs. Jacklyn's dad was one of those unlucky people. Luckily for her family, he soon got another job to help make money. Unluckily for me, the new job was in Florida.

"I can't believe you're moving away!" I remember crying as I hurled myself onto Jacklyn's bed.

"I know it's awful!" she replied, dropping down beside me and patting me on the shoulder. "But I can't argue against it. I mean, my dad said–"

"I know, I know. You need the money." My voice was sad. How could you argue with that?

"I'm so sorry, Audrey." She gave me a melancholy look and I suddenly felt bad about complaining, so I avoided looking at her eyes by shifting mine down and searching for something else to stare at. "Eighth grade," I began softly, sighing, "I really, really wanted it to be awesome."

"So did I. But it still can be awesome!"

I sighed again. "How?" Jacklyn hated being sad, so she was trying to make the situation seem better. That quirk of hers was nice most of the time. But just this once, I wanted her to accept the truth. As the sigh rushed out of my mouth, I looked over at her hopelessly. Her eyes were a crystal clear blue so pure that they would look appropriate on an anime character. Her features were so soft that you'd think they belonged to a baby; they were just so adorable that you had to smile.

"You still have McKenna!" As Jacklyn said this, she waved her hands as if it was not only a huge revelation but also just about the best news in the world.

I pulled a pillow over my head to hide my cringing face. My relationship with McKenna had not always been perfect. McKenna seemed to hate me at the beginning of sixth grade, even though we became friends later that year. Honestly, the beginnings of our friendship had felt like an apprenticeship to me, where I had to learn the how's and why's of McKenna's world: how to treat a too-eager girl who is stalking you, how to get rid of an annoying boy. McKenna put up with me only because she wanted to be friends with Jacklyn. I knew that, I had just never admitted it to myself. I wasn't sure that Jacklyn knew, though. The girl was a magnet and she had no idea how she affected people. It drove me crazy.

My relationship with McKenna continued to function like that until the first volleyball practice in seventh grade, when McKenna skipped up to me out of the blue and chirped, "I like you this year. I didn't last year, because you were so immature. But I like you this year!" I was on my guard, because her usually gleaming eyes had turned as hazy as gravy, and I couldn't see into them clearly. So I just smiled awkwardly in return and said, "Thank you!" It didn't seem worthwhile to try to figure it out. If I said the wrong thing, I could have accidentally ruined everything.

The rest of that year was full of fun and laughs, but I never forgot how McKenna had clung to Jacklyn in sixth grade. And I couldn't help my insecurities breaking through and causing me to worry now: *what if everything's different when Jacklyn's gone?*

I tossed the pillow away and tried to smile at Jacklyn, but she seemed to notice my hesitation. She frowned but didn't comment.

"And there are other girls too, Audrey. Think of this as an opportunity for our class to get really close. Remember how you always wanted that?"

Jacklyn was right. I had always hated how our class was divided by gender. It was like there was an invisible fence between us and the boys, built up by differences in opinions regarding the coolness of farts and video games and those awkward feelings that swim through you whenever you're standing in front of the opposite gender. Much to my annoyance, this fence existed even though we had known each other since we were six! I'd always felt that people you see so often, no matter what gender, should feel like a part of a big family. Maybe eighth grade could make that happen.

"But Jacklyn, as good as that sounds, you're wrong about there being more girls. There aren't. It was going to be you, me, and McKenna. That's it. So now that you're going to be gone..."

...it's going to be just me and McKenna. I finished the sentence in my head. I couldn't bear saying it out loud, for fear that I'd really start getting worried. And I couldn't get worried about eighth grade, because it would be my last year of middle school. There shouldn't be anything to worry about, and I certainly shouldn't let the class size bother me.

The eighth grade class at Eastwood Private School is notoriously small. Most students at our school go on to eighth grade at Oasis Academy, a prestigious high school. Getting admitted to Oasis is a big deal to some people, and the application process is really hard, with essays and everything. You even have to take an entry exam. It's like training for college!

I must have been spacing, because Jacklyn was staring at me and looking very confused.

"No... I thought there was going to be another girl there. What was her name?" She flopped back on her pillow and looked up at the ceiling as if the answer was written on the painted drywall. "Emmaline Adams?"

I cringed and looked up too, making sure Jacklyn couldn't see my eyes. I had no idea what they looked like, but it couldn't be pretty.

Emmaline was a serious girl in our class with round green eyes who worried too much about grades and personal relationships and not enough about hair or what to do over the weekend. McKenna hated her. And we never exactly treated her well. Jacklyn and McKenna laughed at her behind her back. I didn't see the point in making fun of her, but I figured that if I questioned it, McKenna would get in my face and start asking what my problem was. And I seriously wanted to avoid any situation where McKenna was trying to get information out of me, because I could guess from what I knew of her pushy personality that she would not give up until she got it.

I bit my lip and winced at the pain it brought, trying to will that pain to overpower the guilt I felt whenever I thought about how we had treated Emmaline. I got a queasy feeling in my stomach when I thought about Emmaline's sharp face with those bright tea green eyes that pierced you like an accusation. I rolled my shoulders to push the feeling away. Emmaline was gone and there was no reason to think about her.

"Ah, no." I replied as I returned my gaze to Jacklyn. "Emmaline moved away."

"Oh! Well, then it is just you and McKenna. That's fine too!" I just stared forward. "Listen, Audrey. You are just over-thinking this. There's nothing to worry about," Jacklyn insisted, and she laughed. "I can just imagine you and McKenna holding your own next year in the schoolyard against those seventh graders." I had to smile. No way were they taking our special sitting spot at the edge of the building! "There you go!" Jacklyn said enthusiastically. "The return of Audrey Bass's smile!"

But the smile didn't extend past my lips. What did I really have to smile for? My best friend was moving away and the likelihood that my eighth grade year was going to be as great as I wanted it to be was dropping like the New Year's Eve ball in Times Square. I felt more like crying than smiling. But I didn't.

Crying is just a form of weakness in the eyes.

— THE START —
c h a p t e r | t h r e e

I woke up with a start on a Monday, three months before the Monday-of-doom. My hand immediately flew to my bedside table to silence the alarm clock, but it hadn't even gone off. I glanced at the clock and groaned. Only 6:20 A.M. I had woken up forty minutes too early on my first day of school.

After lying in bed for ten more minutes and debating whether to try to go back to sleep, I decided I might as well use the time to get ready for school, to make sure *everything* was perfect. I needed to start the year off on the right foot.

I realized then that it was absolutely ridiculous to feel that nervous. I mean, one of my best friends was going to be there! We had hung out all summer, going to the mall and seeing movies. Why should Jacklyn's absence make our interactions any different?

The clock to my right now read 6:40. Another ten minutes had gone by. *Crap.*

With a new burst of energy, I jumped out of bed and sprang towards the bathroom, already combing out my stick straight hair with my fingers.

Twenty minutes later I was downstairs in the kitchen, sitting at our tile-topped dining table eating a fried egg. Or trying to eat it. My stomach was doing more somersaults than an award-winning gymnast.

"Good morning, Audrey," my dad said as he walked into the kitchen and kissed me on the forehead, all the while staring at the screen of his Blackberry.

"Dad," I responded, "what's on your agenda for work today?"

"Oh, you know, a couple of meetings, piles of paperwork, the usual." My dad shrugged as he sat down across from me and started checking the grapefruit in front of him for bad spots.

My mom's whimsical laugh floated through the air. "Your father is such an overachiever, Audrey. Promise me you'll never become like him," she said jokingly. I tried to laugh in response, but the sound that came out of my throat was more like a choke.

"Audrey!" My mom walked over and patted my arm. "Are you all right?"

"Yes, Mom. I'm just a little bit nervous."

She sighed. "Oh, Aud. Look, I know you've always wanted this year to be the best of them all. And I'll tell you right now that it probably won't be as great as you want it to be, but there is no reason for you to be so worried! You are going back to a school full of people and teachers that are like your second family. You're very lucky to have had the joyful experience that middle school has been so far."

I groaned at my mom's attempted pep talk and kissed her on the cheek. If my school family were to be as annoying as my parents sometimes are, I probably would have dropped out a long time ago. As I pushed my chair back to get up and pack my things for school, my mom gasped.

"Audrey!" she exclaimed.

"What?" I twisted around so suddenly that my ponytail whipped around my neck and went in my mouth. I spit it out and stared at my mother's horrified face.

"Audrey, you can't wear that outfit!"

"Why?" I frowned and looked down at the outfit I had prepared: blue jeans that had been cut off a bit above the knee, and a stretchy white knit tank top.

"That top completely washes you out!" My mother's voice was overly dramatic, but I couldn't help but panic as I thought about having to pick out an entirely new outfit.

My mom stood up and clamped her hands down on my shoulders, directing me towards a mirror. When my eyes met my reflection, I frowned and tried to stop the lump in my stomach from rising up into my throat. My mom was right. The white shirt almost matched my pale hair and completely washed out my face. I threw my mom's hands off my shoulders and turned to rush up the stairs to my room. I mentally flipped through all the good shirts in my closet, trying to pick out a new one as fast as possible. After I emptied about half of my drawers onto the floor and studied myself in the mirror a few times, I found a shirt I liked and sighed with relief. I had averted disapproval from not only my mother, but also McKenna, who was very fashion forward, even though some of her outfits were a bit out there in my opinion. However, my satisfied feeling evaporated as I once again looked at the clock on my bedside table. It read 7:45.

"Mom!" I screamed down the stairs as I scrambled to collect my stuff. "Get the car ready! Come on!" I swung my backpack over my shoulder and immediately hunched down from the weight. Summer was definitely over. "We're going to be late!"

Through some miracle I got to school on time. I managed to calm myself down during the ride over, so that when we arrived I could act confident and nonchalant. Eastwood's principal, Mrs. Darwin, was standing by the front door to greet the arriving students. When I swung my backpack out of the car and started to walk towards the door, she smiled familiarly at me.

"Welcome back, Audrey. Are you ready to help carry the eighth grade this year?" she said. I didn't know if she was joking, but something about the way she said it gave me confidence, and I smiled back as I hugged a first grader I knew.

"Of course, Mrs. Darwin," I replied as I swung open the first pair of doors and walked through the waiting area and into the main part of the school. At once the familiar sounds and smells washed away the morning's tension. This was where I felt at home.

As I walked down the long main hallway to the lockers, I surveyed the clusters of people and noticed that most of the students had already separated into their usual groups. Except for a few lone sixth graders who were probably new and didn't know anyone yet, most people were already chatting away with their respective same-grade-and-gender buddies. I caught the eye of two seventh graders, Larken Brielle and Grace Mana, who I had talked to a few times last year, and smiled softly. I waved to a few of the boys in my grade as I continued to weave my way across the tiled floor through clusters of chattering students. Danny DiAngelis, who I was pretty close to a few years ago, actually waved back at me. I smiled. That at least was progress, and I thought about how maybe there was a chance we could become good friends again.

When I reached the back wall of metal lockers, my eyes fell upon a tall girl in a skirt and furry boots, with brown hair twisted at her neck. It was none other than McKenna Marcum.

"McKenna!" I called out as I approached. "Boots, really? This is New Mexico, not Minnesota!"

The tall girl turned around, and her familiar laugh made me smile. Thank God I could still make McKenna laugh.

"Oh, Audrey, you never change, do you?" McKenna asked as she wrapped me in a hug. "You do know these are in style now, right?"

"Whatever you say, McKenna," I teased as I loaded my backpack into my locker and started looking around for my schedule. "Can you believe we're the only two girls? This is going to rock, and it's only just the start! I mean, we have definite rule over everything girly. It's not like those boys are going to give us any competition, so –"

"Oh, haven't you heard, Audrey?" McKenna asked, interrupting my optimistic prepared speech. She sounded excited.

"Heard what?" McKenna opened her mouth to reply, but just as she started to speak, a high pitched voice interrupted her.

"Good morning, my dears!" the voice said from right behind me. Annoyed by the interruption, I prepared to turn around to deal with whatever clingy person it was, but then I noticed that McKenna was just standing there smiling. My annoyance melting into wariness, I slowly turned around.

Standing next to me was a girl of medium height with olive skin and eyes the color of an old penny. Her long neck led to the gathered neckline of a summery dress. After a few awkward seconds I recognized her and internally groaned.

"McKailey!" McKenna squealed at an equally high pitch and jumped in front of me to squeeze her.

McKailey Harp started at Eastwood around the same time as McKenna. At first they were really good friends and always stuck together, maybe because of their similar names. McKailey had disappeared from the picture after McKenna, Jacklyn, and I started to hang around together. Although Jacklyn and I were both lanky with the same long hair, while McKenna looks completely different, McKenna never seemed to feel awkward with us.

Then at the end of seventh grade, McKailey applied to Oasis Academy and got accepted. I thought she would be at Oasis this year, but here she was now.

"McKailey," I began as pleasantly as possible, "I thought you were going to Oasis!"

"Yeah, I got accepted to OA," she replied, flipping her hair over her shoulder, "but I decided not to go at the last minute. I don't want to spend all my time doing homework, so I decided to come back here instead." She grinned at both of us.

"You mean you felt like you were too good for them," I said before I could stop myself, and McKenna stared at me in shock. McKailey just twisted her head to the side as if there had been some mistake.

"I mean, you felt like we were *so* much better here at Eastwood and you just couldn't resist!" I exclaimed, trying to patch up the situation. *Why* had I said that?

"Ha, of course," McKailey said as she looked around. "I mean, why would I not want to come back *here*?"

"I do *not* know," I replied through a fake laugh and gritted teeth.

Thankfully, the bell saved me from more acting practice. McKailey turned away and started to dig through her locker, which was right next to mine. I took this opportunity to pull my schedule out of my backpack. I looked down and started to study my class list as people shuffled around me.

"Oh my God, you're getting out your schedule too! We think the same!" I heard McKailey exclaim, and I looked up to see that she also was in the process of pulling her already crumpled schedule out of her backpack.

"Oh yeah! Ha, ha!" I replied. *Ugh,* my fake laugh was just getting worse and worse. "What classes do you have, McKenna?"

"Um, first I have Science, then Math second. Then I have English, with Social Studies being last."

"Oh my goodness, mine is the same!" McKailey started flailing her arms at her sides in excitement. "And what's your order for your foreign language and PE?"

"PE first and then Spanish."

"Same, same, same!" McKailey squealed even louder as my gaze clouded over.

I had been looking over my schedule while absentmindedly listening to their conversation, and I realized that I was in absolutely *none* of the classes they were discussing. None at all.

"W-wait, guys!" I was starting to panic; this couldn't be happening, "You mean you have Science first and Social Studies last? Are you sure it's not the other way around?"

"Um, no. I think I can manage to read my own schedule," McKailey responded, sounding a bit insulted.

"Why?" McKenna asked. "What do you have?" She grabbed the paper out of my hand before I could fold it back up and started scanning it. I just stared straight ahead.

"Goodness gracious, you look petrified!" McKailey observed in a voice that sounded almost dreamy. I quickly snapped my gaze away and acted like I was very interested in my nail beds.

"Oh Audrey, we have none of the same classes!" McKenna said, as if I didn't already know it and wasn't trying to convince myself that it was not true.

"What?" McKailey grabbed the sheet and held it super close to her face, as if it was a very important document that had to be broken down bit by bit. "Is that even possible?"

Well, obviously it is, McKailey, seeing as it is happening to me.

That's what I wanted to say.

But I didn't.

Instead I slowly closed my locker and cleared my throat. "But don't sixth and seventh graders have classes together? And eighth graders have classes together, right? So how does this work?"

I could've sworn I saw a tiny smirk on McKailey's face before she shrugged and innocently replied, "You must have classes with the boys."

Great. Classes with the boys, who ignored me as much as possible, and when they did talk to me liked to tell me things like how my hair looked fat, which didn't even make sense because my hair was stick straight. Not only that, but my best friend was gone and the one person I'd always been suspicious of had returned.

Definitely not the best start to the first day, I couldn't help thinking bitterly as the bell rang, and people all around me started to move to their first class like a clan of overly-excited birds. *Definitely not.*

— ICEBERG —
c h a p t e r | f o u r

My first class was Social Studies, and as McKenna and McKailey said goodbye to me, I wrapped my arms around my body and walked towards the classroom with a slew of questions chaotically whirling through my head. What were the chances that I would have none of the same classes as my friends? *How could the teachers do this to me? Couldn't they have figured out a way to keep us together?*

I tried to look as calm as possible when I made my entrance into the classroom, but the sight in front of me made me panic a little bit more. I was obviously the last person to arrive, as the lab tables were full except for one spot. The room was filled with the boys in my grade, plus me.

Class ticked by as I tried to interact as much as possible with the boys, asking them about their summers and such. But I found it too difficult to get them off the topics of skateboarding and video games, so I just gave up.

Partway through class, just about when I usually start staring at the clock to see if I can make it go faster, Mrs. Darwin poked her head in through the door and cleared her throat. All the boys in the class immediately shot straight up in their seats and started to stare at their books.

"I'm sorry if I'm interrupting something, Mrs. Krashaw, but I am in need of Audrey Bass," she said in her strong voice.

"Go ahead," Mrs. Krashaw responded. Then she turned to me and said, "I can catch you up afterwards."

Me? I felt strangely suspicious as I approached the frazzled looking woman. Why would Mrs. Darwin want me? Mrs. Darwin deals with the people who have been shoving kids in the hallways or playing games on the computer during class. Usually it is the boys who are lectured by her. I immediately wondered if I had done something wrong, but quickly made the notion go away and slapped myself on my leg. Where had all my confidence gone? There was definitely no way I was in trouble. It was only the first day of school.

"Come on, Ms. Bass," Mrs. Darwin said as she waved her arm and slipped back out of the door. I quickly followed, realizing this meant I got to escape the rest of Social Studies. When I got out of the door, Mrs. Darwin was already striding down the hallway to the wall of lockers. I had to almost jog to keep up with her pace as I followed. When I reached the end of the hallway, I looked around to see if I had dropped something on the floor there or if she had a poster she wanted me to help her tape up on the wall, but I saw nothing that I could obviously help with. When I returned my gaze inquiringly to Mrs. Darwin, I caught sight of a girl who was standing with her back against my locker. My head rotated back around as I zeroed in on her.

The girl had large eyes; that was the first thing I noticed. I could tell by where the top of her head reached on my locker that she was short, and I saw that her frame was curvy. As I moved closer, her eyes fascinated me. They were a reflective brown, that much was obvious, but they were so mysterious. I didn't want to stare too hard, so I pulled my eyes away from hers and concentrated on the rest of her face, which was framed by wavy nearly-black hair.

While I was dissecting the girl's appearance, Mrs. Darwin had glided over to the two of us. "Audrey," she said with a nod as if we were just getting acquainted for the first time, "you are going to be this girl's guide today."

"I take it she's visiting?" I replied. Probably some girl whose mom was already unhappy with the school they'd picked for her. Most people come to Eastwood in situations like that. Our school has relatively few discipline problems.

"No," Mrs. Darwin responded. "She's new. Today is her first day of school."

Well, it was everyone's first day, but this news shocked me because I hadn't heard anything about a new girl coming in. She must have been a last minute addition. Like, really last minute, because if I was her guide, it must have been the first time she'd ever been to the school. She was diving in without testing the waters first, quite a daring choice.

Mrs. Darwin nodded at me once more and then spun around to stride back down the hallway. I smiled as she stopped to give warning looks to a few younger boys who were giggling around the drinking fountain and splashing water on the floor. Mrs. Darwin might seem really intimidating to the average person, but it was just an act she put on most of the time to make sure order was kept. She could actually be quite sweet if you kept on her good side. My smile turned into a laugh as she continued to stride down the corridor like the perfect businesswoman.

I then turned around to see a look of absolute terror on the girl's face. I immediately stepped forward and said to her in the most soothing voice I could conjure, "Don't worry. She's not really like that when you get to know her."

Her face twitched a little bit as she stepped to the side of my locker, looking just as terrified as before. Maybe I didn't seem friendly enough. I decided to try a different tactic. I reached out my hand, set aside my years of putting unwanted people in their places, and brought out my nicest smile.

"Hi, I'm Audrey."

The girl didn't respond. She didn't even shake my hand. She just continued to stare forward, as if the white wall behind my head was extremely interesting. *Okay...that failed.*

"What's your name?"

"McKinley." She responded with a single word. Her voice was wispy and made me feel self-conscious.

I knew it probably wasn't the right thing to do, considering that she was already frightened, but I burst out laughing. Her name was McKinley. As in M-C-K-inley. Our school had been handed another M-C-K. What were the odds?

"I'm... sorry...," I tried to explain through a burst of uncontrollable laughter, "... it's... just... your... name." She looked so horrified that I quickly pinched myself to make the laughter stop. "I... mean... I'm sorry." I was still having a little bit of trouble making my breaths come out even, so the words were all disconnected. "No, I'm so sorry. It's nothing personal!" I felt awful as I stuttered along, trying to make sure McKinley understood that I wasn't making fun of her. "My two friends," I began, trying again, "have names just like yours. McKenna and McKailey. I just find it amusing that your name is so similar."

"Oh," McKinley finally responded. But then she became silent again. Quiet and even cool, although it didn't make me uncomfortable. Her coolness was like that of Grandma's refrigerator cookie dough, which becomes all nice after you heat it up in the oven. At least, I hoped it was that kind of chill.

I didn't know how to respond, so I just smiled again and tipped my head in the direction of back up the hallway. McKinley actually smiled back and started to follow me.

I made sure I was always there to help McKinley during the next period. It was all going well until I learned halfway through that she actually had all her classes with McKenna and McKailey, and was just following me for today. I tried to hide my grimace at this news and stay positive, for her sake. Surprisingly, as time went on, her shyness actually started to grow on me. She didn't seem awkward. She always looked like she knew what she was doing, but never spoke aloud. It was actually kind of refreshing. Amusingly, she was the complete opposite of me, as I was not known for being quiet. I decided there was no reason to feel self conscious about my level of talking, which was way larger then hers, and continued on naturally.

It wasn't until after the class was dismissed and we started walking towards the lockers to put our stuff away for first break that I realized I had become almost *protective* of our friendship... if you could even call it that at this point. Since it was now break, McKinley was going to have to get used to the throngs of other students that would blanket the schoolyard. More importantly, she was going to have to meet McKenna and McKailey. I took a deep breath as I struggled with the idea of how to approach that.

"Do you guys have recess now?" I heard McKinley ask. Her question caught me off guard. I think it was the first time she had said a complete sentence to me. I noticed then that her voice was actually quite deep, not the high-pitched sound I'd imagined hearing before.

"No, not exactly. What we have now is called break. We just go outside and stand around the playground or the soccer field or wherever we want to go. I mean, I guess you could consider it recess, we just don't use that word because, well, we're not exactly in elementary school any more and so it seems kind of st–"

"You talk a lot," McKinley stated. I turned to look at her. "You use a lot of words."

I had to smile because it was true, and my attempted answer to her question was proof. My sentences always ran on and provided lots of unnecessary details. How annoying someone as quiet as McKinley must find that.

"So, um, remember my friends that I told you about?" I said hesitantly as I started leading her through the now crowded hallway and towards the door to the outside. "Well, you're going to meet them now." I was suddenly worried of what McKinley might think of McKenna and McKailey. Or what they might think of her. "Don't worry," I swallowed hard, "they are nice."

I hope.

Once outside, I led her towards the side of the soccer field and saw that McKenna and McKailey were already out there, standing near the sidelines. McKenna was twirling a soccer ball in her hands. I wondered if McKinley felt as nervous as I did at that moment.

"Hey, guys!" I yelled forward as we approached them. "Look!"

"Uh, hey!" McKenna responded tentatively. She looked at me and then tilted her head before looking at McKinley. "So are you going to tell us about the new girl or is she your secret?" McKenna teased.

"Guys," I began, giving McKenna a glare, "this is," and here I paused again, preparing to cringe at their reaction, "McKinley."

"Oh... my... God!" McKailey responded in a squeal that was becoming quite familiar to me and I reared back, checking to see whether McKinley was disturbed by this. Her face looked quite calm, and the odd reflectiveness of her eyes prevented me from forming any idea of how she was feeling inside. Instead of changing to show different emotions as a normal person's would, they were the same cool reflective brown as when I had first met her.

"Your name is *McK*inley? As in M-C-K? That is *so* cool! We're like twins or something!" I stifled a laugh at McKenna's less than brilliant remark. Names that start with the same three letters don't quite add up to twin-hood. Plus, McKinley could probably stand on a kindergarten chair and still not be as tall as McKenna.

"Guys, we're all, like, matching!" McKailey managed to hook all four of us together with her arms. "Who would have thought it would come together like this?"

My heart was beating fast in my chest and I suddenly hated my blonde hair. McKenna reached out and rubbed my arm.

"You fit in with us too, Audrey," she said as she smiled. "You know, what with your amazing sense of style and all." She winked at me. As much as I appreciated the gesture, the connection was superficial at best. Not that hair color, eye color, or names were exactly deep similarities either.

The sense of being different gnawed at my stomach and I felt self-conscious. I didn't like it, and really hoped that this wasn't just the tip of the iceberg of uncomfortable feelings that I never *used* to feel.

McKinley and I had seemed to be getting along so well. And McKenna and I had been on great terms recently. McKailey... I hadn't decided about yet. But the combination of the four of us shouldn't be giving me these uneasy feelings. I squeezed my eyes shut, trying to command the sensation to leave, but a small part of me whispered that it was no use. I tried harder, telling myself how ridiculous this was. *You're not one to feel awkward with yourself, Audrey*, I thought. *Get a grip!*

As the initial surprise of McKinley's name died down and small talk resumed between us, I continued to have this back-and-forth with myself. Once it had become quite repetitive, I settled it by reminding myself that I wasn't one to have to constantly worry about friends. So I pushed the superfluous worry behind me and put on a smile, laughing along with them.

— THE BOYS —
c h a p t e r | f i v e

At first, having classes with the boys was just depressing. As McKenna, McKailey, and McKinley all went off to their classes together, I was left with people that I didn't really want to be around for eight hours a day. I had known all of the boys forever, but I felt awkward around them. Weren't girls supposed to be all over boys whenever they saw them? McKenna and McKailey certainly were. I wasn't.

The boys bantered easily with each other as they sat down in Social Studies class on the Wednesday of the second week of school. They had been friends for as long as I had known them: Ronnie Morano, Ian Camil, Danny DiAngelis, Johnny Price, Reese Jordan, Eliot Hazuki, and Trey Remington. They were a clique, always sticking together and doing things the same way as each other. They were all troublesome in one way or another, and had all had frequent visits to Mrs. Darwin's office. Some were smarter than others, and Danny was probably the smartest of them all. Not that he didn't break the rules every once in a while, but he knew when and how to be discreet.

"Can you believe we've been assigned homework already?" I heard Trey say as he jumped up to sit on the edge of his desk, something that all the teachers hated. We had more than a full week of school now, and the boys seemed to already be getting antsy. "It's so stupid. It's almost like the teachers actually expect us to do something productive right when school starts! I don't know about you guys, but my body is still in summer mode."

Trey leaned back with his hands folded behind his head and kicked his feet up on the opposite desk so that he was lying flat. The boys at Eastwood thought Trey was cool because he never did his homework. The girls at Eastwood thought Trey was horribly lazy.

"Come on, it's not that bad," said Eliot as he jumped up on the opposite side of the same desk. "I already did the assignment. It only took about twenty minutes."

"Yeah." Ronnie started laughing. "Eliot was such a nerd this weekend, finishing the assignment while *I* was having tons of fun jumping on Danny's trampoline."

"Hey, at least I got my assignment done so my mom won't get mad," Eliot retorted. "You, Ronnie, on the other hand, will probably get grounded by the end of the month. Maybe you and Trey can be under house arrest together." Eliot was grinning hugely now.

"Ah, shut up," Ronnie said, presumably annoyed that Eliot had gotten him back.

"What about you, Audrey?" Danny said. I jumped in my seat, startled that they were bringing me into the conversation. While faintly listening to them, I had been daydreaming about what McKenna, McKailey, and McKinley were doing at this moment. Probably laughing over something their teacher was wearing today and having a ton more fun then I was.

"What about me?" I asked, trying to seem uninterested. I thought that looking uninterested might make me seem cooler. I knew from experience that it worked on girls, but I had no idea about the boys.

"Did you do that assignment already?" Danny was referring to a paragraph we had been assigned to write in Science about three different kinds of bugs we could find in our own backyards. I had done it, and struggled with myself for a moment to decide whether I should tell the truth.

"Yeah, I did it. Eliot is right. It only takes about twenty minutes."

"See guys," Danny said in a loud voice, "even the girl did it. So you all shouldn't be bragging about not doing it."

The girl. Was that who I was? I was *the girl* just like they were *the boys*. Was that how we were going to address each other for the entirety of this year? How family-feeling.

"Yeah, we should," Trey said nonchalantly. "Because the fact that Eliot isn't bragging makes him a *girl*." He gestured at Eliot and they all started laughing. The sound was joyful, but it didn't improve my mood.

"At least that would be a step up," I muttered to myself. I then sat there with my arms crossed and thought about the fun my friends were probably having right now, as more boyish laughter reverberated throughout the room.

"Mrs. Mirielle!" I heard Ronnie exclaim in a warning voice, and I turned to see that our teacher had entered the room. I covered my mouth to stifle my snort of laughter. Now Trey was going to get it.

Mrs. Mirielle swung her head in Trey's direction and almost groaned. "I highly suggest that you stop laughing like a hyena and get your butt and feet *off* my clean desks, thank you very much," she said in a voice with no hint of thankfulness in it at all. They all stopped laughing and Trey swung his legs off the desk, moving down to sit in a chair. "Ah, ah," the teacher said, interrupting his movement. "I wouldn't bother getting settled there. We are just about to set up our seating chart."

A seating chart. Great. Everyone groaned.

The desks in the room were arranged in pairs, so that everyone would have a built-in lab partner for when we did experiments. Mrs. Mirielle walked around the room slowly, tapping each desk with her finger, as if thinking where to place us so that we would pay the most attention. "Ronnie!" she called out once she reached the desk in the back left corner. "You and Ian will sit here." Ronnie and Ian picked up their books and moved to that side of the room as the teacher continued. "Reese and Eliot, please move your stuff over here," she said, tapping the two desks in the right corner of the room. I frowned. Reese and Eliot were going to be an interesting combination. Who knew if they were going to get along. I never really saw them talk, and they looked quite different, what with Eliot's Japanese background and Reese looking like the common surfer boy. Maybe that was why the teacher had put them together: they probably wouldn't distract each other.

Now the teacher moved over to a set of desks in the middle of the right side of the room. "Danny and Trey," Mrs. Mirielle stated, "these two seats are for you. I hope you can handle them," she said, as if the desks were a set of weapons. As Danny and Trey moved to their seats, I counted the number of people who were now seated and my stomach seized up. One, two... three, four... five, six... six people were seated. There were only two people left. Me and ...

"Johnny and Audrey," the teacher said, giving voice to my thought. "You two will sit at the final set of desks, in front of Danny and Trey." I clutched my books and moved to the spot she indicated as Johnny Price did the same.

"Nice, Cash," Ian giggled quietly. "You get to sit next to the girl."

Cash. That's what people called Johnny. Obviously, his name wasn't really Cash. I was sure no parent would actually be cruel enough to name their child that. No one called him Johnny though, except the teachers. Since he shared Johnny Cash's first name and also had a money-related last name, at an early age he and his peers decided that the similarity was so cool that he should henceforth just be called Cash. It stuck, and I think I heard that even his parents call him that now.

I smiled tightly at Cash and sat down, placing my books neatly in the corner of the desk. Cash smiled back at me and sat down as well. We had known each other since Cash had started at Eastwood two years ago. Cash had fit in well, quickly becoming friends with all the boys in our grade. His best friend, Sam Lorenz, had gotten into Oasis Academy last year, but Cash seemed to be adjusting to the change well. Better than me, anyway.

I wasn't exactly thrilled about having to sit next to Cash. I had always avoided him as much as possible. He was probably the stupidest of all the boys when it came to getting in trouble, and honestly, he had freaked me out the first time I met him. On the first day of sixth grade, I had been walking down the hall with Jacklyn, amazed at how much older I felt now that I was out of elementary school. Cash was walking down the hall in the opposite direction, and when he reached us I stopped him and introduced myself, because I knew he was new.

"Hi, I'm Audrey," I remember saying, "and this is Jacklyn."

"Hi," Jacklyn had said too, her pure blue eyes welcoming as always.

"What's up?" Cash had responded in a smooth voice. His eyes were green.

"So how has your first day here been?" I had asked, trying to start a conversation.

"It's been all right." He shrugged, and then grinned. "But it was a pain to get here this morning."

"Oh?" I had asked, confused at the statement. "Why?"

"My dad made me read the sexual harassment part of the student handbook three times before letting me come."

I avoided him like the plague for weeks after that.

Later, Jacklyn assured me that he had just been trying to make a joke to break the ice. I understood, but I still didn't exactly want to be around him. Anyone who would say that for *any* reason just creeped me out.

I flashed back to the present, and noticed Cash was still smiling at me. I cleared my throat. "So," I began, "I assume you didn't do that homework assignment."

"Nope," he responded, grinning even bigger. I noticed how white his teeth were, and the light reflecting off them blurred my vision for a second. I smiled back.

"Nice. You should really do it tonight. Otherwise you'll just be starting off the year with a missing assignment. And that would be –"

"Bad?" he interrupted. "I know."

"Okay," I said, reaching over and grabbing his assignment book. "Then how come you haven't written the assignment down?"

His mouth was still stretched into a grin, and I wondered if it was normal for me to be seeing flashing lights. "I said I knew that would be bad. I never said I was actually going to do it." He grabbed the assignment book back and stuffed it into his overflowing backpack, which for some reason he dragged to every class instead of using his locker.

My mouth opened, but no words came out. Just a breath of air that rushed through my lips, leaving them cold. "Well," I managed to say, writing down an assignment in my own homework journal, "good luck with that." I gripped my fingers tightly around my pencil as the words came out, frustrated with the ridiculous and rather stumbly way my senses were reacting to this conversation.

Cash was about to respond when Mrs. Mirielle stepped in front of the class, signaling that we should start to fill out the worksheet she had put in front of us, in silence. I started working on the questions, and thought about how Cash probably knew none of the answers, since most likely hadn't done the homework for this class either. I realized that I actually had just had an enjoyable conversation with him, without even worrying about what I was missing with my friends. I decided then and there that I could work on Cash. That would be fun. I could work on all of them. Danny wasn't too bad, but the others needed some serious help in school work and attitude. I could help them. I felt better, knowing I had a master plan. *Maybe having classes with them isn't going to be so bad*, I thought as I tried to concentrate on the charts on the piece of paper in front of me. I found myself grinning to myself as I thought that, possibly, it could even be fun.

— SMILE —
c h a p t e r | s i x

At break the following day I found McKenna, McKailey, and McKinley by the soccer field again. I hated having to search for them every day at break time, an unavoidable reminder that they all had classes together while I was stuck alone with the boys.

We stood in a circle again and talked and laughed about funny things we had seen the younger kids do and how amusing it was that the sixth graders were already freaking out about writing a 500 word paper. It was refreshing to still be able to laugh about normal stuff like that. The previous day I had felt as though my worrying nerves were eating away every carefully formed facet of my personality.

"God, I *hated* gym today," McKailey whined.

"Yeah, I feel the same. What we had to do was so stupid," McKenna agreed, rolling her eyes in a snippety way that she had picked up since the end of summer. It was quickly becoming her new trademark.

"What?" I asked. I was curious about what aspect of P.E. could make them get so uptight.

"Today, the teacher decided to let us choose what game we played. And what did the people in our class all decide to vote for?" McKailey leaned in as if this were really important gossip. "Duck, Duck, Goose!" she exclaimed. I gave McKinley a confused look, but her face looked innocently blank, per usual.

"I mean, come on, I can't believe how immature the kids are in this school. We're thirteen years old and we're playing *Duck, Duck, Goose?*" McKenna offered to me as a form of explanation. I looked to the side and tilted my mouth into a tight line, shrugging my shoulders in a gesture that could probably be seen as sympathetic. But inside I was a bit annoyed that McKenna and McKailey felt this way. Especially considering the fact that we also played Duck, Duck, Goose in my P.E. class and I'm *fourteen* and *I* had fun.

A part of me wanted to say something sarcastic or reach out and slap them on the cheek, telling them how silly they were. Part of me wanted to say, *Geez, why do you have to be so negative?* It wouldn't have killed them to let go and just have fun for a while, and it would not have killed them to smile. But another part of me foresaw that I would then have to try to defend myself and my opinion, which was different than theirs, and I suspected that the resulting discussion would not turn out well. The situation was difficult to handle. I sighed to myself, not pleased that I was just letting the point go, but also proud of myself for choosing to shake it off.

Though still, it was annoying that at thirteen they felt that they had to grow up so quickly.

And it was annoying that I didn't feel the same way.

As the first weeks of school wore on, the interactions between the four of us started to fall into a pattern. At the beginning of break, or *recess* as McKinley always called it, we would meet near the edge of the soccer field and stroll around, talking about funny things that had happened that day and bouncing new ideas back and forth.

I noticed that we spent most of our time together laughing. McKailey in particular liked to tell funny stories and then immediately break into an uncontrollable, loud, and rather contagious fit of laughter. You could identify McKailey's laugh from miles away. It just hit you in the ears and kept knocking at your skull until you were laughing either at her or along with her. It always got me laughing, and usually five minutes into break we would all be laughing and smiling at each other. I liked that feeling; it allowed me to believe that we still had a good, real friendship.

As we strolled and laughed, now and then a soccer ball would fly past us. McKenna, wanting very much to show off her skills, would run after it and punt it back. McKailey would at some point follow her, and then they would run around in the center of the soccer field.

"What are they doing?" McKinley asked the first time this happened.

I smirked. "Flirting with the boys who are playing soccer." McKinley actually laughed, which was nice. Then I realized that now the two of us were just awkwardly standing by the soccer field. "Hey, want to go sit down on that bench over there?"

"Sure." Then McKinley smiled. Either her face was finally unfreezing or I was getting better at this. We walked over and sat down on the picnic table benches just past the right edge of the soccer field. I leaned back and stared at McKenna and McKailey as they flirted with the crowd of boys, mostly in our grade. I was worried at how willingly McKailey had bounced off to follow McKenna onto the soccer field. I convinced myself that maybe McKailey had some radar that told her McKenna was heading for the boys, and she wanted to join in. That *would* be like her. But McKinley and I were different – we didn't have to turn every interaction with the boys into an opportunity to flirt. I turned away from the field, half smiling, and struck up a conversation with her.

As we sat on the picnic bench together day after day, I found more and more similarities between us. McKinley's quiet and shy nature and my more outgoing personality complemented each other well enough to create a very comfortable atmosphere.

"So, how have you liked Eastwood so far?" I asked one day as we comfortably lounged across the bench. We had just finished talking about the odd shapes that we saw in the cloud formations that the wind was pushing across the sky. She saw vampires and rabid dogs. I saw a banana split sundae.

"I've enjoyed it," she responded. "I mean, it's nice that the teachers seem to actually care whether you get good grades or not."

I laughed, "Yes, that is usually quite important."

"They're all very involved in making sure the school runs well," she continued, bringing her hand up to free a wisp of dark hair that had been pushed into her mouth by the wind. "Especially Mrs. Darwin." And here she looked at me pointedly. "You seem to know her pretty well. Is she always so business-like?" I noticed when she was speaking how curiously flat and dull her voice could be at times, with almost no emphasis or differentiation on any of her words.

Curious, I thought, not knowing exactly how to use this observation. But soon I shook that away, and a smile curled the edges of my lips as I leaned toward her slightly. "Only when she has to deal with troublesome students," I replied. Then I looked out at the soccer field. Out of all the eighth grade classes I could remember at Eastwood, mine contained the most students who liked to break rules... or at least do things that Mrs. Darwin didn't think should be done on school property, such as seeing how many times you could hurdle over a trash can.

"People like McKenna and McKailey?" McKinley had been

following my gaze. She looked at me inquiringly and asked, "Do they break the rules a lot?"

"Not exactly break the rules, but they have quite a lot of self confidence built up in their little heads and they like to wave it around in people's faces like an American flag." McKinley laughed.

"Are you like that too?"

I hesitated before I answered. For some reason I felt compelled to tell McKinley the truth, but I didn't know how to phrase it. "I try as hard as possible to avoid it. I've ... I've done some things in the past that I'm not really proud of. So now I've been trying to be better about that." I *had* been trying, as of really recently. Now that I thought about it, I had started trying right around the time I met McKinley.

"I'm used to people trying to avoid trouble," McKinley said. She stared straight ahead as her dark hair waved around her face and wrapped itself around her neck.

"Oh? From what?"

"I used to go to a Catholic school. Everyone there was always really uptight."

I nodded. "Well, that makes sense." It was nice to hear about some of McKinley's background. It was hard for me to imagine where this reserved girl came from. "Did you like it there?"

"The school was all right. I was never really happy with the friends I had, though."

"That sounds… awful," I said, struggling to find the right word. I wanted to let this girl know that I was completely willing to be her friend, despite any hesitations I might have had earlier. "Did you just never make any, or ...?"

"No, I made friends. I mean, I had a group of people that I was friends with and they were always there for me and stuff, but they were really different from me, you know? They were really preppy, like Catholic girl school preppy. And I just wasn't like that, so it kind of annoyed me."

"Oh," I said. For some reason I found myself trying to act as nonchalant as possible. Maybe it was because McKinley was speaking as if this wasn't even that big a deal – and to me it seemed quite heavy. "I see."

I was relieved that the bell rang then and we started packing up to go back inside, because I had no idea where to take the conversation from there. I needed some time to think about what she had said – to try to understand this girl better.

Although I was happy to be able to be with McKenna, McKailey, and McKinley during breaks, I couldn't help noticing little things that frustrated me, little worries that I had to constantly shake away. Their constant complaining bothered me most. At first it was just McKailey, and I would tell her to stop or would even argue against her, which would get her really mad.

"Geez," McKenna said quietly one lunch period after McKailey had gotten up to throw her food away. "I swear you guys are going to bite each others' heads off some day or something! I mean, seriously!"

I laughed, "Sorry, McKenna. She just bothers me sometimes."

"Yeah, I can tell. But you guys are still friends." She shrugged her shoulders. "I'm not worried."

Worried about what? I wanted to ask. But I didn't. The question stayed in the back of my mind. Was there anything to be worried about?

As the weeks wore on, McKenna began acting more and more

negative herself, as though McKailey was rubbing off on her. Or maybe I was being unfair to McKailey. Maybe the return to school brought on McKenna's unhappiness.

McKenna's outbursts were most often about her family, specifically the way her parents were treating her. And I would have been worried, if I had believed that her tales were true. But I didn't – it was very obvious to me that her stories were dripping with exaggeration.

For example, one day the teachers were nice enough to let us spend homeroom sitting outside and enjoying the weather. McKenna was late, which was normal, and when she came outside the first thing she said to me was, "Sorry I'm late. My mom was being *such* a pain this morning."

"How?" McKailey asked before I was able to.

"I didn't want to get out of bed this morning. So my mom comes up into my room and is all 'I swear if you don't get out of bed right this minute you are going to regret it.' And I just thought she was going to throw some cold water on my face or something. But, no, she turns around and *slaps* me on the face!" McKenna exclaimed. At first I believed her and was too shocked to say anything. But then McKenna and McKailey burst into a fit of laughter.

"Geez, what a pain!" McKailey said in an amused voice.

I was not amused. But I didn't say anything. I knew better than to try to explain how, in my opinion, it was not at all funny. Although it felt odd to be telling myself that it was better not to say anything, I knew that it was necessary to preserve this nice, comfortable, routine friendship. However, I couldn't help worrying about the fact that our friendship was being built on this fragile territory of being careful not to express certain things; it felt almost dangerous.

No matter how hard I tried to ignore the little differences between us, I found myself getting annoyed when we were together. The way they looked at the world – it was different than my outlook. I certainly didn't think they should be laughing about how their parents had to hit them to get them out of bed in the morning. That wasn't something to be joking about. Not something that serious. And I found myself sincerely hoping that I wouldn't be standing there on the day that their jokes hurt someone – an event that seemed, unfortunately, inevitable.

— DEFECTIVE —
c h a p t e r | s e v e n

Every year the flu sweeps through schools all over the city, sending a new batch of kids home sick every day. Three months into the school year, the flu season hit Eastwood hard. Sick notices went home with us nearly every day, and the parents of the younger children were panicking at the number of kids being sent home with fevers. The school board decided that something had to be done to calm the parents down.

So, the following week, dispensers of hand sanitizer appeared near every entrance and exit to the school. Our teachers told us that we had to spread sanitizer on our hands when we entered and left our classrooms. As if that weren't enough, Mrs. Darwin came in and gave us a lecture on how this was a very important rule, and not one to be joked about.

I personally found the whole thing ridiculous. I had gotten the flu every year since I started at Eastwood. It had become a tradition. I didn't see why they were freaking out about it so much this year. McKenna, McKailey, and McKinley shared my opinion. For once, I enjoyed their complaining instead of being annoyed by it.

"I think the consistency of the skin on my hand has changed from actual *skin* to something more like pickled flesh," McKenna groaned one day as we flung our bodies down on the couches in our homeroom.

"Why are they making us do this? It is so annoying, and I'm pretty sure the only thing it is killing is the parents' worries that the school is going to turn into a hospital ward." I stretched out and sighed into the couch's rough covering, which was shredded from years of abuse by hyper middle school kids.

"Plus," McKailey added as she swung her backpack down to the floor like it was full of anvils, "don't they realize that it's the .1% of germs that aren't killed by hand sanitizer that's getting us sick?"

"Why do you think that is?" I asked as I traced one of the particularly large rips in the couch with my finger. Stuffing was starting to leak out of the torn seam, like blood from a wound.

"You mean, why is hand sanitizer somehow able to kill all the germs in the world except the ones that matter? Who knows!" McKenna said as she slouched even farther down into the cushions.

"Maybe those germs are defective," McKinley said quietly. We all turned to look at her. McKenna and McKailey looked confused, but I knew what she was trying to say. Her choice of words was interesting. I liked it.

Despite knowing that I would probably get sick, I tried my best to take good care of myself. And I did use hand sanitizer quite often, although I admit I did not apply it to my hands as many times throughout the day as Mrs. Darwin would have liked me to. After peaking in late September, when more than two-thirds of the middle school was at home sick, the flu season dragged on into October.

Just when I was thinking that maybe I had escaped this year, the germs struck and I started to feel a little bit under the weather.

"Are you all right?" McKenna asked one day as we were walking down the hallway. "Your face looks a little flushed."

"I'm not feeling the best today," I admitted as I pressed a hand to my forehead, feeling the pulses of heat that were sweeping through my entire body.

"Maybe you should go home, Audrey," McKenna suggested as she gave me a concerned glance.

"I'll think about it," I responded. I never liked going home in the middle of the day, and if I did then I would just be sealing the deal that I was definitely sick. I was still hoping that it was just a passing bout of feeling under the weather.

Break came around, and McKenna told me again that I should go home.

"No use stressing yourself, Aud," McKailey agreed. She gave me a hug before continuing, "We wouldn't want it to turn into something worse."

"Thanks McKailey, I hope so too. But I don't want *you* catching it either, so think before you hug me again!" I smiled as I playfully swatted her hands off my shoulder. "No worries, guys. If I really start to feel bad, I'll tell Mrs. Darwin to call my mom."

"All right, Audrey. You know I'm just looking out for you. And," McKenna said, grabbing her windbreaker and throwing it over her shoulder, "don't take this the wrong way, but you don't look too good. I'm worried that flush is going to spread everywhere and ruin your lovely skin!"

I laughed again, loving the feeling of having friends who cared so much. Their acts of concern continued throughout the morning. McKenna worried about the fact that I looked so unwell and McKailey joined in, pressing her hand against my forehead to test the temperature of my skin and giving me hugs to "keep me perky." Even McKinley stopped in the middle of the hallway to give me a sympathy hug, which surprised me because I hadn't thought of her as very much of a touch person.

I felt worse and worse throughout the day, even with their hugs.

By the time I reached Social Studies class, I was about ready to collapse from the beating force behind my forehead.

"Mrs. Krashaw," I began quietly as I snuck up to the front of the class while the other students completed a worksheet, "I haven't been feeling well today and my head is really hurting. May I call my mom?"

The teacher barely scrutinized me before nodding and pushing her chair back. "You don't look so good. I think that would probably be a good idea." She shuffled some papers on her desk together before turning towards the door. "Come on, I'll get the school nurse to call your mother."

I spent the next school day and the weekend that followed at home, fighting off an annoying cold. First I had a headache, then a fever that made me super hot, then a sneezing fit, and finally I got so stuffed up that I couldn't smell anything. To make it worse, I had to spend the entire three days working on a poster project for social studies. I usually went *way* overboard on posters, and being sick didn't seem to slow me down.

"My goodness, Audrey," my dad fussed one night as he stared down from the staircase landing at my oversize and overly embellished poster. "Most kids stay home when they're sick so that they can rest and slack off, but you are working harder than anyone I've ever seen before!" my dad joked. "Are you sure this even counts as missing school?"

I laughed, and the pressure made my head hurt. "Yes, Dad, it does. After all, I *am* missing a social studies quiz," I teased.

My dad laughed joyfully and kissed me on the top of the head. "That's my little student." My mom walked into the hallway and my dad turned to her and said, "She's always keeping track of everything!"

I smiled to myself, loving how my school work made my parents so proud. I tried to ignore the pounding pressure in my head and continued cutting out shapes and taping them onto my poster board. "You know, Dad, you're right about me working harder than other people. I bet McKenna and McKailey haven't even started on theirs. They are so lazy! They will probably have to do theirs in a rush on Sunday night," I giggled.

"Audrey!" my mom scolded. "You shouldn't talk about your friends like that!"

"Why not?" I shrugged. "*They* talk about *themselves* like that." My mom rolled her eyes and sighed one of her *I give up!* sighs. But it was true. McKenna and McKailey were always bragging about their procrastination and last-minute feats.

On Sunday night I felt well enough that I decided to go to school Monday. I got my parents to agree to this by telling them that there wasn't any point in me lying around and missing any more assignments. In reality, my biggest motive was that it felt weird that I hadn't seen McKenna, McKailey, and McKinley in so long. I was used to being with them every day and then chatting online during the weekend, but this weekend they hadn't been online at all. Who knows, maybe they *were* working on their posters in advance.

On the following Monday morning, Mom decided at the last minute to let me sleep through homeroom to make sure that my bug didn't come back during the stresses of the school day. She woke me up just in time for me to get to school by first period, which I found a bit annoying. I felt that if a parent was going to let you sleep in, you should at least miss some of an actual educational class. I was surprised when I arrived to see that most people, at least most of the boys, had recovered from their illnesses and were now discussing the level-ups they had acquired while they were at home on the couch all day, playing non-stop. *Great.*

Social Studies was my first class, but the teacher wouldn't let me make up the quiz right away because we were presenting our posters, so she told me I had to stay after and complete it during break. This made me mad, because I wouldn't be able to look for McKenna, McKailey, and McKinley right away. I would just have to rip through the quiz.

Luck seemed to be on my side that morning, because the quiz was easy enough that I could quickly complete all the questions. Soon I was out the door and on my way outside for break. As I approached my locker, I stopped and took a detour to the bathroom. Call me a classic teenage girl, but I wanted to check my hair before I went outside. If any wispy hairs had escaped my usually slick ponytail, McKenna would complain that it needed fixing. I didn't really care what McKenna thought, but I always felt like her hair looked a little bit flat and oily in the morning, so I wanted to prove to her that I could take her criticism to heart and make mine look better.

I primped a bit in front of the mirror and then swung through the doors again and out to my locker. Books were pushed aside as I rummaged for my jacket and then I was dressed for success and on my way to see my friends again.

And here's one of those not-really-funny-points in the story where, as I tell it months later, I can't help but laugh. For, if I had known what was waiting for me on the other side of the door, I would have never gone outside.

— JOKE —
c h a p t e r | e i g h t

I knew something was wrong the moment I set foot outside. The air felt weird, different. I can't explain it. All I know is that I could feel the difference, almost even smell it swirling around me. Something was definitely wrong.

My first thought was that maybe someone had been injured on the field or gotten into a fight. Then my thoughts immediately went to McKenna, McKailey, and McKinley and I scanned the grounds for them. They weren't by the side of the soccer field, or on the bench. When I finally spotted them I saw that they were standing near the *middle* of the soccer field, closer to the goal where no one was playing at the moment. I strode toward them quickly, half because I was excited to see them, half because I was trying to escape the heavy feeling in the air.

"McKenna, McKailey, McKinley!" I said as soon as I arrived, and then stopped short. That was the first time I had ever said all three of their names together out loud. I had never realized how *ridiculous* they sounded together before. They really were so similar, and it made me even more uncomfortable. To make things worse, none of the girls turned to acknowledge me when I arrived. They just continued walking in circles around that area of the soccer field.

Finally, McKenna said, "Hi." But I didn't sense any real emotion, and she was looking down when she said it.

Why was this all so awkward? I slowly walked past McKenna, McKailey, and McKinley and stared at them as they continued. I realized that they weren't necessarily walking in circles, just continually moving around each other and spinning around. They looked a bit like animals who were trying to keep warm in the winter.

Moments passed as I stood there and stared. Nothing seemed to happen, and not only were they not saying anything to me, they weren't saying anything to each other either. So I decided to join in with their odd walking pattern. Maybe there was some point behind it that I just couldn't see. I walked around with them for at least three minutes, with my hands stuffed in my pockets and my nose tucked down in my jacket to try to escape from the cold breeze our movements created. Eventually, I just couldn't take it any more, and tried speaking again.

"Why are we walking in circles?" I asked.

"To escape from the bugs," McKenna said, still without looking at me.

That confused me even more. I looked around me in the air. There were no bugs anywhere. None at all. I didn't see any point in trying to tell them this, so I decided to see if I could get one of them to actually *look* at me.

"Hey," I stepped forward into McKenna's personal space, "did anything really happen while I was gone?"

"Nope!" McKenna replied in a cheery voice. She continued to look down.

I groaned and turned away, because she hadn't even looked at me. This was getting frustrating, and on top of that a nervous feeling was building up in my stomach, and I was really starting to get annoyed by the way the air felt. Pressure was closing in on me from all sides. Was I crazy for thinking that? The atmosphere is not exactly something you can grasp.

The dynamic between us was wrong. It wasn't apparent in what they said to me, but they still hadn't looked me directly in the eyes, and they continued to walk in random circles. For a second I wondered if the shapes they were tracing on the ground meant something, but decided that that sounded too much like something out of a murder mystery movie. And we hadn't laughed about anything today. Usually McKailey tells some ridiculous story that sends us all into hysterics, even McKinley.

It was then that I noticed that *McKinley* was *giggling*. She must have started while I was thinking to myself. Actually, they were *all* giggling. All three of them. They were trotting in circles around me and giggling like little kids. And I had no idea why, or even what was so funny. And the air around me *still* felt awful and weird and uncomfortable, like something was terribly wrong. I felt like I was in a nightmare.

McKenna started swatting at the air around her like she was trying to escape a swarm of bees. "Ugh! There is this huge ladybug that just won't stop following me!"

"I know, it's awful!" and here McKailey started spinning around super fast and pushing her palms out in the air. "It just *won't go away*."

I looked around in the air once again, to see if maybe there were bugs around and I was just going crazy. After all, I was claiming to be able to sense in the air that something was wrong... but nothing *seemed* to be obviously wrong. However, all around me McKenna, McKailey, and even McKinley were jumping around and slapping their legs as if they were being bitten, and there were absolutely no ladybugs on me or anyone else around the soccer field either.

"And it is not even a normal ladybug," McKenna said, her words vibrating because of her constant movements. "It has got these *long* wings that are *super wispy* and absolutely *never* stay in place. I don't even know how it can fly with wings like that!"

My stomach knotted even more and only my years of practice at never letting an outsider know when something got to me allowed me to keep my face blank. I couldn't be hearing this. My ears had to be tricking me.

"It's like a demon ladybug!" McKailey said as they all burst into laughter again. Did they even remember I was there?

I took a step back and breathed in and out slowly, trying to slow my heart. I felt dizzy. Maybe I shouldn't have come to school today. I was hearing things wrong and twisting people's words and movements.

The tiny rational parts of my brain tugged at my attention and whispered to me that I needed to *leave now while I still could.* Those parts of me knew the truth.

I was the ladybug.

Despite all the signs pointing towards that awful fact, I continued to take deep breaths and stepped back into the circle of girls, which had stopped moving for the time being.

"Audrey," McKenna said to me, and I was so startled by her saying my name that I almost tripped. She looped her arm through mine to stop my retreat. "Let's go over and see how the boys' soccer game is going." She dragged me towards the center of the field. I stumbled along and McKailey and McKinley followed.

"Hey, boys!" McKenna called out in a flirtatious voice. A goofy boy named Ronnie looked up and smiled a toothy grin.

"Hey! Come to play?" he asked.

"You betcha!" McKenna then spun around in a circle, carrying me with her, and let go of my arm, sending me toppling to the ground. I got up and tried to regain my balance, and stood there for a few moments as McKenna competed with another boy in our class over who got to try to punt the ball into the goal. I realized there was no use in standing there, as I couldn't play soccer, and turned around to ask McKailey and McKinley if they wanted to do something else. I blinked for a few moments and then realized that they were both running in the opposite direction, towards the other goal, laughing so hard they looked as though they were having problems breathing. My stomach contracted again and that rational part of my brain started to panic.

This had to be a joke, one of those things we'd laugh about later because McKenna and McKailey would find it so funny that I actually believed they would try to run away from me.

I realized then that if this *was* one of their jokes, then the one person who most likely wasn't fully into it was McKinley. True, she had been laughing and acting weird along with them, but we had a special connection from all those weeks of talking on the bench together. I could get her to help me.

"McKinley!" I yelled as I started running after my friends. She didn't stop running, and I had to dig into my inner sporty side to run fast enough to catch up to her. At that moment I was so thankful for the fact that she was quite short and I therefore had longer legs than her. "McKinley!" I yelled again, more desperately, and I was shocked at the vulnerability I could hear in my voice. I sounded weak.

I grasped McKinley's shoulder as if trying to keep myself up in the social structure, not slipping down into whatever was waiting for me. I spun her around, and reared back when I saw the fierce look on her face. It was completely un-McKinley, un-everything that I had learned about her during the past month. She looked wild, and I saw a hint of desperation there too. But maybe it was just my own, reflected in her eyes.

Her eyes. For the first time ever, they were transparent, no cloudiness at all. I could see right through the pigment of her dark brown irises. I found myself getting lost in a never ending circle of brown unlike any I'd seen before. I knew a lot of people with brown eyes: my mom with her comforting brown, McKenna with her shallow brown, and McKailey with her gorgeous but flat brown; but none of them had ever been this open. At this moment I could see right into the core.

I saw insincerity.

"What?" McKinley almost snapped, tucking her wavy hair behind her ears. I tried to keep my voice from wavering. "Do you want to go over and sit by the bench?" Her eyes pierced into mine and I saw her ball her hands into fists before responding.

"Why would I want to do that?" she asked like I'd just offered her the most disgusting option in the world. "It's cold, and it's windy."

And with that she flipped back around and continued running in the opposite direction, joining McKenna, who had run up and around us as we were having our conversation.

I just stood there and stared back darkly, not even trying to catch up. There was no point. McKinley had been the last chance, the last hope I had, and her words had broken right through that barrier.

The bell rang and I made sure to keep my head down as I slowly trudged to the door and back inside.

— THE CROWD —
chapter | nine

The first thing I did when I got home that afternoon was email Jacklyn. I had spent the rest of the school day in a haze, trying to shut out everything that had happened during break and just concentrating on the present. I even laughed at the boys' pointless jokes during class. I think that made them happy, because they smiled at me and I smiled back. It was nice.

On the car ride home I dodged my mom's usual questions about how my day had gone, and instead thought about how to phrase my email to Jacklyn. I couldn't afford to try to make it sound better than it was, I decided. Not that I knew exactly what was happening here, but I had to describe it to her just like it had seemed to me when it was happening.

When I sat down at my computer it was easy to type the first sentence.

Dear Jacklyn,
Something weird happened at school today.

Weird. That was the only word I could find to describe it.

After I finished writing the email and sent it off, I buried myself under the pile of fall blankets on my bed and tried not to think. *Thank God we have a field trip tomorrow*, was all I could think. *So I won't have to deal with any of this.*

Morning came soon, and I had pushed everything from the

previous day behind me. I was relieved not to have it on my shoulders any more. Maybe it was all a fluke. I could start over today.

When I entered the school, I saw McKenna, McKailey, and McKinley huddled on the bench next to the front entrance, talking intently. I thought about waving, but stopped myself at the last second.

When homeroom started, our teacher said that we would be loading onto a bus at 8:30. I was depressed that it only took one bus to take our entire middle school to a museum.

During homeroom I sat at the table with all three of them. It seemed all right, no weird laughter or confusing riddle-like jokes. But then they started talking about how they had gone over to McKenna's house last night, and been there for seven hours. Then they discussed Halloween, which was two days away. We had previously planned to go trick-or-treating together. I guessed that plan was off, because they were talking about renting motor bikes and riding down the streets like a gang of toughs, in a triangle shaped formation with McKenna in the front.

They talked to each other like I didn't even exist, like they didn't even care.

Our homeroom teacher, Miss Theresa, soon called for us to line up for the bus.

"Eighth graders first," she said in an over-chipper morning voice and all the sixth and seventh graders groaned. McKenna, McKailey, McKinley, and I were the first in line, with Ronnie Morano and Ian Camil right behind us. In previous years, Ronnie had been incredibly goofy, to the point of being annoying. This year, he'd been flirting constantly with McKenna, which was equally annoying. I just hoped McKenna's sudden change in behavior hadn't rubbed off on him.

"Now there are some rules to go over first," Miss Theresa continued after everyone had lined up. "There will be no rough-housing inside the bus. You all must remain seated at all times, and to make sure no one gets injured, there will be no pushing or arguing over seats. To make sure of this, there is a rule that the maximum number of people per seat is three."

My stomach dropped, for the first of what I was beginning to suspect would be many times that day, and I silently cursed the teacher. Three, seriously? Why not two? Why not *four?*

"So," she continued, "please respect this rule. If you do, everything on this trip should go smoothly." She pushed up the sleeve of her cardigan to check her silver watch. "Now, onto the buses!"

People actually cheered in response to this. I suspected they weren't planning to obey the rules that had just been dictated. As we ran through the classroom door and began our way down the hallway, I was planning how to handle the seat situation. McKailey was first in line and I was second, followed by McKinley and then McKenna. If I was lucky, then McKailey and I would sit on one seat and McKinley and McKenna on the other. That seemed the best way it could work out. I had to hope for the best.

The line turned the corner and I became more nervous as we approached the bus. The feeling was familiar. Back in sixth grade when I was still establishing myself, I often worried obsessively over social situations. For some reason, I never found it worrying that I would freak out over things like where to sit on a bus.

As we stepped outside and made our way past the curb to the bus door, I heard McKenna and McKinley whispering feverishly behind me.

"Go, go, go!" I heard. And then McKinley bolted forward and leaned into my side, pushing me to the ground and running ahead to the bus. McKenna followed, and they both jogged up to meet McKailey. I sat on the ground with my mouth open as I watched the three of them climb onto the bus, giggling the whole time.

"Are you all right?" I heard a voice ask. I looked over to see Ronnie crouched down next to me. Ian was standing a little bit farther away, staring at the bus door where McKenna, McKailey, and McKinley had just been. Then I looked to the side and, horrified, realized that the first of the seventh graders were crowded around the door to the school with their faces pressed tightly against the glass, no doubt due to a desperate urge to get a seat on the bus as soon as possible. They were also staring at me intently. I spotted Grace and Larken at the front, their arms wound around each other as always, their gazes emitting more sadness than interest. I tried to shield my face with the cuff of my sleeve and suddenly envied their friendship greatly.

"Um, yeah, I…" I looked down at my palms, which were scraped from abrasion on the sidewalk, and tried to answer the question that Ronnie had posed earlier, "…I fell." My eyes felt red, and I resisted rubbing them with my dirt-clad hands.

Ronnie shared a look with Ian before helping me up. "Uh, sure. Well, be careful?" He said as if he wasn't exactly sure whether to believe me or not. I smiled while still looking down and wondered if I should thank him again. I had known him since kindergarten, after all, and he seemed to be genuinely worried about me. But I felt too embarrassed to continue standing in front of him. I didn't want to get him too wrapped up in memories of this less-than-good day, because he was in all my classes and I'd have problems feeling comfortable around him. So I settled for another smile and then ran to the bus, brushing off the dirt on my jeans.

As I climbed on, I saw my friends sitting together on one seat, as predicted. I walked down the aisle slowly and saw that the seat across from theirs was still empty. I realized this was perfect, and actually not a bad way to fix the problem. If I sat across from them, we would not be squished and I could still talk to them by turning toward the aisle. I had done this many times last year on field trips with Jacklyn and McKenna, and it had worked out great.

I settled in and watched as the other kids got onto the bus. I imagined pointing out to McKenna the kids who had tripped getting on. Then we would laugh about it so hard that McKailey and McKinley would just have to join in. The daydream sounded so nice that I just had to turn to the side and try to talk to them.

"What's so funny?" I asked immediately, because they were already laughing quietly.

All three went silent. McKinley opened her mouth as if to say something, but then ended up just wetting her lips with her tongue. McKenna just stared at me, her face never changing. After a few awkward Mississippi-seconds, they turned their faces back to each other and started laughing again. I slumped into the seat, then swiftly yo-yo'd myself up straight again. I wasn't about to give up.

I turned into the aisle again and thrust my body forward, invading the space of their seat and pushing my way into their conversation.

"Hey, guys!" I said. I didn't know what else to say. I wasn't worried about sounding stupid any more.

McKenna turned her eyes to me and looked my awkward position up and down. "Hey," she said.

"What are you guys laughing about?" I asked, repeating my earlier question, now that I had their attention.

McKailey shared a glance with McKinley before answering. "See our bus driver?"

I craned over and was able to catch a glimpse of the driver's eyes in the rear-view mirror. His were algae green, with specks of a darker pine-needle shade in them. They reminded me of a pond, cool and lively. I felt sorry for those eyes, stuck behind a glass windshield all day.

"Sort of," I said, tilting my head. "Why?"

McKailey started laughing again. "He has so much fat on his waist that it comes out over his pants in *rolls*." She was half-whispering, and then all three of them burst into laughter again, louder than the time before. I didn't find that remotely funny, actually more gross and depressing, but I laughed along anyway. It was harder than before, I noticed, to act like I was so amused. I was beginning to wonder how much I had sacrificed over the years for my friendships.

After I was done with my fake laugh, I noticed that I felt a little bit better about the situation. Satisfied, I smiled at all of them, even McKinley, who I had been considering shunning, and leaned back in my seat. Soon the bus started to rumble forward. I closed my eyes and let my heart continue to slow down as the movement calmed me. Maybe I could handle this. I was fixing…whatever needed to be fixed.

I kept my eyes closed until I felt my resolve to be who I wanted to be come back. I couldn't stay this desperate. It wouldn't look good to people watching from the outside. I thought back to the sad, almost sympathetic look that had adorned Grace's and Larken's faces as they stared at me through the streaked glass of the school's front entrance. *No,* I thought, *not good at all.* They might have realized how weak I felt.

When I turned back to continue talking with McKenna, McKailey, and McKinley, the horror that I'd forced down inside burst out like an overextended soap bubble. McKailey had completely twisted her body around so that all I could see of her was her back, and then had propped her right elbow up so that it rested on the back of her seat. My view of the girls was completely blocked; all I could see was McKailey's back. I had been completely and, not so subtly, cut out.

I slumped back into my seat again, and automatically brought my hands up to my eyes. I rubbed them over the skin there, which was already dry and abraded, and thought about what to do next. I thought about trying to force them out of their little huddle, but then I looked back at the way McKailey was positioned and realized that that would be nearly impossible. For the first time in my life I was outside the crowd. I was the one sitting alone on the edge, at a loss for words and with no idea of what to do.

I wondered how many people *I* had made feel this way.

My eyes darted to the seat in front of them. Ronnie and Ian were sitting there. I wondered if maybe I could lean forward and spend the rest of the bus ride trying to talk with them. At least maybe they would make eye contact with me. And maybe smile.

But I quickly discarded the idea, because I found that I was just too exhausted. And I felt hopeless. For the first time in my entire life, I just didn't care. It was like a part of me had died yesterday, when all of this started.

What *had* started? All I knew for sure was that my world was shattering around me. And I didn't even care how melodramatic that sounded. *Was this something I'd had coming?*

The bus continued to bump its way along the road, and the people around me continued to laugh and joke, and meanwhile I sat low in my seat and tried to cover up the wounds I felt opening within.

— SAVIOUR —
chapter | ten

The field trip went by in a blur. I didn't pay much attention, which I hoped wouldn't lower some stupid participation grade that the teachers planned on giving us. At first we toured the museum, which was boring to the point of death because our tour guide spoke in a complete monotone. Then one teacher announced that there would be a scavenger hunt to test the knowledge that we had gained from the tour. I highly doubted that any of us had taken away much knowledge from hearing a retired guy speak in a voice that should belong to a robot, but most people seemed pretty excited. It was, after all, an opportunity to run around a museum like crazed teenagers.

"First, a few ground rules," began my homeroom teacher in the same chipper voice she had used earlier in the day to explain the bus rules. "In a moment you will be splitting yourselves into groups. After you have formed your groups, we will hand you envelopes that contain clues as to what you are to find. You will have an hour to complete the task." People all around me immediately started whispering about who would be in their group and whether they thought they could win. I was standing next to McKenna, McKailey, and McKinley, as I had throughout the entire tour. They had never talked to me, and were always huddled together, or managed to angle their bodies so that I was completely shut out.

"Oh, and one more thing," the teacher added as she scribbled down some notes onto a clipboard. "There should be a maximum of three people per group."

My heart sunk. *Three* people. Great. It was now official. The world was just out to get me.

Even though I knew what was going to happen, I turned to face McKenna, McKailey, and McKinley. They all immediately had grabbed onto each other's elbows.

"So, I guess I'll go find someone over there," I pointed in the opposite direction from where we were.

"I guess so," McKenna said to me, and I felt even sadder because her voice sounded so cold. We had been such good friends just a few months ago, and even the best of friends in the months before that. I felt desperate because, no matter how hard I tried, I wasn't able to grasp onto the moment when this had suddenly changed.

I didn't fight the fact that I wasn't going to be with them. Instead I walked over into the throngs of people and my mind whirred, trying to think about which group I could possibly join, while still replaying the past moments of the day over and over again. I found myself walking over to where the seventh graders were standing together. Soon enough I found myself standing next to Grace and Larken, muttering something along the lines of *Can I be with you guys?* and trying not to look at their eyes, through fear of what I might find there. I knew from my past conversations with them that they were kind and open, and I desperately hoped that meant that they wouldn't mind if I tagged along with them.

Grace looked a little shocked when I asked if I could be in their group. Larken stared into my face and I could imagine it looking like a lost little child's.

"Sure," she said with a smile, and I had never been more grateful.

When I went home that night, I again dodged all parental inquiries about my day and locked myself in my room for the rest of the afternoon, trying to heal my wounds and push away all memories of what had happened and all hunches as to what was going on.

You're fine, I convinced myself. *You just need sleep.*

But even while I slept, my mind was still digesting the things that had occurred over the past two days. Something had happened while I was sick, I was certain of that. Maybe a meteor fell from the sky and hit all three of them on the head. Now they didn't want to talk to me or even look at me. And when they did talk to me or look at me, I felt like I wasn't *really* there. Instead they were just talking to the space where I was standing.

Strangely, when I was alone with one of them, everything would change. During the field trip tour, there were moments when I was walking just with McKenna because the other two were off giggling somewhere. During these moments, McKenna would randomly just jump in front of me and hold up her hand for a high five, or grab my shoulders and pull me into a hug, taking a moment to smile into my eyes. I would look into hers as well. They were flat, completely two dimensional. I used to love brown eyes, but slowly the ones around me were becoming more and more unlovely.

It was not just McKenna. Even McKinley came up and gave me a hug during random moments when we were alone, much like she did on the day I was sick and she was telling me she thought I should go home.

I dearly wished that I had never gone home. Maybe then everything would be different, and I wouldn't have to be fighting my way past their force field. Who knew that three days of being sick could make such a difference?

I stayed in this mind trance all night, and when I woke up in the morning I didn't feel rested at all. Not only that, but the bad feelings were still churning around in my stomach like I had just gotten off a rollercoaster. I felt exhausted, not just from the lack of good sleep, but from keeping up my sort-of-good attitude and normal disposition over the past few days. *Why can't Mom and Dad tell that there is something wrong? And couldn't the people in my classes at least do more than just smile tentatively at me when I approach them for company?*

I mulled over my prospects and soon was wavering between believing that everything would be fine and having to keep up this façade forever – all while silently begging to be relieved. Not that I believed McKenna, McKailey, and McKinley would act this way forever. No, I was certain that after a while this stage would pass and it would all go back to normal.

But what if it doesn't? In that case, sooner or later I'd need a savior, otherwise I was going to go crazy.

It annoyed me that no *other* people's lives were changing. Why did it have to be only mine? In all my classes the boys were acting just as out there as normal. None of *them* seemed even remotely tired.

"Hey, guys, check out Cash's new haircut!" Danny said as he dropped his backpack onto the floor and settled down in one of the computer chairs at the side of the Social Studies room.

"Nice spikes, dude!" Ronnie exclaimed, jumping forward out of his desk chair to the couch where the boy with the hairdo in question was slouching. Ronnie and Danny had been best friends almost since birth, and Ronnie was Danny's sidekick. He would agree with *anything* that Danny said, and was really good about backing him up.

The boy they were fussing over, Cash, was sitting on the couch with his arm over the back, smiling to himself. I was sure he was enjoying all the attention.

"Thanks, Ronnie. I had to practically pull my mom's arm off to make her let me get it done," Cash said proudly as he ran his hands through his newly spiked hair.

"Well, I think it's awesome!" Ronnie said as he sat down next to Cash.

"Yeah!" Ian agreed as he ran and jumped over the back of the couch and landed on the cushions. Like Ronnie, Ian was goofy and always joking around. I looked around nervously, making sure Mrs. Mirielle wasn't in the room already and hadn't seen Ian vault over the couch like that. It would've surely gotten him sent to Mrs. Darwin's office. Once I realized the teacher wasn't there, I made my way over to the couch as well. I sat down slowly and stared at the boys as they continued to discuss Cash's new spikes.

"It is pretty sweet, Cash," repeated Danny. "I've always thought about doing that to my hair, but never got around to it."

"You could pull it off too, Danny," Cash said. "Hey, maybe you should ask your parents to let you get it done. We could all do it! It could be our new thing!"

"I like that idea. We would all match during our classes. Our teachers would be like, 'What the hell is going on?'" he said. I rolled my eyes at Ian's wonderful communication skills.

"I agree," Danny began, and then he smirked, "but that still leaves the problem of Audrey."

My eyes darted up in shock that they had mentioned my name. Since the beginning of the school year, I'd spent my class time waiting eagerly for class to be over so that I could see McKenna, McKailey, and McKinley. Now I no longer felt eager for class to end. Maybe I could actually spend some time interacting with the boys. *Maybe then they wouldn't seem as annoying*, I thought to myself.

"She can do it too," said Cash with the same smirk on his face. "Come on, she's a girl. It's not like the teachers actually notice anything except for her hand when she waves it in the air to answer every question." Cash then proceeded to mimic me raising my hand, waving his around in the air and saying in a high squeaky voice, "Oh, me! Call on me!"

Then again, maybe not.

"Wow, thank you, Cash, for that wonderful interpretation," I said, rolling my eyes.

"You are so welcome," he responded enthusiastically with a slightly raised eyebrow.

"So when are you going to cut off your hair, Aud?" Ian asked, leaning forward and propping his elbows onto his knees. "All those beautiful blonde locks are going to need to go somewhere."

"Oh! Oh! I'll take them!" said Ronnie, patting down his short slick chocolate brown hair with his palm.

"Oh yeah, because my hair is going to look lovely hanging down your neck like the silk from an ear of corn that has been *ripped apart*." I grinned as I teased him, liking the feeling of having a light conversation with someone.

Ronnie, Ian, and Danny all laughed in unison, saying things like "Nice joke, Audrey," and "Wow, she really got you, Ronnie!"

I laughed too. It had been a long time since I had interacted with them, and I liked it. They didn't care about any of the stupid stuff that girls did, and probably wouldn't get upset if I did things like make fun of their hair.

As the laughter rippled out of my throat, I noticed that I didn't feel like I had to worry about anything else happening anywhere else in the school. Who cared about what people were doing in other rooms, when I was sitting on a couch laughing with people who seemed to just simply care that I existed. It was a simple gesture, but at that moment, it was enough for me.

— A GAME —
chapter | eleven

During the following week, it became harder and harder to get out of bed and go to school. McKenna, McKailey, and McKinley continued to avoid me at break and were not really talking to me. If I tried to jump into one of their conversations, they just turned their gaze to me and stared at me like I was an alien. After a few seconds they would return to whatever they were talking about, leaving me just standing there. Although it was stupid and annoying, I got used to it, so I could be around them during every break and lunch period without hurting all the time. Life was bearable as long as I could pretend that this whole ordeal wasn't happening to me.

During one lunch period, McKenna, McKailey, and McKinley weren't sitting in their usual spot. Confused, I sat there alone and ate my sandwich, getting up every now and then to walk around the cafeteria, surveying the other tables. I felt like an idiot, walking around looking at people's faces like I couldn't find my friends. It shouldn't be so hard to find three people in a middle school of sixty. I felt stripped of everything, like every face I passed was looking back at me, thinking *why does she look so lost?*

I eventually discovered that they were sitting with Grace, Larken, and their friends. I found that very odd because I knew how they hated those girls. I guessed that now they hated me more.

Thankfully, that was the only time they played hide-and-seek with me in the cafeteria. Unfortunately, after that, they started trying new things.

So I created a game to help me navigate through the day. The game made me feel like I still had some control over my life. It was kind of fun. It put some excitement into my day, and made me feel like I was living some other person's life. A spy, maybe, who had to deal with annoying and foolish people and trick them into thinking they were winning, even when they weren't.

The game made it easier for me to tell everyone that school was going well. I didn't feel like I was lying. One night my mom came into my room and sat down on the edge of my bed, straightening out the creases her weight made in the sheets. "Audrey," she said, "tell me that you're all right." I was pleasantly surprised at how easy it was for me to say, "Yes, everything is all right."

Everything was fine.

I had turned my days into a board game. I would see McKenna, McKailey, and McKinley for the first time during first break. They would rush out of their class early and try to get outside before I did. I could *also* rush out of my class, therefore getting to them before they were able to find a hiding spot, or I could take my time and go outside once I was ready. Then I would spend time looking for them. I would walk slowly along the soccer field, surveying the sidelines and looking to see if they were standing and giggling behind one of the clumps of bushes. I tried to avoid feeling idiotic when I did this, which was a challenge. Usually, I would find them, and then the usual antics they reserved for our face-to-face interactions would resume.

On a typical lunch day they would sit at their usual table, and I would come in and join them. Lunch was odd, because except for a few funny stories told now and then by McKailey, we would sit in complete silence, with the only noises coming from our side of the table being the crinkle of foil and opening of containers.

They rarely ate more than half of their food. The first to finish would stand up and throw the remains in the trash can. Then she would turn around and say, "I have to go to the bathroom." It would be odd to really and truly have to go to the bathroom every single day after lunch, but of course this was all a set-up.

Five minutes later, a second girl would declare herself done. *She* would then go and throw out the remains of *her* lunch. She would say, "I'm going to head out to break early," and give some pathetic reason why. As she said this, she would nod at the remaining girl, as if confirming something before walking away.

The third girl then sat with me and ate slowly. During the first few days of this ritual, I thought that unlike the others, she wanted to enjoy the taste of her food. By mid-November I knew better: it was nothing but a planned out game.

While we sat in silence, I knew that the first girl to leave was now in the girls' bathroom at the end of the hall. The second girl to leave was making her way down there too. They would meet while I sat calmly with the remaining girl, who would still be chewing with a purpose. I would look down at my lap while the remaining girl quietly finished her lunch.

"Where are they?" I would ask, looking around as if I was confused as to why the two girls hadn't come back from the bathroom. I always asked that. It was part of the game.

"Oh, I think they already went outside," she would say. "Let's go meet them."

And then, as we walked outside, the final and remaining girl would walk behind me. A little too far behind: far enough to lose herself in the crowd of fourth and fifth grade students, and far enough that she could sneak away without my noticing.

At this point I could change the routine. I had a choice. I could draw cards, pick different directions to go on the board.

Some days I would walk outside and sit on a rock, waiting for the girls to sneak out through the door on the opposite side of the school and find their hiding spot. I waited for them to hide, because if I was going to play the game, I was going to play fair. Then I would walk up to random people and ask them if they'd seen the other eighth grade girls. I would ask anyone and everyone, trying to keep any hint of desperation out of my voice. Normally, people just shook their heads no and gave me an apologetic look. Eventually, some innocent sixth grade boy would tell me where he had seen them, perhaps hiding behind the playground equipment. That particular time, I found them lying in the grass behind the playground, which was on a slightly raised piece of land. The girls were lying flat on their stomachs to hide behind the low gray concrete retaining wall that held the playground dirt in place. With their faces and bodies pressed into the grass, you couldn't see them if you were standing more than a few feet away.

Some days I would walk outside and not wait for the girls to hide. I would walk with purpose to the end of the yard and stand a few feet away from the door that let them sneak out without being noticed by the teachers surveying the schoolyard. I would stand there with my hand on my hip and a perfectly casual visage. That way, when they popped out a few feet away and started running for the nearest cover, I could immediately run after them and say, "Hi!" Their responding smiles were always forced and fake. News flash, so were mine.

Some days, I wouldn't go outside at all. I would stay in the lunch room until after the third girl got away from me by melting into the crowd of students, and wait until all the fourth and fifth grade kids had gone outside. Then I would innocently tell lunch lady that I'd left something very important in my locker and that I simply *had* to go get it. But after I had walked to the end of the hallway and retrieved the non-existent item from my locker, instead of walking back up the hallway to go outside, I would approach the girls' bathroom. I learned quickly that that was where they were meeting. I would always walk inside to find them standing in front of the mirrors and fixing their hair. When one of them turned around and saw me standing there dumbly, she would say something like, "Well, *hello* there," in a shocked voice. The other two would greet my presence with a shout of obscenity.

"What on earth are you doing here?" one of the girls who seemed angry about my sudden appearance would ask.

"I have to go to the bathroom," I would reply, hoping my innocence wasn't fleeting. And then I would walk to the stall, looking down to avoid their poignant stares, and close the door behind me.

Once inside, I would sit on the toilet, lean my head against the wall, and listen to their giggles of joy as they whispered, "Go, go, go!" and ran out of the bathroom, ditching me.

Usually, after that, I would just open the stall door, walk out, and go outside as if nothing had happened. I was never once shaken by their behavior. After all, it was just a game. So, I never once shed a tear.

Until one day, however, I stayed in the stall.

That was the day that Mrs. Darwin found me crying in the bathroom.

— CRY —
chapter | twelve

I hate the light snowfalls that New Mexico gets in November. After the initial flurries, the beautiful snow quickly melts away, leaving muddy ground resembling a painting done by a blind artist.

On especially muddy days, the teachers insisted that it would be too much of a problem when we came back inside, and forced us to stay inside for break. I did not see how this could be much better, because instead of messy carpets, the teachers had rooms full of hyper, noisy middle schoolers who were not able to run around and vent their energy.

After the first snow that fall, our homeroom teacher announced that we would be staying indoors for our first break of the day. McKenna, McKailey, and McKinley groaned dramatically. "Yippee," McKenna muttered sarcastically, "now we can all sit cross legged on the floor like third graders and play a friendly game of Monopoly. Totally my idea of fun."

I tuned McKenna out as the teacher continued. "Oh, and remember that we will have a Code Red drill today. When the alarm sounds, we ask that you all follow your teacher's instructions and file into the room that he or she asks you to, in an orderly manner."

Kids around me started murmuring about how cool it would be if there actually was a Code Red alarm and an enraged killer tried to break into our school. I didn't think that would be cool at all. Just the thought of some creepy guy with a gun in his back pocket targeting our school made my stomach feel like it was being rampaged by a herd of gazelles.

Come time for break, instead of going to our lockers and getting ready to go outside, everyone in the middle school was asked to come to either the Social Studies or Science room. I chose to go to the Science room. Well, actually McKenna, McKailey, and McKinley chose to go to the Science room and I followed them there. A part of me knew how pathetic it was, but another part of me, the part that controlled my feet, just didn't know what to do any more.

Inside the Science room, the girls commandeered a table and I followed them there, sitting a little bit farther away from the table than they did.

After ten minutes of watching the girls play Apples to Apples, I decided I needed a break and got up to go to the bathroom. I didn't bother announcing where I was going. I knew they couldn't have cared less.

I snaked my way through the crowd of people and out into the hall. The closing arc of the classroom door swept my pent up stress away from me and back across the threshold into the Science room. I sighed and blew out a huge mouthful of air. When the door clicked shut behind me, I stood for a second with my back against the door, reveling in the fact that I could now breathe. I was away from McKenna, McKailey, and McKinley, and seemingly just because they weren't there, the air was clear to breathe again.

I didn't honestly need to go to the bathroom, but that's where my feet led me as I pushed away from the classroom door. I walked slowly, knowing that moments like these were my only escape. I wondered why I was letting myself live like this.

You could make all of this stop, an inner voice whispered to me, but I foolishly pushed it back. Fooling myself into thinking that I could change it was dangerous, was causing me to slip further down the slippery slope of this game. And the further I slipped, I knew, the longer it was going to take to get out.

My inner knowledge didn't match what I allowed myself to know on the outside as I walked towards the bathroom. *Changing it would require understanding what is happening, and you don't understand,* I told myself. I tried to silence the thoughts in my brain that were actually starting to. Somewhere along the way my mind had made an executive decision that the truth would be too painful.

I ran my hand along the wall as I walked, as if holding myself up. The plaster felt cold and clammy. These walls used to hold together a place where I felt at home. I didn't feel at home here any more. I felt like a stranger, pushed into this new place of horror day after day, just for the laughs of some evil being. When I came back to school that dreadful Monday, I had stepped into a parallel universe where everything was different. I felt like I didn't know anything, like my entire being had just been disconnected from the life I had led before.

Once I reached the bathroom, I turned inside and stood there, staring at the stalls. I didn't want to go inside a stall. The stalls were where I went when I followed McKenna, McKailey, and McKinley to the bathroom. The stalls were where I went to hide while I listened to them laugh and felt them slip away. I shouldn't have to go to the stalls when I was on my own. I shouldn't have to hide like that.

Instead, I walked over to the sinks and washed my hands, letting the soap and water run over my skin and feeling their coolness. I looked at the sign above the sink for the elementary school kids that said *Continue to wash your hands until you have said the ABCs in your head.* I smiled and closed my eyes, repeating the ABCs to myself slowly. I felt myself being taken back to elementary school. Those had been the good days, because it had been so easy for me to keep myself protected. There wasn't all this drama and seriousness. I didn't have to worry about anything in elementary school. Even in seventh grade, I had still had Jacklyn. Now she was gone, and I hadn't even heard from her after I sent her email on the day this all started. It was as if Jacklyn had just disappeared.

After I finished washing and drying my hands, I slowly began my journey back down the hall. The girls were probably still playing Apples to Apples, laughing over the stupid cards they were putting down. I thought again about the pressure that would fill the air as soon as I entered the Science room. I suddenly felt very tired and did not want to have to face it again. If things never returned to normal with my friends, I was willing to settle just for a neutral atmosphere, so that I could sit there in peace.

Just then, as I was thinking about how uncomfortable the air would make me feel, a loud *brrrring* filled the air, making me jump back as my head immediately began to ache from the sudden volume. It kept ringing, louder and louder, and for a moment I didn't know what was happening. Then I remembered: *the Code Red drill.*

I ran down the remainder of the hallway as fast as I could and pulled at the handle of the door to the Science room, but it didn't budge. It was locked. I stuck my face right next to the glass in the middle of the door and tried to wipe off the condensation on it. The lights were off in the room, and I couldn't see anyone. I was gasping for a reason that I couldn't name as I banged my hands on the glass, trying to get someone to come and unlock it for me. But there was no one in sight. *Why hadn't they waited for me?*

I imagined this being a real Code Red alarm, with the creepy guy with the gun slithering down the hallway, looking for the one kid who was stupid enough to get herself locked out of the classroom. He would see me and think, *Oh, they forgot to make sure she was inside before they locked the door. She must not matter to them at all. I might as well kill her…*

"Audrey? What are you doing out here?" I whirled around at the sound of the killer's voice. Then I remembered that the shooter had just been in my imagination, and as my eyes cleared I saw that it was Mrs. Darwin. "You're supposed to be inside," she continued.

"I-I'm sorry," I said. "But they… they locked the door and I can't get in so—"

"You shouldn't be out here," she said in a hurried voice, grabbing my arm. "Come on."

I protested and tried to hang on to the handle of the door, but she dragged me away and led me down the hall. "Here," she said once she reached the Math room. I thought she had the key and was going to unlock the door for me, but instead she dragged me the other way, and I turned around to see that she was opening the door to the closet used to store extra desks and textbooks.

"Mrs. Darwin," I began, but she just pushed me into the closet and slammed the door behind me, leaving my words hanging. I could hear the click as she locked the door and left.

I was stuck inside a closet. The dim glow around the edge of the door illuminated a small wooden table, presumably once used as a desk, that occupied the center of the room. Two bookcases lined the walls to my left and right. I filled the remaining space.

As I stared at the tiny dark room in front of me, I slowly realized that I was still gasping for breath. I felt the air close in on me. With nowhere left to run, I felt my resolve break down as the reality of all the events and bad feelings that I had been trying to push away with my stupid game crashed down on me at once.

"No." I heard the word come out of my mouth and pierce the air. "No, no, no."

Why was this happening to me? It wasn't *fair*. I never did anything to deserve this. *Did I?*

"What did I do?" I whispered to myself. "What did I *ever do?*" And as I said those words, the gasping increased until all of a sudden my face was hot, too hot, and I felt as though my cheeks were on fire. I reached up and touched my face but quickly pulled my hand down when I found it was wet.

I was *crying*.

"No, no…" I turned around and pushed on the closet door with all my might but it wouldn't budge. I was trapped. Not only that, but I was trapped in a closet while everyone else in the school was safe and sound and together. I had been locked out. Just like McKenna, McKailey, and McKinley were locking me out of their life.

I couldn't take it any more. I lurched forward and slammed my hands down on the table. I spun around and slashed my arm out at a bookcase, knocking it off balance and causing books to slide off its shelves. As the books toppled around my feet, I clenched my fists and suppressed a yell, letting the tears fall as I doubled up over the table. This wasn't crying; it couldn't be. I couldn't be this weak. There was no reason for me to be acting like this.

I was about to slam my fists down on the table again when I

stopped myself. Why was I always beating down on myself for how I was acting? I wasn't being *weak*, I was simply reacting to the way I was being treated by *them*.

Was that weakness, I wondered idly, *letting yourself feel?*

I realized then that I was having a breakdown. At *school*.

The thought was enough to stop me mid-slam, and I felt myself slide down off the table and onto the floor. Voices reverberated down the hallway as I grabbed my stomach and gasped for air, air that wasn't coming.

I'd been trying to deal with this by myself the whole time, and it had become too much. The calming thoughts, the constant questions, the game, they were all just ways of dealing. Dealing with the fact that there was really only one way to describe what was happening to me. I was being bullied. Not only this, but I was being bullied in a place that I had thought of as my second home since kindergarten, and by a group that included two girls I had considered to be my friends.

It was depressing. Awful. Sad.

Suddenly everything seemed so clear, as if everything that had happened to me during the past few weeks was being magnified inside my head. I felt stupid. There was no point in fighting it any more.

The dark that surrounded my crouching figure was suddenly broken by a beam of light from outside; someone had opened the door. I quickly turned to the side and wiped my face.

"Audrey? Are you in here?" It was Miss Theresa, the math teacher.

"Yes, I'm fine," I answered, even though it wasn't what she had asked.

"I heard some noise coming from the closet and… why are you in here?" she asked, seeming very confused. I breathed out very slowly before answering, to ensure my voice sounded normal.

"The alarm went off, and I was in the hallway. I guess my teacher didn't realize I wasn't there and locked the door, so Mrs. Darwin threw me in here."

"Oh my gosh! That's awful!" Miss Theresa approached me and gave me a hug. "Are you all right?"

"I'm fine," I repeated again, although I realized how untrue that was. "Everything's fine."

As she pulled away from the hug I looked up straight into her eyes and watched her stare at mine. I wondered if she noticed the bright red rings that were most likely there. I wondered if she could see in my eyes that everything was *not* fine.

"Audrey," she began, and I was suddenly afraid that she *had* seen, so I jerked my eyes away. "Do you need to go to Mrs. Darwin's office or...?"

"No," I snapped. "I just... I just need to go to the bathroom."

"All right then, hurry up. Class is going to start soon." She smiled kindly at me before taking my hand and leading me out of the closet. I stood there and stared as she locked the door behind me again. Then I turned and retreated to the bathroom where I had been before the alarm went off. I could feel the tears coming back.

I walked into the bathroom quickly, prepared for it to be empty and planning to walk straight up to the mirrors to inspect my face. I was looking at the floor as I entered and heard someone gasp. I looked up to see *them* standing in front of the bathroom mirrors. Of course.

"Audrey!" McKenna said as she put down her tube of lip gloss. "Where were you?"

My eyes darted around as I stared at each of their faces. They were all inspecting me as well. "I went to another classroom," I lied. "I was just going to get something, but then the alarm went off."

"Oh, well, we were looking for you," McKinley began.

"Sure you were," I interrupted. I didn't have time for this. I walked straight forward past them and into one of the stalls. After I locked the door and sat down on the toilet, I cried. I really and truly cried, for the first time ever at school. I had accepted so many things today; I might as well accept that too.

"What is her problem?" I heard McKailey whisper to the others.

"I don't know," McKenna said. "Come on, let's go." She said that a little bit louder, no doubt so that I could hear it and know that they were ditching me. Again.

As soon as they were gone I burst out of the stall and grabbed some paper towels, dabbing at the damp spots on my cheeks. I knew that I should leave the bathroom now. This was when I had always left. That's how the game worked. *Screw the game,* I thought and scrubbed viciously at the pools of water that were still beneath my eyes – so viciously that I created red abrasions on my flushed skin. I needed to stop crying. I needed to get to class. But my body just wouldn't comply; it continued to shake and more tears pooled in my eyes and dripped down my face, soaking the paper towels and making them useless.

"Audrey?"

I whirled around and covered my face in horror as I saw Mrs. Darwin standing at the bathroom door.

"No, I'm fine," I repeated for the third time before she even said anything.

"Come with me," Mrs. Darwin said in a soft voice, and I felt her hand close around my wrist. I tried to pull away but she just looked me straight in the eyes, and I noticed hers were brown. Brown, just like McKenna's, McKailey's, and McKinley's. But unlike those other brown eyes, I saw nothing but complete kindness and care in her gaze. I started crying even harder, and she let me hug her as she led me out of the bathroom, hiding my head with her arm.

— STOP —
c h a p t e r | t h i r t e e n

Being in Mrs. Darwin's office felt awkward. Normally, only students who were in trouble for breaking rules were brought in here. I had never imagined that I'd be brought to the principal's office for having a breakdown in the bathroom.

Surprisingly, the office didn't look too intimidating. Against one wall stood a desk that was absolutely covered with papers, with an Apple computer poking above them in the center. One chair sat under the desk, most likely for Mrs. Darwin, and another against the back wall, probably for students to sit on. Next to the chair was a miniature fountain, which filled the room with the soft rhythm of falling water.

"You can sit there," Mrs. Darwin said, motioning to the chair by the fountain. I slowly moved to the chair, still wiping my eyes with my hands. A part of me hoped that I could trick her into thinking I had not been crying. The other part of me knew I needed to give up on that.

Mrs. Darwin sighed deeply as she sat down. I noticed she looked just as nervous as I felt. "Tell me what happened, sweetie," she said in a voice that sounded withered, tired.

"Nothing happened, Mrs. Darwin," I said, looking down. "I've just been having a bad day."

"So this has nothing to do with the interactions between you and the other eighth grade girls?" Mrs. Darwin said suspiciously, looking down at me with the riveting gaze that I'd seen her unleash on other people many times before.

"Yes," I replied. I fiddled with my hands.

"Audrey," Mrs. Darwin said in a strong but understanding voice. "I know that you like to put on a strong face in difficult situations. You've been that way ever since you were a kindergartener. You never liked to be weak," Mrs. Darwin stated, smiling at what I assumed were memories of my kindergarten self. Inside I was appalled at how spot-on she was. "But I *beg* you to talk to me. There's obviously something bad going on here and it is not good for you to keep it inside. You're obviously already very upset about it, and it could just get worse."

I stared at the fountain as I listened to Mrs. Darwin's words. They made sense to me. I knew they were true. I obviously wasn't strong enough to go to someone responsible, like my parents, on my own. I needed help before I completely deteriorated. Mrs. Darwin stared at me as we sat in silence for a long time. I heard her sigh, as if she felt that we weren't ever going to get anywhere. I heard her push her chair back, as if she was going to get up and dismiss me.

"I just don't know what I ever did." I spoke in a harsh whisper that was followed by a new wave of tears. I had been waiting to ask about that for weeks. That was the question that continued to confuse me the most.

"You didn't do anything," Mrs. Darwin said in a soothing voice, although she didn't even know the situation. Or maybe she did.

"You think that there's something odd about the way the eighth grade girls are interacting?" I managed to get out. She shrugged softly.

"I've noticed some weird vibes."

"They started excluding me all of a sudden!" I said. It felt great to finally say this, but at the same time old feelings from that very first day flooded back, making me feel more distressed.

"In what way?" Mrs. Darwin asked. "What have their tactics been?" She said this with a perfectly straight face, and in the back of my mind I was filled with wonderment at how odd that formal word sounded in this conversation.

I gulped, preparing myself to look back on it all. "Well, at first they just wouldn't really talk to me, or made me feel really awkward whenever I tried to jump into one of their conversations." It was still hard for me to speak calmly, and I paused between almost every pair of words. I stopped and stared at Mrs. Darwin. She nodded her head for me to continue. "And then it just continued to escalate and get worse until at certain points they would be straight out running away from me or always angling their bodies away from me and cutting me out by standing in little circles. The second day was when we went on that field trip. On the bus they all sat on one seat and I sat on the one across the aisle from them. McKailey twisted her body away from the aisle and propped her arm up so that she was completely blocking my view of them and all I could see was her back and..." I slowed down again to wipe my face and breathe deeply as I felt myself growing more hysterical with each word. I sensed that my sentences had become less a cognitive arrangement of words and more a scrambled cry of desperation. I had been clenching the arms of the chair as I talked, still on edge, though my body was slowly relaxing as I talked to Mrs. Darwin.

"That is awful." She spoke almost in a whisper, and reached out to take one of my hands. I let her.

"And I just don't know what I did or why they started do this all of a sudden and I... I just want it to stop!"

"Well of course!" Mrs. Darwin agreed with me firmly. She let go of my hand, leaned back in her chair, and sighed again. "Well," she began in a *what are we going to do now?* voice, "I'm not foolish enough to think that I could just have a talk with the girls and make this all go away. In fact," and here her voice got darker, "getting them into trouble would probably only make it *worse*." I nodded in agreement. I had always known this as well. I hoped Mrs. Darwin had some kind of solution, because I had none.

She scratched her chin and leaned forward in her chair before speaking again. "I think we can agree to keep this a secret from the other teachers. If any of them found out, they might contact McKenna's, McKailey's, and McKinley's parents without thinking it through."

I nodded. "So, you promise not to tell the teachers?"

"Yes. I promise that I won't tell any teacher as long as you keep the same promise to me."

"I promise," I said desperately and swallowed hard, knowing that I'd do absolutely anything to keep any bigger damage from being done.

"But," Mrs. Darwin's voice was dark again. She was back in businesswoman mode. "But, if we aren't telling anyone, then that means it's up to *you* to do something about it."

"What do you mean?"

"You need to get yourself away from them, Audrey." I felt her words ring in my ears. That was the problem; I didn't have the strength to leave, because then I would be completely alone.

"I can't," I said simply.

"Even though it's so miserable to be around them?"

"I…I just…I've figured out ways to be able to deal with it."

"What ways?" she asked, her face on the verge of skepticism.

"Like, I usually know what they are going to try to do to me at each time of the day, so I'm prepared for it. So when it happens I can just play along, you know? I can feel like I'm just acting along, and that way it doesn't hurt as much."

"So you mean you'd rather stay miserable and let them continue to break you down?" Mrs. Darwin really was staring me down now. It made me mad that she wasn't seeing my point. I retaliated.

"No! That's the point! It helps me *not* be miserable!"

"Audrey, today I found you crying in the bathroom like you had just been notified that the world was about to end. Do you really think I'm going to believe you're not miserable?"

I breathed out, frustrated, and wrapped my fingers tightly around the sides of the chair again. Mrs. Darwin didn't understand that my world had already ended, so there really was no point in exerting all this effort.

"You're not making things any better for yourself by playing this game," Mrs. Darwin said, leaning forward and speaking softly again. I looked away, not sure if I wanted to accept her point. I wiped the remaining tears off my face and tried to calm my breathing.

Mrs. Darwin stared at me as I did this, her elbows propped on her knees. Eventually, I dared to look straight ahead again. Her eyes looked straight into mine, and again I saw kindness and care. I also saw wisdom. And deep down, within the depths of her dark pupils, I saw worry.

"You do realize," she said softly, "that by continuing to do this you're letting the bullies win?"

I tensed up and looked away again. That was the first time any word relating to bullying had been spoken out loud. It hurt, cutting away at my heart. I still felt the stinging shock that this had happened at all, and now I couldn't help but wonder why I had let it get to this point.

Mrs. Darwin seemed to sense that I didn't feel like talking any more. I expected her to tell me I was excused and could go on to my next class, but instead she stood up. She stooped down and rummaged around on her messy desk until she found a grey sheet of paper. Her hand reached out to grab a pen and she scribbled on the sheet to make sure the pen was working before she started to write out her message. Silently, she handed the paper to me and began to exit the room. I looked down and read:

> *Please excuse Audrey Bass from being tardy to class. She was having a personal discussion with me.*
>
> *Signed, Marina Darwin*

As I read the words in her curly script, Mrs. Darwin made her way around my chair and left her office. I followed her with my line of vision as she stepped onto the tiles of the main office, her heels beginning to click on the floor. When she was halfway across the office, she very slowly turned back around to face me, as if all her limbs weighed too much. I thought I saw a sigh escape her chest before she looked directly into my eyes.

"You've got to stop doing this to yourself, Audrey."

Then she turned back around and finished her journey out of the office area and into the main hall. I was left sitting in her office, alone.

chapter | fourteen

I spent the rest of the day in silence: a nice silence, a good silence. For the first time in so long, no bad thoughts or worries plagued me. I felt like my head had been banged against a wall and then emptied, leaving me at peace while at the same time with a slight migraine.

When the school day finally ended and I arrived home, I collapsed in my room and turned on my laptop, trying to distract myself from the day's turmoil. I was shocked to discover that I had an email from Jacklyn, finally. When I saw the familiar email address, my stomach filled with warmth. I clicked to open the message and started reading.

Dear Audrey,

I am so, so, so sorry that this reply is so late. It has just been absolutely crazy adjusting to a new school. I hope you understand and will forgive me.

Oh. My. Gosh. What you just described sounds horrible. Are you sure that they are doing this to you? I mean, I find it shocking that McKenna would do something like this...but I believe you if you say it's happening. I don't at all believe that you are going crazy. After all, you have always been very much a keen observer.

Well, it's just horrible for them to be doing that. But know one thing, Audrey: you are way above their level. Like way, way above. So promise me, that no matter what happens, no matter what they do, you won't sink down to where they are. Because if they have to stoop down that far, then there is something really wrong with their view of life. They need to grow up and snap out of it.

I hope that by now this has stopped, but if it hasn't, just remember that they are not worth your time with that kind of negative attitude. Promise me that you will try to still be the wonderful person you have always been, even with the way they are acting. I don't know how busy my life is going to be here, or how much I'm going to be able to talk to you, so just promise me that you'll continue to be your strong, social self.

I miss you a lot already.

Love,

Jacklyn

I stared at the email for a long time. It was amazing how just that page of words could make me feel so much better, make me feel like someone out there still understood me and knew how my mind worked.

Some sentences in the email really stood out to me, especially the ones about not sinking down to their level and continuing to be myself.

My strong, social self. I certainly hadn't been acting that way. Not strong, and certainly not social. Being strong was something that I was going to have to build back up to. But being social – I already had opportunities for that. Interactions had been getting better with the boys, even before this all started. I had spent so much time recently being depressed that no one had magically noticed something was wrong that I hadn't really taken advantage of my opportunities to interact with the boys. I saw them eight hours a day, so I might as well try.

But where should I start? With a new burst of confidence, I opened up my assignment book and flipped to the school calendar, looking to see if anything special was happening soon. I scanned forward to the box for this Friday, November 20. The first middle school dance of the year would start at 7 PM. I remembered how nervous I had been for my first middle school dance back in sixth grade. I soon learned that the dances were not that big a deal. In fact, I wasn't even planning to go this year. *Actually,* I realized, *it was the other girls who were planning not to go. I was just going to follow along with them.* I scrutinized the facts: a dance where McKenna, McKailey, and McKinley wouldn't be there, but the boys certainly would, because they would never miss out on the chance to dance with girls. It was the perfect opportunity, the perfect place to start being myself again.

"Mom," I yelled, running out of my room and to the edge of the stairs. "Start getting the car ready, we're going to the mall."

"Why?" she asked. I could hear the clanging of dishes, as if she had just finished cooking something.

"Because," I said, walking down the stairs, my vitality returning with each step, "I need a dress."

The eighth graders were supposed to set up the decorations for the dance, but I was the only eighth grade girl who showed up. So I decorated the gym myself, since the boys weren't capable of even deciding where to put a balloon.

At 7 PM the doors opened, and people of all grades and genders piled into the small gym (we didn't need a big one, given the size of our school). It amused me how widely people's outfits varied. Most of the girls were dressed up in wonderfully poofy pastel dresses with ribbons tied around their waists. Most of the younger boys were wearing jeans and T-shirts. However, most of the eighth grade boys had changed into a nice white or plaid buttoned-down shirt, which was a relief, even if they were still wearing jeans. I was wearing a white and green spotted dress, which I had scavenged out at the mall for a great price – though my mom had made me pay since it was so last minute.

In reality, our dances were quite lame, with teachers chaperoning at every corner of the room and another teacher acting as DJ. But if you ignored all that, it was possible to have fun. You just had to talk to your friends. The first few songs were fast upbeat ones, probably to help calm the nerves of the sixth graders who were freaking out about having to dance with boys. I walked over to chat with Grace and Larken, who were sitting on a bench and eating Skittles. They seemed super-shy until you got to know them better. Maybe we'd never become the best of friends, but I was grateful that they allowed me their company and kindness. I was surprised to discover that they were still nervous about the slow dances, and I tried to reassure them as much as possible. But as I did, I discovered that even *I* was still a bit nervous. It wasn't the dancing part that worried me, it was the awkward moment when the first slow song came on, before people actually started dancing.

For the past two years, Sam Lorenz and I had acted as the slow dance icebreakers, with Sam coming up to me and loudly and over-dramatically asking me to dance, and me over-dramatically accepting. After we broke the ice, the awkwardness in the air melted away and other boys would ask girls to dance. Most boys were afraid of being teased if they were part of the first couple dancing on the floor.

This year, however, Icebreaker Sam was at Oasis Academy, and I had no idea whether anyone would volunteer to do the task. If no one did, it could get really awkward. If no one started to slow dance, the teachers would intervene and pair us up themselves. Anything was better than that.

I walked away from Grace and Larken and stepped over to the DJ table, where a list of the requested songs was posted. I tried to scan down the list in the darkness to see how soon the first slow song would come on. Unfortunately, it was too dark for me to see anything, and I was just about to ask the teacher when the beginning notes of the first slow song filled the room. Groans came from every corner of the room. I continued staring into the blackness in front of me, my mind spinning from the rhythmic combination of instrumental and voice, not wanting to turn around and have to face the awkwardness of no one starting to dance. As the first notes rang into the gym, I started counting the seconds that passed.

One Mississippi, two Mississippi—

"Audrey!" My thoughts were cut off by someone yelling my name. I could tell by the voice that it was a boy, and I slowly turned around to see Cash leaning against the snack table, the same nonchalant look on his face as always. I also noticed that all of the white in the room was glowing with a slightly hypnotic shade of light purple. When the slow song came on, one of the teachers must have turned on black lights.

Cash's white dress shirt was glowing so strongly that it made his earth-colored skin look abnormally dark, and the glow outlined the contours of the features of his face, making them look almost threatening. I, on the other hand, was probably being washed out by the glowing sections of my white and green dress. The black light on my pale skin and even paler hair would reduce them to almost the same shade as my dress, making my entire figure look continuous and two-dimensional. The black light was turning us into visual opposites.

Cash was still leaning against the table, one of his hands buried in a pocket of his jeans. "Audrey!" he repeated. "Dance with me!" It wasn't a request; it was an order. I frowned. That was no way to ask a girl to dance.

"Why?" I asked, proudly crossing my arms across my chest.

"Because you are the first girl I saw," he replied, shrugging. I rolled my eyes as he began to walk towards me and reached out his open hand. Ignoring his hand, I just stood there. He then grabbed my wrist and I let him tow me to the center of the floor, where we adjusted ourselves to the slow dancing position and started to step back and forth to the rhythm. I swiveled my head and saw that no one else was dancing yet. Instead the two genders were separated and standing at opposite sides of the gym. I smiled to myself; *we* were the icebreakers. When I turned my head back, I noticed Cash staring at me with an unreadable look in his eyes. I immediately felt self-conscious. Superficial thoughts fluttered through my head, and I was tempted to lift a hand to check whether my hair had frizzed up and come out of its neat ponytail.

"*What?*" I asked, a bit annoyed, partly at him and partly at myself. I shouldn't have had to worry about my hair when *they* weren't around.

Cash tilted his head. "Your lip is bleeding."

"Oh, that," I said, relieved. "Yeah, it's been bleeding all day. It was way worse earlier today, hurting every time I opened my mouth."

"Then why didn't you just *stop* moving your mouth?" Cash said in a smart-aleck voice, as if that were the obvious solution.

I rolled my eyes. "I don't know if you've noticed, but it's kind of hard for me to stop talking point blank."

He snorted. "Yeah, I've noticed. I knew from the moment I first laid eyes on you in sixth grade that you were going to be one of those hyper, talkative girls."

"Thank you!" I said brightly.

"It wasn't a compliment."

Cash's attempted insult amused me and only made me brighten my voice more, because I knew it would annoy him. "Oh? Why not?"

"Because," he said in a grim tone, "the way girls act is always so *pretty.*" He spat the word out as if it was poison. "From the way they talk, all the way to the way they write – all curly script with those little hearts over the letter *i.*" He shook his head to the side and grimaced as he growled, "I. *Hate.* Pretty."

During his little diatribe, I listened with my mouth partly open, beyond amusement at his honesty. I didn't know whether to burst out laughing or nod in sympathy. He seemed to still be distracted by his hatred of prettiness, so I zoned out of the conversation and into the atmosphere around me. I realized that this had been a mistake when the song playing in the background finally registered with my ears. After taking in the mushy words that made up its chorus, I felt a flush begin to creep up my cheeks.

I briefly caught a few words, such *green eyes* and *baby* and *sparks* and I cringed at the sappy love lyrics, trying to tune them out. I didn't like music at the best of times, and the saccharine sweetness of this song made my head ring, obliterating my logical thoughts and replacing them with dust. As I tried to shake the feeling away, I noticed a growing pressure on my side. I went into full alert. At the beginning of our dance, Cash's hands had been exactly at my waist, and now they had moved up to the bottom of my rib cage. At least, that was what it felt like. I didn't want to look, for fear of making it even more awkward, so I just gulped and convinced myself that I was imagining things.

I looked back at Cash, who was frowning so hard that the skin around his eyes and nose had bunched up. "I hate this song," he whined.

"I picked it out," I answered in an amused voice. It was partly true, because I had contributed a CD of random songs for the dance. I try not to listen to music because I don't like how the notes assault my mind with a blur of colored images, so I had put together the CD by pulling tracks from mix CDs that Jacklyn had given me. "I'm sorry, is it too pretty for you, Cash?" I hated the song too, but I couldn't help teasing him.

The corners of his lips turned up and he nodded his head. "No offence, Audrey, but it's a horrible song."

I shrugged. "None taken."

Cash rolled his eyes. "Of course. You never get insulted." He looked amused. "I swear it's impossible to get you down."

My mind instantly raced over the past few weeks. *If you only knew, Cash*, I thought bitterly, and then I tried to shake the unsettling feeling off.

As we talked and the song droned on, I found myself being pulled more and more into his eyes. He really did have pretty eyes. They were electric, almost a combination of jade and lime. I could almost imagine his eyes as gemstones, except they looked lively enough and so full of energy that I thought for a moment there was a possibility they might actually start buzzing, sending out real-life sparks.

I was pulled out of my trance by the realization that Cash's hands had continued to rise up my sides throughout the conversation, and I wondered if it was truly an absentminded action. Soon they were only inches below my breasts and I felt beyond uncomfortable. I still didn't want to say anything, out of fear of making the dance even more awkward, but I couldn't stand it any more. I slid my hands down from his shoulders and jabbed my elbows into his hands.

They didn't budge. I tried again, pushing down as hard as I could, and meanwhile making sure that I was smiling at Cash as kindly as possible. He was doing the same. We were both standing there, an arms-length apart, smiling as if we were the best friends in the world, while his hands and my elbows battled fiercely.

"So, what do you think about the dance so far?" I asked, desperate to find something to talk about.

"Yeah. Um, it kind of fails," he said. I had to admit that he was right.

"I agree," I said sadly. It wasn't often that I sank so low as to agree with Cash. "The problem is that our class is full of procrastinators. And when you put a bunch of people like that together, you get nothing done. Plus, we have people like Trey who don't give a crap."

Cash laughed. "Yeah, I'm shocked he even came."

I shook my head. "The only reason he's here is to eat the food. Even you must realize that."

Cash smiled. His hands were *still* fighting upward, even against my sharp elbows. We were in a wrestling match, my arms no stronger than his hands. I was on the verge of tiring out.

It's probably just because I'm so short compared to him, I decided. *Cash doesn't realize that his hands are so far up. Or maybe he got yelled at by the teachers before the dance for always having his hands too low and now he's being extra careful. He's trying, that's all.*

Cash continued to throw little insults at me for the rest of the song, but it was funny, and I smiled the entire time. Strangely, I didn't feel as afraid of him now. I felt like he'd actually shared a part of himself with me. Maybe that was because his eyes were so striking. They were like a pool; I could swim in them, getting lost in the different waves. I discovered that they weren't just green, his eyes had flecks. As we danced I counted the colors in his eyes: teal, yellow, turquoise, chartreuse, a little bit of purple…

In the middle of my counting, the song came to an end. Cash stopped moving his feet and removed his hands to fiddle with a tie that wasn't there. The absence of his grip was a shock and a cold breeze from the ceiling fans instantly froze the sweat from his hands through my dress. I shivered and crossed my arms, making sure Cash couldn't put his hands back. Not that I thought he would try.

"Thank you, Audrey, for letting me dance with you." He gave a fake bow, and I smiled.

"You're welcome," I breathed out quickly before darting away, searching for someone, anyone, to talk to, desperate to describe what I had just experienced. I spotted Grace and Larken standing in a corner and figured that, as on the day of the field trip, they were unlikely to reject me. As I approached, I heard them raptly chatting about the boys that they had danced with. I jumped in.

"That was the most interesting dance of my life," I said, breathing out fast. It was true.

"Why?" Grace asked eagerly, leaning in as if me coming up to them like this was completely normal. "What happened?"

"It… I was dancing with Cash, and I think his hands were moving up my body."

Larken gasped. "You were dancing with Cash? He creeps me out a bit."

I smiled. "Yeah, he creeps me out too, Larken, but it was actually fun to get to know him. And I'm not worried about the hand thing. I mean, he probably just didn't realize he was doing it, right?" My sentence had started out as a statement but turned into a question. I was convinced that it was true, but I just wanted to share it with someone. I couldn't let it boil inside of me.

Larken's face split into an amused look before she started *laughing* at me. Grace's small features just looked horrified.

"Audrey, you do realize he completely knew what he was doing, right?" Larken said through her laughter. She was looking at my feet, and I grabbed her face and made her look right at me.

"What do you mean?" I asked, annoyed that I didn't know why she was laughing.

"Cash is a *boy*." Larken said as if that explained everything. "You can't take his actions with a grain of salt and then make excuses about them. He's not an angel. He doesn't have a halo over his head. At least, if he does, I can't see it." She started laughing again, and I stared at her, horrified. I didn't want to believe I was *that* naive.

"Audrey." Grace's voice was soft. "Cash is a bad idea. I mean, he's *bad*. He prides himself on that."

"I know that," I said, slightly annoyed that I was getting schooled by two girls younger than me, about a boy who wasn't even in their grade. "I'm just getting to know him – it's *fun* getting to know him. I was always so spooked before that I never tried. Now is my perfect chance. I mean, I have nothing better to do!" I held my arms out in explanation, but then realized that Grace and Larken did not know about my situation, and therefore could not understand what I meant.

"All right, all right," Grace said, patting my arm, "calm down." I frowned. I hadn't realized I needed to calm down. Grace continued, "I believe you." Then she stared at me for a few seconds before her face split into a smile and she started laughing. "I just can't believe you thought that he didn't mean to make his hands keep going up!" She said, setting down her cup of punch and doubling over. Larken joined in, her smile carefree. "I know! You really need to work on trusting your instincts, Audrey!"

I stood there as they laughed at me, confused and annoyed at first. But then I remembered how I had stared at Cash's eyes and convinced myself that I was imagining his encroaching hands because I was scared of making things more awkward. I smiled. They were right. I smiled wider and then I started laughing. Then all three of us were collapsing on the bleachers in laughter. I was a fool, and not just about Cash. I had spent the last month trying to convince myself that nothing was happening with those three girls, that they weren't bullying me. I had been ignoring the signs, turning everything into a game. That was going to change.

I let myself grin at Grace and Larken – and was then caught off guard at how good it felt to just grin at someone. I was certain my lips were stretched out way too wide to look attractive. However, that was the least of my worries as they laughed at me and I laughed back, because I realized that suddenly I was so glad I had come.

— ENEMY —
chapter | fifteen

After having so much fun at the dance, I was disappointed to discover that it didn't change how I felt when I was around McKenna, McKailey, and McKinley. I had spent a long time thinking about what Mrs. Darwin had said in her office, and I didn't know if I could do what she wanted. If I stopped "doing this to myself," then that meant completely cutting the girls out of my life. *How do I even start doing that?* I couldn't help but wonder. And, at this point, was I really doing this to myself? I wasn't completely convinced yet. All I knew was the persistently nudging, slowly awakening realization that I needed to start digging myself out of the hole that I had somehow been buried in. It had all happened so fast. Like clouds scattering before a storm front, the carefully crafted friendship that I had with the other eighth grade girls had suddenly been ripped apart. I was left behind, buried under piles and piles of snow that fell all too fast for me to comprehend.

Indeed, I slowly felt my strength return. I decided that there was a fault with my game, in that I needed to stop sitting around and watching them play their little games with *me*. I needed to play *with* them, interact more. As I decided this, a part of me poked at my conscious with an outstretched finger, saying *I'm not really sure if that complies completely with what Mrs. Darwin meant.*

Baby steps, dear, the other part of me said as a way of defending my actions. I knew that it would be best to separate myself completely from those three girls, but I was going to take the opportunity to show some strength first. It was time for me to get down and dirty, to walk behind enemy lines.

I started with lunch. They were still doing their vanishing routine, which amused me. I realized now how stupid it was. *Had they actually spent time coming up with this stuff? Had they actually spent time figuring out how to hurt me?*

One day, when McKinley got up and said she had to go to the bathroom, I also got up. I slowly threw out the wrappers from my lunch, and then I told McKenna and McKailey that I needed to go to the Math room to get some tutoring. It was really amusing to see their confused faces. For the first time in a long time, I had power. For the first time in a long time, I almost felt okay.

As I stepped out of the lunch room, I saw McKinley run down the hallway until she reached the end and turned the corner. I knew she was going to the bathroom; that much I had learned from walking in on them there. Now I found it funny that McKinley thought she was being so discreet when she ran. You could tell from the little smile she wore on her face and the shine in her eyes, a shine that she'd stolen from mine.

On another day I waited until McKinley and then McKailey had left, leaving McKenna as the last one at the table. I found it hard to lie to McKenna, because we used to be such good friends, yet many of those fun memories had been burned out of my heart over the past month. I barely remembered what it had felt like to interact with her before the bullying started.

I got up and threw away my lunch flotsam, taking time to think through how I was going to phrase my lie. When I returned to the table to pick up the final piece of plastic, McKenna grabbed my hand.

"Have you got another Math study session?" she asked in a thick voice. The weight on my hand pulled me down until I was leaning over the table and at her eye level. I looked into her flat dark eyes, which were as muddy as brownie dough, only splotched with suspicion instead of chocolate chips.

"Nope," I said, trying my best to keep my voice light despite the fact that she was staring me down. "I'm heading down to clean out my locker. I – uh – got in trouble with Mrs. Darwin because of how messy and dirty it was." I attempted a chuckle. "You know me! I can just *never* keep stuff clean." McKenna continued to stare at me and wouldn't let go, so I began to pull. She flattened her hand, gluing my forearm to the table. I pulled with all my might, gritting my teeth. Eventually I succeeded, and my arm flew up too fast for me to control it, whacking McKenna in the chin in the process. I quickly turned around and strode out to the hallway. At one time, I would have apologized for the accidental collision, but not any more. She was my enemy now.

As soon as I entered the main hallway, I saw McKailey standing in front of the drinking fountain, looking from side to side. As I watched her jerky movements, I found it amusing that even though I was standing plain as day in the hallway, she didn't seem to be aware of my presence. I watched her make her way down the hallway and rush into the Math room. I held my breath when the door shut behind her, wondering if that was actually her final destination. But then, after about fifteen seconds, she opened the door and ran down the hall and into the Science room.

I started to walk down the hallway, staring at the unmoving door that she had just slid through. Suddenly it opened and I screeched to a halt as McKailey stood with her back towards me, looking from side to side again before tip-toeing over to the room for kindergarten and first grade. She stood with her back flat against the door, like a spy, and a look of pure excitement on her face.

I covered my face because I absolutely had to laugh at her behavior. She was *sneaking* down the hallway from room to room, like she was being chased by an assassin. Unknown to her, in a way she was. I was learning the secrets of their wicked game. After taking a few heaving breaths, she darted to the English room, then the Social Studies room, and then all the way down the hall to join McKailey in the bathroom.

As I waited outside that day for them to find their hiding place, I realized that also, in a way, I was still playing a game with them. And I wasn't sure this game of observing how they managed to ditch me all those times was any better – I was just being drawn in by a combination of amusement and curiosity. After struggling with this thought for a bit, my feet seemed to decide it wasn't worth it and I found myself heading for the basketball court, where the boys were running around, the basketball crunching on the half-frozen blacktop.

"You guys are crazy," I said, walking over. "You just need to accept the fact that it's way too cold to still be playing basketball."

"No way," said Reese as he made another hook shot. "The basketball doesn't go away until my mom makes me stop wearing shorts to school." I looked down to see how Reese was dressed. He was wearing a graphic tee and plaid knee-length shorts. I was wearing jeans, gloves, and a marshmallow jacket.

"Again, you're crazy," I repeated. "You do realize you don't live in California any more, right?" I asked. Reese spent the first six years of his life living in Orange County, and he still goes back there every summer.

"Shut up, Aud," Reese said, passing me the ball. He looked over my shoulder for a bit. "Hey, so why aren't you over there waiting for McKenna, McKailey, and McKinley?"

My face froze like the ice below my feet. I threw the ball at his chest and said, "Wait, you know about that?" Reese's eyes darted and I swear he looked panicked for a second.

"Know about what?"

"You know about them hiding from me?" My voice was shrill. Was it possible that the boys had been looking out for me?

Reese stared at me for a second and then looked over to the other edge of the blacktop, where Danny was standing with Ronnie and Ian. I followed his gaze before he looked back at me. "What? No," he said. "I was just, uh... I mean, you know you guys are always playing that game? Where you stand out here with us and they hide, so you guys can bond by having to find each other? I was just asking why you weren't playing it today."

I stared at Reese and felt the hope drain from my face. New thoughts attacked each other in my brain, all vying for my attention. Was that what had been going on? It seemed absolutely ridiculous for this to be their idea of a bonding game. Yet fears were beginning to slip into my head again, like those stupid insecurities that you can never get rid of. I wondered if I had just imagined the look in McKenna's eyes. And then a worse thought struck – was I making the *whole* thing up?

Am I crazy?

I walked away from Reese without even saying goodbye and sat on a rock. The excitement and anticipation of the past two days were gone, and now I felt raw, as though the cold air had dried out my skin until it hurt. The hurt was back.

The next day I didn't do any snooping, which was probably a wise move. They all looked like they expected me to play the game, and McKenna stayed until the end of lunch. I assumed that they had caught on that I was trying to break the pattern of their game, and they wanted to make sure I stopped. They couldn't afford to lose their power. I understood. Over the last two days I'd been on a high by stealing just a little bit of their power. That's how strong it was.

I made sure to let McKenna know I'd given up, by staring down at my feet the entire lunch period. I didn't even answer her when she asked whether I was feeling all right. Whether she was checking to make sure I had stopped trying to defy them, or was having one of her sudden nice moments, I didn't care. I just wanted to be left alone.

McKenna left lunch early. One moment I looked up and she was gone, so I walked out to break on my own. I sat on the same rock and stuffed my hands into the pockets of my trench coat jacket. I wasn't sure of anything any more. All the confidence I'd gained from the dance was gone, pushed away by Reese's one little comment.

I thought about how Reese's eyes had kept darting around, and about all the time he spent looking at Danny. It was almost as if Reese was hiding something too.

A fire lit inside me again and I stood up, looking over at the door at the end of the school. I knew McKenna, McKailey, and McKinley would appear down at that side of the field, but I never knew *how* they got there. That was my last bit of snooping to do.

I had started this journey of figuring out the secrets of their game, so I might as well complete it. I walked with a purpose across the frozen grass and over to the door. I stopped when I was standing a few feet away from the door, behind a low hedge.

I noticed that the door was slowly being cracked open. I stared at the entrance, waiting for someone to come through the opening door. But no one did.

So, very carefully, I stepped slowly forward. Trying not to crunch on the frozen grass, I peered over the hedge at the sidewalk that led to the door. I couldn't believe the sight in front of me.

McKenna, McKailey, and McKinley were crawling, that's right, *crawling*, out the door on all fours.

"Hello," I said. I couldn't help myself.

McKenna looked up and I saw the scorching fire in her eyes; the brownie dough was now burnt. It was ridiculous. It was hilarious. It was humiliating. McKinley looked up at me, and her eyes showed her embarrassment. McKailey kept her gaze on the sidewalk as she slowly stood up. When she looked at me, her eyes were dull amber. I looked away. They were too boring for me to waste my time on.

"Hel-lo," she responded slowly, rolling each syllable on her tongue.

I smirked, the thrill slowly returning to my heart. I had caught them crawling out of the back door of the school, on all fours, just to ditch me. It wasn't just stupid. It was pathetic. I wondered how I could have ever let someone who thought that *that* was a smart move make me feel weak.

I smiled. "I am going to go over and watch the boys play basketball. You three can join me if you want." And then I turned on my heel and walked away.

— ESSENCE —
chapter | sixteen

That night I reveled in my new sense of success. I liked the feeling; it meant I had some power again. I had some choices about what to do, and this time they were real – to me at least. I tried to ignore the fact that the feelings of success had been engineered by nothing more than me manipulating my own made up game.

For the first time since she had moved, I called Jacklyn. My life had moved so far from where it had been before Jacklyn left that I wanted to make sure I was still in the same *universe*, one where Jacklyn existed.

"Hello?" I said into the receiver of my phone, wondering if she would even remember what I sounded like.

"Audrey? Is that you?" Jacklyn sounded shocked, excited. I couldn't really tell what she was feeling. That's one of the bad things about telephones; you can't see the other person's eyes.

"Yes, the one and only," I said, smiling. "Can you talk right now?"

"Yes, of course! Just hold on a second…." Jacklyn's voice slowly faded away and I heard other voices faintly exchanging words in the background. "Back," she said a few seconds later.

"What was that? Are you at someone's house?"

"Yeah, I'm with a friend," Jacklyn said. My heart sank. Jacklyn already had friends – of course. She never had to worry about losing or not having them. That frustrated me, but at the same time I was glad for her and relieved that I didn't have to worry about her being happy. She was always able to turn her life right side up. "But it's okay," she continued. "I'm here to talk to you."

I breathed out a sigh. "Thanks."

"So, what's happening with the girls? Is everything all right?"

Yeah, it's fine. I'm dealing with it, I wanted to say. But I had to remind myself that this was Jacklyn, my best friend. This was a chance for me to help myself instead of just sugar coating it.

"It's getting there, I guess. I don't know. I've definitely made progress," I said.

"Oh? Progress how?"

"Like," I blew out air, trying to figure out how to phrase it, "I'm starting to let myself have fun again." She didn't reply with words but I heard her breaths of understanding, so I continued. "When I'm in a situation where the girls are bringing me down, I can just go over to Danny or Ronnie or Ian and talk to them, and then I can have fun. I'm proud of myself." I giggled, realizing how ridiculous that sounded.

Jacklyn straight-out laughed. "I'm proud of *them*. I mean, I'm proud of Danny and all the boys for being nice to you. I mean, wow, *nice* – that must be a new one for them!"

I smiled and laughed in agreement. It wasn't so much the boys' niceness that surprised me, but the honest emotions I sensed coming from them. You don't usually expect honesty to be radiating from a group of boys that age. It a new, surprising, lovely thing to experience – it was just plain *nice*.

A few weeks ago I had reflected on my knowledge of bullying tactics, gleaned solely from the fifth grade film fiasco, and had dug a point from my memory that created a new fear. I had been afraid that McKenna, McKailey, and McKinley would try one of the most obvious tactics: try to make other people at Eastwood dislike me.

But it was now late November and the boys were still talking to me and treating me as they normally would. And that fact, the realization that *that* fear had not come true, just made their niceness all the nicer. Now I realized how advantageous it was that boys did not get sucked into petty drama; they would not be involved in something as stupid as friends suddenly ostracizing someone for no reason.

"Speaking of Danny," I began, wondering if Jacklyn could help me figure out why Reese was acting so weird that day, "I was wondering recently if maybe he knew, you know, about them bullying me." It felt weird saying that word out loud to Jacklyn, but she didn't stop me to acknowledge it, so I just kept going.

"Why, has Danny said something about it?" Jacklyn said in a distracted voice.

"No, but there are certain moments where I feel like maybe they just know... like they feel bad and are trying to take me into their group. And then earlier today Reese asked me why I wasn't waiting for McKenna, McKailey, and McKinley, to find their hiding spots like I usually do, and then he acted like it was a slip. He covered it up with this weird excuse, and before he said it he spent a long time looking at Danny. It all just makes me wonder."

"Um, Audrey," Jacklyn interjected, "I don't know exactly when or if I'm even supposed to say anything about this, but..."

"What, Jacklyn?" Now I felt like I was getting somewhere. "What is it?"

"Danny and I have been texting lately. It just started all of a sudden – and we started talking about how his eighth grade year was going and stuff."

"Oh, wow! Has that been awkward for you?" Jacklyn and Danny had dated for a while in sixth grade. It was stupid – one of those relationships when you've just gotten into middle school and you start dating for the sake of dating – but it was the reason Danny and I became good friends. I had been the go-between in their relationship. I would talk to them about each other whenever they felt too afraid, or thought it would be awkward. I never felt awkward in situations like that.

"No, not really," Jacklyn said, laughing. "Those feelings have mostly faded away. But it's been nice, he's told me about how annoyed he is at how uptight all the teachers are and stuff."

I let out an easy laugh. "That bothers some people a lot. Me? Not as much. Of course, maybe I've just been too preoccupied to really notice."

"Maybe," Jacklyn laughed with me, and I noted joyfully how easily our laughs and smiles had come in this conversation. Jacklyn was so good at making me feel better – there was no reason to fake happiness when I was around her. "Anyway, he asked if I'd been talking to you recently. I said yes, and then I… oh, well… I asked him if he knew about how you, McKenna, McKailey, and McKinley were getting along. I'm sorry; I know you wanted to keep it quiet! But I really wanted to know, so I was trying to spur a response and –"

"It's okay, it's okay," I said quickly. I might've been a bit mad, but at the moment I was more interested in what Danny's response was.

Jacklyn continued, "And he was like, 'I don't know, it seems like the others have broken off from Audrey and haven't been treating her the nicest lately.' And I was like, 'Oh! It's worse than that!' I told him all about how bad it was and how much they were bullying you. He didn't realize the worst of it, Audrey!"

"Oh my…" I said, lost for words. So Danny knew, which meant

the others knew, which meant that *Reese*...

Jacklyn was continuing her story in true gossip style. "And then he was like, 'I knew something had changed and that they were being mean to Audrey, but I thought she just didn't care.' " I couldn't believe it. Danny had thought that I didn't care? I must have been better at the whole poker face thing than I had thought. But Danny had also noticed that something was wrong. If only I'd known that before, then I wouldn't have had to worry that maybe I was just making the whole thing up. "I told him how much it was hurting you, Audrey. He told me that if it ever gets bad you can just hang out with the boys, because they like you. As a person, I mean." I smiled to myself. I knew what she meant, and suddenly my heart felt a little bit warmer on the inside. Danny had offered me companionship.

"So, that's probably why Reese was acting so weird. He wasn't sure whether he was allowed to say that Danny knew," Jacklyn said, concluding her story.

"Thank you so much for telling me this!" I said. "If I could, I would hug you through the phone right now." Jacklyn laughed.

"I love you, Audrey. I have to go now, but try to just enjoy yourself, okay?"

"Okay," I said. "I'll try." And I meant it, but inside I worried that something new would happen and mess up everything I'd accomplished. I needed to watch my back, watch out for a clue as to whether anything was going to change. I knew that becoming confident was a risky process. My skin wasn't anywhere near as thick as it used to be, so those three girls could knock me back down.

At break during the next few days, I watched the boys attempt to play basketball. I sat with my back against the wall of the school, where it was warmer, and watched them run around on the crunchy blacktop. McKenna, McKailey, and McKinley usually sat with me. Since the day I caught them sneaking out of the school on all fours, I had gotten out to recess before them, and watched as they marched out of the school in single file and over to me, where they sat down.

The way they treated me didn't change. I noticed smaller, more kinetic details about their behavior. The girls snickered at certain things I said and motioned to each other with their eyes. As the days went by, another routine started: one of them would get up and pull one of the boys to the side. They seemed to be asking the boys for some kind of favor, but every time the boy's answer was the same: *no*. I wondered what the girls were asking for.

As much as I tried to ensure otherwise, these little details started to get to me again. Even though things were better, my emotions were very up and down. My old feelings of loneliness would come back at times, flickering on and off. The initial high from changing my attitude about what I could do in these tough situations had evaporated, leaving a dreary world to deal with. I made sure not to think too much when I heard a giddy giggle from the girls or when an ominous feeling permeated the atmosphere. I no longer thought too hard about the fact that when one-on-one, McKenna, McKailey, and McKinley were very nice to me, almost clingy, but when all together they became a pack of people who didn't care about my existence. I decided that not thinking too hard was the best way to keep my sanity. I wondered if I was selfish for continuing to want more of a change in how they acted around me. *Is it okay to want an even bigger improvement than the one I've already gotten?*

One day, I entered the school yard at break time to be met with a surprise: McKinley and McKenna were already sitting down at my usual spot, watching the boys dribble their ball. At first I was suspicious of this change. Was this a clue that I should be wary? I stood and took in the scene, trying to absorb the essence of the situation. This was new territory for me, and I wanted to make sure my senses were still working well enough to be aware of everything that was happening. Maybe the girls were trying to get on top again, to get an upper hand. But I shook the worries away and decided to just enjoy my break. I was too tired to get tied up in little things like that.

As I walked over and started to put my snack down next to McKinley, I was met with another surprise. McKinley looked me right in the eyes and started *talking* to me.

"Do you want some of my pomegranate, Audrey?" she asked, holding half of the red fruit up to me as if offering it to a deity.

"Oh, no thanks," I replied. "I don't really like fruit." McKinley nodded and I stood there awkwardly for a second, not sure what to do.

"Would you like some of my chips?" I asked awkwardly, feeling like I should give something back in this situation, be the bigger person. Maybe I could let them learn by example. I leaned down and picked up my bag of chips that I had previously set down on the cement and held it out to her.

"Thanks!" she said cheerily as she reached out to take some. Her brown eyes sparkled at me, and I frowned. It wasn't a good spark, like I'd seen with Cash. That much I was certain of.

In a distracted daze, I started to sit down, concentrating solely on the way the light had reflected off her irises. What emotion had been there? Kindness? Greed?

"Oh!" I exclaimed suddenly as I felt something dig into the back of my jeans, causing me to roll over onto the right side of my butt. "What was that?"

"Oh, sorry," McKinley said, leaning over. "That was my pomegranate! I didn't realize you were going to sit *there*," she said with a laugh that then grew, turning infectious. At first I was a bit annoyed that she had let me just sit down on her food, but then her laugh was ringing in my ears and it sounded so real that I couldn't help but laugh along, turning to watch the boys make fools of themselves on the icy basketball court. I wiped the pomegranate seeds off of my backside, not worrying about it.

The eighth graders had study hall during the last period that day. Mrs. Krashaw had been assigned to sit in the room and watch us work, and she was so impressed with how studious we were that she decided to let us go early so that we could spend some time getting refreshed outside. We weren't too pleased about this, since it was cold outside, but anything was better than spending another ten minutes trying to concentrate and do our homework.

As we walked down the hallway to the exit door, I enjoyed the peace and quiet and flashed over memories from the day. It had gone well; at least nothing terribly awful had jumped out at me from the shadows. Worries had nagged at me all day, but I had continued to push them away and I was glad, because it had all worked out okay.

I was staring at my feet, walking in my own little world, when I heard some giggles coming from behind me. I knew immediately that the giggles were from *them*. They were walking directly behind me, seemingly taking their time as well. Mrs. Krashaw was walking in front of me, and in front of her were the boys, who were eager to get outside and get moving. My brain froze up, wondering why they were giggling and what was so funny. No doubt it was something relating to me, and I wasn't thinking that in a selfish way. Believe me, I would have preferred their giggles to be about anyone else. I just rolled my shoulders back and kept walking, wanting them to know that they weren't getting to me.

I spent the rest of our break ignoring the nagging little feeling in the back of my head telling me something really was wrong.

Afterwards, we all retreated out of the cold and walked back to the classroom, gathering up our books and preparing to go home. As I started to exit the classroom, Mrs. Krashaw stopped me and motioned towards the hallway, pulling me aside.

"Is there something wrong?" I asked, voicing the fear that I had haunted me for the last half hour and thoroughly confused as to why she was not letting me go home.

"No, not really. It's just…," Mrs. Krashaw sounded terribly awkward for a teacher, which was unusual. "I was wondering," and here she looked from side to side and leaned down to my height, lowering her voice, "did you by chance get your period today?"

I immediately started to panic, but managed to keep a cool-sounding voice. "No, why?"

"Oh, I'm sorry," Mrs. Krashaw said, immediately backing off. "Well, then, it's nothing." She straightened up and smiled as if she had done her duty. "Have a nice day, Audrey!"

I kept a smile on my face until she had passed me and started to walk down the hallway. Then, I ducked my head down and darted into the nearest bathroom, which just happened to be the same bathroom I had taken refuge in after the Code Red drill incident. I ran inside and slammed my books onto the floor, turning around and examining my backside in the mirror. To my horror, there was a round spotty red splotch on the lower edge of my left butt cheek. Humiliation slowly reddened the cheeks of my face, while familiar feelings of hurt found their way into my stomach. I felt so foolish.

It had been the pomegranate. *McKinley's* pomegranate, which I had sat on.

I unzipped my sweatshirt and wrapped it around my waist. I turned around another time, making sure no one could see the spot, and trying to ignore how ugly the sweatshirt looked, hanging limp at my knees like the skin of a dead animal.

Humiliation still coursed through me. I was shocked. Mostly, I was embarrassed that my teacher had been the one who had told me. That's how alienated I was. I didn't even have friends who would let me know that some evil girls had lured me into sitting down on a pomegranate.

The cliché thought that *I just want to crawl in a hole and die* entered my head, but I settled for crawling into the nearest stall. I curled up into a ball and tried my best to not think about anything but how I needed to control the liquid now pooling at the corners of my eyes.

— SANITY —
c h a p t e r | s e v e n t e e n

I couldn't believe that I was crying in the bathroom at school *again*. As I sat on the floor of the handicapped stall, I pressed my hands over my eyes like patches, trying to keep the tears from coming. "No, no," I whispered to myself. "It's not worth it. Why can't you see that it's not worth it?"

Great. Now not only was I crying, but I was talking to myself.

I sat up straighter and groped around the wall of the stall until I found the toilet paper roll and ripped off enough to dab my eyes. I could hear people walking down the hallway, talking loudly as they headed outside to be picked up by their parents. I didn't want to go out and join them. I just wanted to sit there, on the floor. I needed the time alone. *Let my mom think I'm missing*, I thought to myself. *Let her have to spend time looking for me. Let her have to come in here and see how down I am. Just let her.*

Okay, so maybe I didn't actually want to be alone. But being alone was better than the humiliating alternative of having someone see me like this. I had already been humiliated enough for one day.

Just as I was delicately dabbing the rough paper below my eyes, I heard the footsteps of someone walking into the bathroom. I panicked, dropped the rolled up paper and scooted into the far corner of the big stall, pressed my head against the back wall and hugged my legs to my chest. I held my breath.

The person – whoever it was – stopped walking and the room was silent for a few agonizing seconds, during which I tried my best not to breathe. I wondered why they were just standing there in the middle of the bathroom, so I slowly moved my head over and tried to get a glimpse from under the stall partition. I realized, in horror, that when I dropped my rolled up paper it had bounced out of the stall and into the main area of the bathroom. The person was now bending down and picking up the ball of tear stained paper. They started walking again – towards me. I tried to remember if I had even locked the stall door. I couldn't remember. I was too frozen, curled up against the wall of the stall, which was probably covered with gross stuff, thinking about how I should have just walked out while I could.

Once the person's shoes were standing right in front of the stall door, I stared at them for a moment and noticed that they did not look like a girl's shoes. *They almost look like –*

But then the door swung open, and I was staring into the eyes of – Danny.

Danny? I was too shocked and embarrassed and confused to point out that he shouldn't be in the girls' bathroom. I just looked down, straightened my body until the wall of the stall supported my back again, and resumed sniffling. I pushed my hair back and watched from the corner of my eye as Danny slowly walked over to the stall. He entered and turned to lean back against the side wall of the stall that was at a right angle from me. Then he slid down until he was sitting in the same position as me, and leaned his head back. He seemed to be looking up at the ceiling as he let out a long slow breath. I just stared, thinking that eventually he would realize he was in the girls' bathroom, get embarrassed, and charge out, and then I could get out of this compromising situation.

"So…what's up?" I heard him say. I turned to stare at him. Was he really *talking* to me in a *stall* in a *girls'* bathroom?

"Nothing much," I responded slowly. He just nodded and looked around, tapping his fingers on the tile floor.

"How's eighth grade going for you?" Danny said, pausing now and then as if he was trying to figure out if that was the best question to ask.

I rolled my head and stared directly at him, my voice low. "It sucks."

Danny let out a combination laugh and sigh, smiling at me. "Yeah, I should've seen that response coming." He was about to say something else, no doubt another question, when I cut him off.

"Danny – what are you doing here? You do realize you're in the girls' bathroom, right? So *why* are you sitting here talking to me?" I asked. It came out a little snappier than I would have liked, but I was on the edge.

"It's called empathy, Audrey," Danny snapped. "I just thought you'd appreciate some."

I didn't know what to say, and I needed somewhere to stare, so I looked up at the ceiling. "You don't even know," I whispered, not really knowing what I meant by it.

I saw out of the corner of my eye that Danny was making gestures in the air with his palm. "I mean, I don't think this year has been that great for anyone, Audrey, if that makes you feel any better."

We were both staring up at the ceiling now. "Really?" I said. "It seems to me that McKenna, McKailey, and McKinley are enjoying themselves enough." I started laughing then and said, half to myself, "God, it sounds so awkward to say their names all together out loud."

"Yeah, I know," Danny said. "But, if it makes you feel any better, you don't have to any more."

"Huh?" I said, confused about what he meant.

"They titled themselves as a group. They made up a name for all three of them and they want everyone to call them that now."

I let out a sharp burst of laughter. "Are you joking? That's ridiculous!" I waited a few seconds before grinning and asking, "What is it?"

Danny responded slowly, as if he was dragging out every juicy syllable. "The M-C-Ks."

We both just laughed, staring up at the white tiled ceiling as if all the answers were up there.

"So really, Danny, why are you here? You seem to be trying to make me feel better. Is that your goal?"

He smiled, leaning forward and pulling his legs to his chest with his hands. With his blond hair and blue eyes, he looked very much like a little boy. "I don't know, I just... I saw that you were upset today and I...," he looked up again, in a search for answers that would never end. "Jacklyn told me she wasn't quite sure how you were doing. If you were convinced you were going crazy or if you felt like you had no friends...." He looked at me then and grinned, his eyes piercing, "I'm really just the messenger."

I smiled. "Well, I appreciate it."

Danny nodded his head, as though confirming something to himself. Then he continued. "So, how are you? I mean, besides the whole eighth grade sucks thing."

I shrugged, drying my eyes a little bit more. "I'm... confused." That didn't seem like the right word to explain it, but it was the closest I could come. "I guess I don't even know what I'm doing here any more."

"Like at this school?" Danny asked, his voice warm. "Or do you mean in general, like on this earth?" He held his hands out in defense. "Are you going to get all deep on me? Because I don't think I can handle that."

I laughed at his very boy-like panic. "I meant I didn't know what I was doing in this stall," I said, grinning at him now. "But we can go deep if you want!"

"No, no, I'm good!" he exclaimed, and then paused. "Well, what *are* you still doing in this stall?"

I sighed, my hands flopping off my legs in defeat. "Being scared," I said, "mostly just being scared." I felt like such a child saying it.

"Why are you scared?" he asked.

"I'm scared to... move on. No, that's not the right word. I'm scared to go out there and be myself again." I looked at him, wondering if he was listening to my indecisive answer. "In fact, I'm not even sure if I know who 'myself' is any more."

"Who do you want to be?" he asked. The timing of his questions was so spot-on that it was ridiculous. The insight flowing from him was so unexpected that I found myself caught off guard for a second, staring at him as if he was a completely new person. I thought for a moment that he would make a great psychiatrist later in life.

"I want to be someone who's not scared," I stated when I could finally talk again, laughing at myself. I was going in circles. I wanted to stop going in circles.

"So, what's stopping you?" Danny asked. "Go out there, right now, and stop being afraid. No one's stopping you, Audrey."

I smiled at him. "I guess not. It's just that sometimes I feel like I'm the only one in the world who feels the way I do. Or even worse – that

I'm making everything up."

"Of course you're not making it up! *I* know that, the rest of the guys know that. Pretty much everyone in the school knows."

I shook my head. It was so hard to hear it. "Are we talking about the same thing?" I asked. I had to make sure.

"I'm pretty sure. We all just thought it wasn't affecting you." Here he looked up at the ceiling again for a second, and then back at me. "But if it is, we're here to help, when needed."

I breathed out through a smile and looked at Danny, thanking him wordlessly. He smiled back, and his blue eyes were flecked with a paler blue that shone with sincerity.

"You know," he said, "I've always wanted to come in here."

I laughed loudly. "Are you serious? You've wanted to come into the girls' bathroom?"

He became defensive. "Well, not for the reasons you think," he said, making me laugh again. "I'm not like that. I've just always been curious. It's so much nicer in here, it's unfair! I mean, you girls have a table, a cabinet, *air freshener*.... Your bathroom smells like strawberries. Ours smells like dirty gym socks."

We both laughed, and then fell into a comfortable silence. True, we were still both huddled on the dirty floor of a girls' bathroom and I had just been humiliated by my pomegranate stained pants, but the air held a warmth that made all of that seem irrelevant. I looked up and thought about how Danny's eyes had seemed so open and true; so reflective. The light fixtures on the bathroom ceiling sent out light rays that danced off the tiles in a similar way, making the normally dirty surface shine like diamonds.

Something that had previously seemed so untouchable was that much closer to me now.

It was another ten minutes before Danny and I got up and left.

— ROLLERCOASTER —
c h a p t e r | e i g h t e e n

I was strangely calm as I finally left the school that day. I felt settled, as if I didn't have as many worries to battle as before. It was similar to how I had felt after the long conversation in Mrs. Darwin's office because, just like then, I had gained more insight. I found it a bit amusing that it seemed I had to be taught my lessons through conversations with other people. Mrs. Darwin has shown me that I needed to have courage, and now I realized that on top of that, I needed to have acceptance. Now, not only was I accepting the newly named M-C-Ks' behavior, I also planned not to let it bother me any more. I was going to make them give up the games they were playing with me through the best, though hardest, way: not caring.

For the first time in months, I was able to get out of bed in the morning without the assistance of my mom threatening to come up with cold water. I was able to load my things into my backpack and walk out the door without dreading the day ahead. I even found myself rushing out of my class before lunch in order to get to the lunch room early. At first I wasn't sure why, but then I realized it was because I was eager to *not* connect with them, to show them that I didn't care. I was eager to be a living, interacting human being again. I finally felt like one again.

It was ridiculous, I knew, to be feeling so high off the ground – so over it. But what I was feeling was so amazing, in a way that I couldn't explain, that I couldn't resist acting on it. The sensation of confidence only got stronger as I walked over and sat down with Grace, Larken, and the other seventh grade girls. I thought about sitting right next to

Grace and Larken, since I knew them the best, but they usually sat all the way off to the side. It seemed to me that if I was breaking away from the M-C-Ks, I might as well make it a point to talk to every single one of the girls at this new table. I was ready to spread my newfound spark.

I was sitting comfortably on the bench and had started to unwrap my sandwich when I felt them enter the room. I couldn't help myself; I looked up. When my eyes focused on their moving figures I got a huge surprise. They weren't going to sit at our – *their* – normal table. Instead McKenna was leading the other two straight towards me. Well, not exactly me, but the table I was sitting at. They were coming to sit with the seventh grade girls. I saw my confusion mirrored in the other girls' eyes as the three older girls sat down on the bench opposite mine. I made it a point not to acknowledge their presence. Amazingly, it was quite easy. It wasn't like they would say hi back, anyway.

They sat down and I carried on. I conversed with Grace about how our moms had made us the exact same sandwich for lunch: ham and cheese with tomato. I laughed with Larken and Lia over how stupid carrots look when they are cut in half. I continued on like this for the first twenty minutes of lunch period. It was nice; it was joyful. I felt fine.

I tried my best not to make eye contact with the M-C-Ks, and I succeeded for a while. However, when I traded food with a girl at the other end of the table, I had to lean forward. As I stretched my body out, I glanced up and my eyes locked with McKenna's. As I stared into her eyes, a jolt of energy swept through me and I knew, in that moment, that she *knew*. She knew I was done with them. She realized that I wasn't clinging onto them any more. I was letting myself be free and be myself.

She was scared.

I stayed in that position as the energy continued to flow, buoying me up. As if I were at the top of a rollercoaster, my stomach was on edge, anticipating the thrill of the descent. It was the same thrill I'd had the day after the dance, only stronger.

As the day went on, the thrill dissolved from a rush of happiness into a nagging responsibility in the back of my mind. I'd built up my courage and talked about being bullied with Jacklyn, Mrs. Darwin, and even Danny. And apparently almost the entire school knew about it or had a hunch something was wrong. However, I felt guilty about the two main people who didn't know: my parents.

Don't get me wrong, I have as a good a relationship with my parents as the next girl, but I've never been good at starting up awkward conversations with them. Awkward, meaning serious. Our relationship had always been fluffy, concentrating on the funny moments in life, not the serious. I felt horribly guilty that the worst of the situation was past and I hadn't yet told them. I knew that I should have done it a long time ago. I needed to tell them soon.

When I got home, the thought was still nagging me like a bug bite that wouldn't heal, itching constantly. I couldn't just walk up to them and start talking. I needed to concentrate first, long and hard. I needed a conversation starter, or a list of ways that I could deal with whatever reaction they had. I needed to go where I could think, with no distractions.

I slipped past my mom's "how was your day?" spiel (I had gotten really good at it over the past month or so) and ran up to my room and into the shower. That seemed like the safest place to escape. I turned on the water and let it run for a while over my hand, watching in fascination as the sensation slowly turned from cold to heat. I stepped forward and let the hot water wash away the dirt; I tried to let it wash away everything.

As I stood under the water, I tried to think of good conversation starters. *Hi Mom, I know you haven't heard about school in a while. It's actually a funny story….*

No. I wasn't going that route. *You know what I've learned from Jacklyn moving away? I've learned that a lot of people in this world suck at being friends.*

No. Too negative. Perhaps something that would immediately excuse her from any guilt. *You know, I went into middle school not really sure what to expect. You helped with that a lot, Mom. You really taught me how to deal with difficult personal situations.*

No. That was an absolute lie. I wasn't getting anywhere.

Nervously, I laced my hands together, alternately wringing and untwisting them, not knowing how to get this conversation started. I stared at my feet and watched as the water ran down my leg in one clean strand and then bounced out into individual drops as it hit the curve at the top of my foot. The drops disappeared, rolling off and onto the smooth tile.

I thought about how much happier I was now; it was almost shocking. I had only needed to take one step away, and the girls' presence no longer pressed on my shoulders everywhere I went. I felt free, like I was in control of my life.

Shouldn't that be all that mattered? The fact that I was happy, or on the verge of being happy? My mom shouldn't have to worry about the stupid things that the M-C-Ks were doing (and they really were stupid). She should only have to worry about me, and my happiness. I should be able to just walk up and tell her what was happening at school, but then tell her that I'm happier – and that's all that matters.

That was what I was going to do.

I shut off the stream of water and dried myself slowly. Stepping out of the shower was easy; combing my hair was easy; approaching my mom, however, was not easy, no matter how much I had prepared. But my burst of happiness propelled me on.

"Mom," I said as I approached the bottom of the stairs and saw her standing near the island in the kitchen, "I need to tell you something." I was surprised at how completely nonchalant and light the words came out, which was probably for the better anyway. No need to make my mother have a panic attack.

"Finally," my mom said with a laugh. "You haven't told me anything in so long, I was getting worried!"

With good reason, I thought, but shook my head and continued on. "Recently, at school, I noticed some odd things happening."

"Oh? Like what?" my mom asked, looking back down at her cutting board. Now that she thought that she wasn't getting any drama or gossip, she had gone back into classic mom mode. Maybe that was better for me, though. I could tell her, get it off my shoulders, and move on.

"It just… kind of seemed like *maybe*…" I was toning it down too much. I stopped myself. I needed to give her the bitter truth. "It seemed like the other eighth grade girls started to kind of exclude me."

My mom's brown eyes shot up and she stared at me, but I couldn't tell what emotion powered the sudden movement. Her eyes were pools of warm chocolate, wise, beautiful in the center but pierced with fear at the edges.

"What do you mean, excluding you?" my mom asked in a fluttery voice.

"They stopped talking to me, stopped really paying attention to me, started running away from me, started insulting me with stupid comments that were really metaphors for some part of my body." I saw the panicked look on my mother's face and backtracked. "But, that's just what I think! I don't really know." When the panic didn't fade from her face, I looked down. *Was this the right thing to do?*

"O-oh my goodness... Audrey!" She couldn't seem to get a full sentence out.

"But it's okay now, Mom," I rushed ahead quickly, holding my hands up as if she was going to faint and I needed to catch her. Actually, was she going to pass out? She stood there, looking straight ahead with eyes that had suddenly increased in size.

"Is it really? Has it gone away completely?" she asked.

"Well," I began, acting as if I was prepared to answer this question. But then I saw the fear in her face and decided she deserved at least the raw truth. "No. It hasn't." I was almost ashamed of that fact.

"Then it's not okay."

"I'm sorry," I said, even though I didn't know why. I spit out those two words whenever I don't know what to say next, because they are good at filling the air. "But I've improved a lot," I said, speaking slowly and looking down at my hands. "I'm not letting it bother me any more and I'm recovering from what they did before."

"I'm sorry too," my mom said, reaching forward into a hug. "Your father and I never thought that... we never expected you'd be forced to deal with something like this." She seemed to be having as much trouble getting words out as I did. "I mean, why should we? You're so outgoing. It's always seemed like you're not one to let others affect you that way," she burst out.

"I know, I know!" I said, amazed that we were thinking the same thing. "That's what I said!" I paused for a moment and said a bit quieter, "I felt like it was unlike me. It's so weird."

My mom almost laughed, hugging me even harder. "Thank you so much for telling me, Audrey. It must have been hard to do that."

"Yeah," I said, closing my eyes. "I had to work to get it out."

"I can't magically fix everything," she said, but I didn't know if it was to me or herself.

That reminded me. "Promise me, Mom, that you won't get involved in this. I promised Mrs. Darwin that I wouldn't speak about this to any other teachers and neither would she, because they would just freak out. Instead we're working through this together in a less obvious way."

My mom pulled back, looking shocked. "Are you sure that's the best idea? I mean, I know Eastwood has no tolerance for bullying but – "

"It's for the best, Mom," I reassured her. "Besides, it's already getting better. I'm learning."

My mom sighed and hugged me again, then pulled back sharply. "Hey, why did Mrs. Darwin know about this before I did?" she said in a suspicious voice.

"Uh...," I began, not exactly ready to tell her about my breakdowns in the closet and the bathroom. She wasn't ready for that yet. "I'm so sorry, Mom!"

"Oh, I guess I should just be glad you told me at all." She hugged me again. "I promise you, Audrey, the bad times will end soon. Just continue being yourself and remember that you are an amazing person." It was such a cliché mom thing to say, and yet it made my insides warm up like they were being filled with warm cocoa.

"Thank you, Mom," I said, sighing into the hug. I wrapped my arms around her tighter and reveled in the support her frame gave me, not wanting to let go. "I love you."

— THE DREAM —
chapter | nineteen

As the weather got colder and we spent more and more breaks indoors, I got used to hanging out with the boys. The transition began slowly, with me sitting next to them on the days when there was a spare seat. Then I gradually began to come over to them more often, getting more and more used to their boyish conversations. Did this mean I was becoming more like a boy? Not at all. However, they did tease me enough on the subject.

"How am I supposed to feel comfortable talking about all my private guy stuff when there's a girl around?" Eliot whined one day. "It's not fair."

"Do you realize how much you sound like a girl just by saying that?" I retorted, amused at Eliot's hurt look.

"No one cares about your whining, Eliot," said Reese, rolling his eyes.

"Well, there's no need to be *rude*," I said back, not liking how mean-spirited Reese could be at times.

"Calm down, guys," Danny said as he leaned back. We were all seated on a big cushion that had been laid out in the middle of the English room for use during indoor breaks. The boys, however, had taken over the cushion before anyone else even had a chance to get to it, spreading themselves out and propping their feet up in the center on a pillow. They had, however, allowed me to come and join their circle, though I was banished to sitting crossed legged in the farthest corner of the cushion between Eliot and Ronnie. I didn't mind; at least I was *in* the circle.

"There's no reason to get uptight around Audrey," Danny continued, sliding his hair out of his eyes with his hand. "She's like one of the boys now." He grinned, knowing how that would get to me.

"I am not!" I said, self-consciously playing with my hair, which I had curled that morning so that it streamed over my shoulders like a cascade of blonde water.

"I agree," interjected Ronnie, sticking his tongue out. "She's *definitely* not a boy. I mean, look at that hair! She obviously spent like thirty minutes this morning doing it."

"Oh, like you don't spend that long on your hair, Ronnie," Ian said. Then he launched into an imitation of Ronnie combing his hair, humming a song to himself like a Disney princess. Everyone laughed. I barely even noticed that the M-C-Ks were sitting off to the side in the area under the staircase to the storage room. I barely even noticed that they were laughing too. Barely.

"I wonder what they're laughing about," I said quietly, mostly to myself, as I shook my head. I couldn't help it. It seemed almost sad the way they were separated from the rest, sitting off in that corner, but there was still that gleam in their eye that made me shiver. They were obviously up to something.

"Who cares," Ian declared, messing with the laces of his shoe.

"Why in hell does it matter?" Trey asked, a smirk on his lips.

"I don't know, I just can't help it!" I leaned forward and pointed at the nook where they were sitting. "Look at how they're squished off to the side with those little grins on their faces. They're so happy for some reason, you can just tell by the excitement in their eyes."

"I repeat: why does it matter?" Trey asked again, separating every word.

"Girls are so weird," Reese declared. "They worry about stupid things like their hair and their nails and what *other* girls are laughing at. It's ridiculous."

"Yeah, why do you have to be such a girl, Audrey?" Trey asked, looking at me accusingly. Danny started laughing, and I wanted to as well, but I managed to keep a straight face.

"Uh, maybe because I *am* one?" I exclaimed, half laughing. "Oh my God, Ian, what are you doing?" I asked in an exasperated voice, ready for some crazy story. During our conversation, he had been trying to tie or untie the laces of his shoe, and now he had taken his right shoe completely off and seemed to be trying to stuff his face inside it.

He looked up, alarmed that I had asked. "My shoe was refusing to stay tied, so now I'm trying to see if maybe my socks have made it smell too bad for the laces to stay together," he said to me as if it was the most sensible thing in the world. Both his face and his voice seemed to belong to a small child. I stared at him with disgust on my face as he smiled guiltily. I tried not to gag at how unintellectual this entire conversation was.

"You guys are *so* gross," I said, throwing my hands up in defeat. They laughed.

In addition to becoming comfortable with hanging around with the boys, I had also made progress in my relationships with each individual boy. It was strange to realize that each had his own personality to bring to conversations, instead of being the lumps of brainless flesh that they seem to be when they're together. I was soon having enjoyable one-on-one conversations with Danny, Ronnie, Ian, and even Cash.

Especially Cash.

In New Mexico, adults apparently think that a little cold wind will cause you to get pneumonia and die. But on the rare days when we were allowed outside for breaks, Cash and I developed the habit of walking in circles around the abandoned soccer field, talking about the most random of things. We were able to do this because the boys had finally given up on playing basketball, accepting that winter was finally upon us.

One day, Cash decided he needed to advise me on how to "further" my friendship with the boys, or at least make sure that it continued to exist.

"Don't get me wrong, we have no problem with you hanging around, but I just think there are a few things you should seriously think about doing," he said.

"Okay," I said, a little afraid of what these things would be. "And what are they exactly?"

"Well," he began, obviously happy that I was going to let him have his moment, "for one, don't talk about girl things so much. See, us guys have a brain capacity that simply can't handle that."

I laughed at the underlying tones of sexism in his comment. "Are you mocking me?"

He cocked an eyebrow. "Maybe. But seriously, think about it. Are you ready for number two?"

"Oh great, there's another one?" I complained. "Is this one actually serious?"

"Well…"

I sighed. "Just go on."

He grinned. "You should chat with us online after school and on weekends. That's where most of our social life takes place."

I gave him a horrified look. "Are you kidding? *That's* how you interact most of the time, through online chatting? Are you at least having worthwhile conversations?"

"Nope." He shook his head. "We mostly play games. Like Twenty Questions or Would You Rather."

"Couldn't you just play those in real life? That way you'd at least be face to face," I suggested. I mean, I was all for enjoying the benefits of being able to communicate online, but these people didn't seem to understand the value of companionship.

Cash shrugged. "I don't know. That would just be weird."

"Nonsense." I looked around, seeing if I could find something that would help me think of a way to prove it to him. None of the other boys were within sight. I turned back to him and smiled. "Play it with me."

"Huh?" He scratched his head and then stopped walking, stuffing his hands into the pockets of his dark blue jacket. "Play one of those stupid question games with me, right now," I continued. "Then you'll see that it's not so strange."

"Uh, I don't know, Audrey –"

"Come on, chicken! Let's play Twenty Questions. Ask me a question!" I grinned. I wanted to win.

He looked nervous for a second, but then grinned back. "Fine. Who do you like?"

My grin instantly disappeared. "*That's* a question you can ask?"

"Yeah," Cash said in the classic *duh* voice, making me feel stupid. "What did you think? Now come on, answer the question."

"No!"

"Why not?"

"Because first of all," I turned around again, this time looking for a way out, "that's not how you play Twenty Questions. And second, I don't feel comfortable telling you that." I could feel my cheeks heating up. I pulled up the collar of my jacket, trying to hide the slowly growing circles of crimson. I wasn't sure if my embarrassment was because of the question or because *Cash* was asking the question. But that was something I didn't want to think about.

"Why not?" he said again. "Just the other day you were talking about how much more of a family you feel like our class is now. So come on, 'fess up. Family members tell each other things like this."

I stuck my chin out. "No, that's ridiculous. Ask me a different question."

Cash sighed. "Fine," he said in a monotone voice. He was silent for a minute before he spoke again. "Who was your first kiss?"

"Cash!" I yelled, hitting him on the shoulder.

"Ouch," he muttered to himself, and then laughed. "Come on, Aud, what did you think these questions were going to be about?"

"I don't know... just something besides boys, or in your case, girls." I sighed. "I guess I should've known better."

"Yeah!" Cash yelled back. There was the *"duh"* voice again. "What did you think? That we would be asking questions about our hopes and our dreams, our most intimate desires?" His voice got higher as the sentence went on. He was obviously mimicking me.

I hit him on the shoulder again. "That would've been better! It gets tiring to be around all this boy talk 24/7."

"Well then, why don't you leave us in the dust and go find some *girl*friends your own age to talk to?" he teased.

I fell silent.

So did he, once he realized his mistake. His face turned neutral. "Hey," he said quietly, bumping my shoulder with his. "I didn't mean that. I meant –"

"It's fine," I said quickly. "I mean, it's not your fault."

"So, let's," Cash said.

"Let's what?"

"Let's talk about girl stuff. I mean, since you don't have any girls around. What should we talk about, our dreams?" he said again, but seriously this time. I just stared at him. He coughed awkwardly. "I'll start. I had a really funny dream last night."

"Oh?" I commented, looking down. This was extremely awkward, but also interesting and, in a way, touching.

"Yeah. Uh – we were both in it. It was me, Ronnie, Ian, Danny, and you."

My eyes popped open wide. *Me? I was in it?*

"We were all on a desert island," he continued, "kind of like in the last *Treasure Island* movie. And we were climbing around on the rocks and swimming and it was really nice. And then something went wrong. I don't know exactly – it was one of those dreams where you just know something is really wrong all of a sudden. Danny, Ronnie, Ian and I got stuck in the rocks, and we couldn't get out and there was no food or water. And you had to run around the rocks in this certain pattern in order to get them to open up so that we could get out. And in the end you did – you saved us and we all got out and… then everything was okay."

We were still standing where we had previously stopped walking –

just standing in the middle of the field. I had been staring at him while he told me his story, but staring had probably been a bad idea. No reason to get caught up in his eyes, which I was now having difficulties not falling into. Had his irises changed colors again? Or were they the same green as before? I couldn't remember. All I could remember was that he had just dreamed about me. Well, not *about* me, but I had been in his dream.

"Audrey?" I heard Cash say. "Are you there?"

"Yeah, yeah," I said, quickly coming back to the present. "Sorry, my head has been in the clouds all day today."

"I can tell," Cash said, chuckling. "So, are you going to answer my question?"

"What question?" I wrinkled my forehead. I couldn't remember him asking me a question. All I could remember was him telling me about his dream, and looking at me in that weird way.

Goodness, this was bad. And then he was smiling again and my vision was clouding over with sparks of bronze and this *really* needed to stop. I needed to get away from his smile, from his eyes, from the way he was talking to me. I wanted to slow it all down, but I couldn't. I could tell that, whatever this was, the damage had already been done. Where was Trey with his crude jokes when I needed him?

"I asked you what you dream about," he said.

"Oh, um…." My forehead was still wrinkled and I couldn't, for the life of me, think of something to say.

Your eyes, I wanted to say. *I dream about being an artist and getting to paint your eyes, having to spend hours picking my colors because it is just so hard to define them.* "Uh…"

And then the bell rang. The bell rang and Cash's head whipped around, and I could've sworn he looked disappointed, which was bad. This was all bad. Why was I suddenly so happy and so worried all at once? *Please stop dreaming about me,* my inner thoughts begged him. *This can't be happening. I just need a friend.* Why was this happening? I did not like Cash. *I do not like Johnny Price,* I told myself.

The bell was still ringing and so was my head, and I watched in awe as Cash walked away without my answer to his question.

Saved by the bell.

— KALEIDOSCOPE —
chapter | twenty

"Well, *duh* Cash likes you!" Larken whispered to me as we sat on the pile of snow that the second and third graders had heaped up during their break.

I breathed out sharply and tried to ignore the warm flutters that filled my stomach. "*No, he does not.*" Larken was staring me down. "He can't. Anyways, relationships like this in middle school are always so pointless because all it does is ruin your friendship. I can't afford that right now. I like being able to hang out with the boys."

"I know, I know," Larken said, patting me on the shoulder and softening her voice. "I like that you are able to hang out with them too. I'm glad the boys are your friends now. You're so much better than *them.*" She said it in a way so that I knew exactly who *them* were.

"Really?" The word slipped out of my mouth without wanting a response. I looked at Larken and she smiled. I suddenly felt so grateful for this kind girl who had been there for me throughout this crisis. "Thanks," I said, smiling back. "And I realize that we're not super-close, so I'm especially grateful that I have you and Grace to talk to whenever I need to get some things off my chest. I mean, the boys are hilarious, but sometimes I just need some girl advice."

Larken laughed, and I was slowly beginning to figure out why her parents had named her that. "You're welcome. I'm glad I've had the opportunity to get to know you better." She looked down for a moment. "To be honest, I was sort of afraid of you last year."

I was shocked. "What? Why?"

"I don't know," she said, looking down when she saw how I was staring at her. It was obvious from her gleaming eyes that she did know. I urged her on. "You and Jacklyn," she began, "you guys had all the power last year. I saw the way you pranced around the school in this happy-go-lucky way, like you never had to worry about anything. And you didn't. You had every inch of each other's backs covered, and it was fascinating, it was intriguing. I wanted to just understand how you were able to build up that atmosphere!" I stared at her with a blank face as she reminisced and her eyes lit up with each memory of Jacklyn's and my effective shield, the one we built and sealed to keep out all aspects of weakness. "But," she continued, "I also saw how you treated the people who got too near to your circle. I saw how you treated the people who didn't seem to be fascinated by you, people like Sarah and Emmaline." My stomach began to twist, wringing all the warm feelings away. That was a past I didn't want to think about. But I couldn't block out the question that was slowly working its way in – *was this true?*

"I'm sorry, Larken," I interrupted. "I have to go." She stared up at me in confusion as I pulled my jacket tight and walked away, my mind on the genuine apology that I had just made, partly because I was leaving in the middle of her story and partly on behalf of the story itself – for the fact that I had ever once been that person. Larken made that person sound horrible.

My friendships with the boys continued to be as wonderful as ever, giving me the will to try harder and harder to completely pull myself away from the M-C-Ks. I had succeeded in removing myself physically from their lives, now I had to succeed mentally. As I slowly built up my confidence to the level it had been before the ordeal began, my attitudes and thoughts were changing. It was weird – despite the happiness, my feelings and thoughts felt all broken and mixed up. Like a kaleidoscope, they rotated from sad to happy, from lonely to loved, from scared to defiant, from circle to square, from green to red.

I wanted to stand up for myself, to make some kind of comment to the M-C-Ks. I wanted to rub something in their faces, to go up and say, *Ha, ha; I won and you lost.* But I *wasn't* going to do that, because that was against everything I had decided I wanted to be. The old Audrey might have done that, but I wasn't that person any more. Especially after what Larken had told me. That wasn't how I was going to deal with this situation.

During the last period of the day, the teachers had started a special class for eighth graders, where they taught us the social and study skills they said we would need for high school. I found it quite interesting, since I didn't have parents who told me about these kinds of things. But it was obvious that other people – at least, people whose names start with the letters M-C-K – found it incredibly boring. *Well, too bad for them.*

When we were lucky, we had a ten or fifteen minute study hall at the end of the period to start on our homework. One day the boys and I were working on an especially difficult math problem, and we were so stumped that we had to get Mrs. Krashaw to come and help us at the white board.

It was really amusing, since Mrs. Krashaw was not a math teacher. Eventually we were all running up and trying to help *her* help us. I was laughing so much I almost forgot we were doing math. As I was leaning against the table with Danny, both of us half suffocated with laughter as we tried to help Mrs. Krashaw figure out how to factor a polynomial, my ears picked up what the M-C-Ks were whispering in the corner.

"Do you hear them over there? Absolutely freaking out about math."

"Yeah, I know, what dorks!"

"Dorks, more like nerds."

"It's not like poly-oli-nomials, or whatever they are called, are that funny."

"Losers."

They all whispered the last word over and over again, overlapping each other and laughing quietly like hyenas. I couldn't help myself. Every blood vessel in my being was at the boiling point. I stopped laughed, stood up, slowly turned my head to the side and stared at them. I gave them the meanest stare that I had ever given in my life. I could feel the hate and frustration pouring out of my eyes in tangible waves. I gave them an *oh-my-God-you-are-so-immature* glare. *Shut up,* I thought. *If you know what's good for you, just shut up.*

McKailey must have been able to feel it too, because she slowly stopped laughing. Their laughs, which at first had been lively sounds, turned into forced syllables that sounded a lot like *"ha."* She held up her hands and made the other girls stop laughing too, dropping them to the table as she looked down and the humor drained from her eyes. I quickly looked back at Danny, suddenly realizing what I had just done. *That was bad. You shouldn't have let yourself slip like that.* It had felt good, I realized. It had felt really good to squelch their merriment. *Well, no harm done, I guess. Just be careful.* I couldn't let myself explode, because I could guarantee that the outcome would not be pretty or good.

One day we were given descriptions of different ways people classify themselves socially in high school, and then asked to divide into groups and dissect the psychological reasons behind the classifications. Each group was then given a list of character names along with descriptions of their activities, and asked to decide what social category they fit best. Unfortunately for us, Mrs. Krashaw didn't let us pick our own groups. Unfortunately for *me*, I was paired with McKenna, McKailey, and McKinley.

We awkwardly sat down on the floor in a corner of the room and sat in silence for a few seconds. The only sound besides the conversations of the other groups was McKailey's sudden eruptions into random hyena-esque laughter. I rolled my eyes and grabbed one of the papers with our descriptions, starting to work on where to place people. I swore to myself that if McKailey laughed one more time I would throw my backpack at her face, but then quickly took it back. *Calm down*, I told myself. *Geez.*

We worked this way, not having any group interaction at all, until McKenna spoke up.

"So, we should obviously put this Tabitha character in the cheerleader group. She's clearly going to be popular, and a leader."

"Really?" I asked, looking back over Tabitha's description. It said that Tabitha was a 14 year old girl who had trained for the last seven years in swimming, gymnastics, and track, and she needed to be constantly moving to be happy. "I think she would fit in better with the athletes group. She could do track and field."

"Not going to work," McKenna said, shaking her head like a dog who doesn't want to let go of a bone. "Female athletes are rarely very popular unless they are cheerleaders, so we have to put her there. She *needs* to be popular," she stated firmly, and then muttered in a mean-spirited voice, "and with that name, she's going to need all the help she can get. I mean, 'Tabitha' sounds like the name of a wrinkly old lady."

So rude, I thought. I felt a pressure – hate – exploding in my head again. I pushed up onto my knees so that I was a bit higher than McKenna and said with a twisted face, "Excuse me, but who died and made *you* queen of everything?"

The entire room went silent. It was only then that I realized how loud I had been speaking.

"I'm sorry," I whispered in a breathless voice, my eyes wide, as everyone's eyes bored into my frozen figure. I was in a state of shock, breathing hard as I stared at McKenna. She had turned white, and I could clearly see the dry patches of skin where she had tanned too much and the places where her recent honey blond dye job had gone off in the wrong direction, leaving dark strands here and there. She didn't look hurt, or even shocked, but her face had drained of every emotion.

"I'm sorry," I said again, and I truly was. McKenna livened up a little bit, twitching her fingers, and she just looked overwhelmed and confused at the fact that I was apologizing. And of course she was confused – she didn't understand. She didn't understand that old-Audrey was different from new-Audrey, because that was not how McKenna lived – she didn't believe in people changing like that. She didn't believe that there was a *reason* to even change, or even apologize for any wrong-doing that had happened in the past. To her it was just that – the past – something that should be forgiven without reason and forgotten. That was so clear to me now. I stared at my ex-best friend as this new clarity helped return the feeling to my body.

Then I gathered up my stuff and walked out of the classroom and to the bathroom.

— CRAZIER —
chapter | twenty – one

I gradually became able to control the rage inside of me as, day by day, it withered away. Even if the anger was only submerged for the time being, it was a relief not to have to worry about it on a daily basis – not to have to worry if one little action by the M-C-Ks would set me off.

As the weeks wore on, my life slowly returned to what it used to be, except that my friends were now mostly boys. But apparently that made a difference not only in my life but also in me. At least that's what my parents said.

"You're different," my dad said, pointing his fork at me as we sat at the dinner table.

"I'm sorry?" I asked with a smile. We had just finished laughing over memories of my mom's failed cooking attempts; she hadn't always been so amazing in the kitchen. True, her chicken casserole was amazing *now*, but once upon a time it had tasted like old rubber and was the reason our kitchen almost burned down. That memory usually sent my dad and me into uncontrollable fits of laughter, making my mom to blush redder then a cherry.

"You're different," my dad repeated, smiling widely, "more lively."

I looked down at my plate, embarrassed. "Thanks?" I said, unsure, and I knew I was blushing.

"It's because of her friends," my mom said, standing up and starting to pile up the plates. "Her new friends," she added, winking, and I began to feel uncomfortable. My dad didn't know that I had spent the past month hanging out almost entirely with boys. I wasn't sure he'd be too thrilled about it.

"Well then," my dad said, leaning forward, "you must tell me all about these *amazing* friends who have brought the light back into my daughter's eyes." I didn't answer and we sat there for a moment in silence. He spoke again, this time in a softer voice. "I know I'm not home a lot, but your mom told me about what was happening at school. I just want you to know that I think you're so amazing and brave for getting through that." He got up and kissed me on the head. "Maybe, one day, you can tell me all about it. When you're ready." He smiled at me one more time and his blue eyes twinkled. They were cobalt, a dark majestic blue shade that I'd never been able to name as a child, but that I loved more than the stars in the sky.

As he walked away and up the stairs, my focus moved to my mom, who was still standing and smiling at me. "You're afraid of what he will think, aren't you?" she said. "Afraid he'll get all upset when he finds out that they are all boys."

I got defensive, even though she was right. "They aren't all boys," I insisted, my voice like a little child's. "I have Grace and Larken too."

"Fine," she said softly as she sat down next to me, "but the ones who are making a difference are boys."

I smiled and looked down again, but not before noticing that my mom's face still wore a bright smile. "I used to think boys were a different species who liked to spend their time joking about immature things and never really connecting with each other," I said, still looking down. "But now, as I spend more time with them, I see that they are all individuals. They just care about different things than girls do." I was speaking slowly, picking my words with care. "And it's great, because they don't care about any of the stupid stuff. The hate, the petty little acts, the drama – they don't get sucked into that. They just let all of that stuff go. All they care about is the fact that we get along. We get along and they have each other's backs and that's it." I smiled wider. "It's so simple. It's so very simple and I never realized it could be that way."

"True," my mom agreed, stroking my hair. "But be careful, because it can also get kind of crazy. Because they're like this and you're like that and together you're even crazier."

I could tell that my mom was picking her words with care, as if they were overripe fruit that could burst. I tilted my head to the side and thought about what she had said. I wasn't sure if it completely made sense to me, but I had gotten the gist of what she was trying to say. She was starting to veer off into delicate territory, and suddenly I was sure of what she was going to say next.

"I bet one of them has a crush on you," she whispered into my ear. Even though I saw it coming, her teasing made me uncomfortable, and I jumped up off the chair, half laughing.

"No!"

"Yes," she stated calmly. She was still calm, and suddenly I wasn't. It was so unfair.

"No," I repeated, placing my hands on either side of my face and hoping that she couldn't see what I was thinking about. I started running away, up the stairs, just to be safe.

"You're just afraid of accepting this, Audrey," my mom called after me in a sing-song voice."

"No, we are *not* talking about this, Mom." I darted into my room and my mom appeared behind me. *How did she get up here so fast?* I thought, but was immediately distracted when she started to tickle me. "Mom, for goodness sakes! I'm fourteen!"

"Which is exactly why I'm doing this," my mom said between breaths. "Everyone can afford to be young once in a while." So I just laughed and my mom laughed and we kept on laughing into the night.

And I couldn't help thinking in the back of my mind about how much I had changed.

The following week at school we had parent-teacher conferences. Every family had an appointment to come in and talk with their child's homeroom teacher. Mine was Miss Theresa, a nice but sometimes timid woman. She let the boys in her class take advantage of her kindness too often. I had thought about telling her that multiple times, but always then decided it would be too awkward.

In preparation for my conference, I had to put together a portfolio of my work from the semester, which I would later go through with my parents, telling them why I was proud of each item. It was tedious work, but I guess it was intended to boost kids' self-esteem. As I went through my portfolio and thought about what to say about each item, I found that I got a large lump in my throat when I tried to talk about the assignments from late October and early November. I cleared my throat vigorously, trying to make the lumps go away. I couldn't have that problem in front of Miss Theresa, because she would most surely notice I was acting strange and want an explanation. I still remembered my promise to Mrs. Darwin.

My conference was scheduled for the 7th of December right after school, which was nice because I could just stay in Miss Theresa's room after we were released from homeroom at the end of the day. I settled down on the old couch with my portfolio on my lap and breathed out. My days had become packed recently, with me being more and more eager each day to come to school. I was suddenly finding opportunities to do things after school with my friends, and I never had to worry about sitting alone at lunch or having to play a game of hide and seek at break. During lunch I either sat with Grace and Larken or the boys. More and more, however, I had been sitting with the boys. They were a relief after the years of girl drama. I definitely believed now that every girl needed to have a guy best friend.

Miss Theresa tried to strike up an awkward conversation with me about how my year had been so far, but was interrupted by the entrance of my parents. I was thankful for their arrival, because I had no idea how I would even begin to describe how my year had been. *I've been riding a rollercoaster of emotions*, I could say, *except I went downhill first.*

I began to go through my most recent pieces one by one: a math test that I aced, an English essay that contained descriptions I was especially proud of, a project from our high school preparation time where I wrote a paragraph about whether I was nervous. Mrs. Krashaw had singled mine out for being "especially sensitive." The guys had found that hilarious. "God, you're such a girl, Audrey," Trey had said, shaking his head. He had said that a million times before, and his comment only made me smile more.

I was pleased at how easy it was for me to go through each assignment. As we traveled back in time through the semester, I found that I was able to get through November's and October's work too, thanks to my rehearsals.

"Okay, so I think we're done," I announced after I had finished telling them about the *How Was Your Summer?* essay that I had written for English at the beginning of the year.

"Wait," Miss Theresa said, her face looking like that of an excited chipmunk, "I have a surprise for your parents, Audrey!"

"Oh?" my mom asked. "What?"

"There was a poem contest in late October. We had a professional poet come in and give the kids a lesson on poetry, and then they wrote their own poems. Your daughter's free verse poem won the contest, and it was so wonderful that I think it would be a crime not to share it with you now." My mom and dad exchanged glances, shrugging their shoulders as if to say, *"All right, that sounds cool."* I, on the other hand, was looking back and forth from my parents to Miss Theresa, my stomach seizing up with nervousness. I wondered if I could call a time out, take my parents to the side of the room, and talk to them about what they need to *not* say during our conversation about the poem. Unfortunately, this wasn't a game of volleyball.

I had faint memories about this poem, but I was sure it was full of some very strong emotions. I remembered that the poet had come on October 30, the day after the field trip and two days after the bullying had started.

Miss Theresa, who had finally found the paper, walked over and held it out in the direction of my parents, but I snatched it away, quickly reading it over. On the crinkled up paper my handwriting said:

A week ago, I was excited about Halloween
I wanted to take part in the horror-filled scene
But now, it seems, I find myself not

Interested in what I previously sought

I think I'll be a heart for Halloween
A heart, split by a big, jagged seam;
Broken.

"That's... beautiful," my mom said slowly after she read it. My dad nodded his agreement in businessman style.

"I certainly thought so," Miss Theresa said. I wanted to wipe that beam off her face and make her realize that she was playing with fire, but she kept on going. "Tell me, Audrey, how were you able to put so much raw emotion and feeling into your words?"

"Oh, you know," I said in a shaky voice that I attempted to make sound modest, "I just dug deep down and managed to pull something out."

"It was because those stupid girls started to bully her," my mom muttered. She was leaning forward with her elbow on her knee and her chin propped on her hand, a frustrated look on her face.

Oh no. I wanted to slap myself across the forehead. I saw a confused look dawn on Miss Theresa's face. *Here we go*, I thought. *That's what you get when you toy with the emotions of a mother who is upset with your school because she thinks they've done an awful job of stopping her child from being bullied.*

"I'm sorry, they what?" she asked, obviously finding it hard to comprehend what was being said.

"Oh, nothing," I quickly covered up, even though it was obviously not nothing.

"No, tell me!" Miss Theresa insisted, looking back and forth between my mom and me. Her head was bouncing in an annoying manner and I just wanted to make it stop. "If s-s-s-something is happening here, I n-n-need to know!" she stuttered.

"Well, um," I began, feeling boxed in and glaring at my mom. Her face was still angry – she didn't seem to understand the mistake she had made or the bad situation I was now in. I breathed out heavily and decided I was not going to be able to lie my way out of this. Anyway, I was tired of covering stuff up. "Around late October the other eighth grade girls sort of started to exclude me," I said, repeating what I had said in telling the story to my mom.

"Oh, no," Miss Theresa whispered. She looked at me and I could feel sympathetic vibes rolling off her. I didn't feel like I needed those vibes any more. I curled my legs up to my chest and made my face look as reassuring as possible.

"It's okay, Miss Theresa. I mean, it's December now and I've moved on since then. Besides, the whole ordeal turned out to be good, in that it forced me to branch out to new friends. I've gotten so much closer to some people who I've been seeing every day since kindergarten, but until now I never actually understood *who* they were." I was surprised at the words that were flowing out of my mouth. And whether they were true or not, I knew that I needed to keep talking, to keep reassuring her until I was certain that thoughts of bullying were not going to keep her up at night. Otherwise – I didn't want to think of the consequences.

"Audrey, I... I can't believe that the faculty at Eastwood has let this slip under the radar. This is unacceptable. We need to call in these girls right away and speak to their parents." Miss Theresa looked more and more determined as she made this speech, and she started to stand up.

"No!" I squeaked, propelling myself forward. Miss Theresa faced me, still not able to comprehend. I could see in her eyes that she didn't understand the panic bubbling up in mine. My parents were still sitting on the couch calmly, not understanding. I tried to send distress signals to them over mind waves, but decided that the chances of our being telepathically connected were low. "Listen, Miss Theresa, I know that you might consider what you just heard to be an abomination that absolutely needs to be addressed," I began, wondering where I was getting all these dramatic words from, "but I assure you that I, with the help of some other people, have it absolutely under control."

Miss Theresa straightened up and stared at me, stony eyed. "Audrey," she said, snapping her feet together and assuming the posture of a soldier. "I know that you may think this is all under control, because you are a teenager and you think that adults shouldn't get involved in teenagers' problems. But I am an adult and I know better. Now, I cannot make you any promises that the school won't get involved." As her intense stare paralyzed me, I realized there was no way of stopping this woman on a mission.

A loud tap came at the door and Miss Theresa peered over my shoulder. "That's my next conference knocking," she said, returning to her cheerful voice. She turned back to my parents and clapped her hands together. "Mr. and Mrs. Bass, I'm afraid that our time is up. I thank you very much for coming. I think that we *both* learned a lot about Audrey. Until next time!" She smiled and waved goodbye like an attentive airplane pilot.

After we left the room I turned and looked at my parents. I could tell by the contented look in their eyes that they *still didn't get it*. So I turned around and walked back to the car in stony silence, a prickly feeling spreading across my skin. I brought my fingers up and stretched the skin under my eyes, trying to get rid of the hated feeling that I was about to cry.

Only after we were on our way home did my parents start to understand that something was wrong.

"Are you all right, Audrey?" my mom asked, a question that I'd heard at least 23,048,374 times in the last month and half. Well, maybe I'm exaggerating. Maybe.

"How could you say that?" I asked, staring out the window. I felt small and vulnerable sitting in the car, having no idea what was going to happen over the next few days or what I was going to have to face.

"Say what?" my mom asked. I could see that she was worried she had caused me more pain.

"Say that they were bullying me," I whispered. My mom twisted around in her seat and stared at me blankly. "You knew," I said, a bit louder. "You knew about the promise I had with Mrs. Darwin and you said it anyway!"

"I'm sorry, but I'm confused!" my mom half-yelled, her voice high. She grabbed my dad's forearm. "Do you understand her, Charlie?"

"Calm down, Blaire, I'm driving," he said calmly. My dad was used to dealing with my mom when she started to panic. "Audrey is saying that she made a promise to Mrs. Darwin, some kind of deal I guess, and by making that comment about her being bullied to Miss Theresa, you broke it."

My mom stared at my father for a while and then back at me. She didn't speak for a while, so I decided that this was my time to make my point.

"When Mrs. Darwin found out about the whole situation, she brought me into her office and we had a talk. Afterwards, when we were thinking about what we needed to do, she told me that telling the teachers would only make it worse because they would freak out and tell *other* people, causing *them* to freak out, and then they would get the M-C-Ks in trouble, which would only cause them to get *furious* at me, which would make them start bullying me *more* and...." Even though I had started out calmly, my voice had gotten higher and higher and my eyes had continued to sting more and more and my parents were looking at me as if I was just getting crazier and crazier and next thing I knew it had turned into one huge run-on sentence.

Then I was crying.

— HOMEBOY —
chapter | twenty–two

My mom spent the rest of the car ride apologizing and trying to calm me down. "I'll fix it, Audrey. Don't worry, I'll fix it," she kept repeating over and over again. "No!" I had sobbed, "you can't say *anything*. Only I can fix this."

I hoped, desperately, that I could fix this.

By the following day of school I had talked myself out of going to speak with Mrs. Darwin, for fear that she would be angry with me. And quickly the subject was driven out of my mind by a new situation that battled ferociously for my attention. The middle school would soon be going on another field trip.

Memories from the last field trip still made me wince. The way I had been so meek and confused seemed pathetic to me now, and I just wanted to go back in time and slap myself. *Be strong, Audrey*, I would tell the old me. *They aren't worth it.*

I was put even more on edge when the teachers announced that for this trip, we would work together in groups to research the museum we were going to visit. The teachers had already decided that our groups were to be organized by grade and gender.

As in my group was going to be the eighth grade girls.

McKenna, McKailey, McKinley, and me.

I was considering the different ways that I could fake being sick when the Social Studies teacher, Mrs. Benz, walked up and motioned that I should come out to the hallway. I followed her, wondering if I was in trouble. I hadn't done anything. But then I remembered my parent-teacher conference and my promise to Mrs. Darwin, and suddenly, being paired with the M-C-Ks for a day was the least of my worries.

"Audrey, I'd like to talk to you about your group arrangements for this upcoming field trip," she said, staring down at her clipboard. I had always wondered why every teacher had one of those – and what the heck they kept on it.

"Oh?" I asked. I hadn't realized there was something to be discussed.

"Yes, about your group?" her voice went up in a way that made it sound slightly like a question. "It's been brought to our attention that you don't exactly *get along* with the other eighth grade girls."

At first I was happy that she was saving me from being with them. Then all her words sunk in and I caught my breath. "What do you mean, it has been brought to *our* attention?" I asked, stressing the one word that was really freaking me out.

"Miss Bass," Mrs. Benz said in a formal voice, almost cutting me off, "whatever has happened to make what has happened happen is none of your business." I leaned back and stared at her in awe. Had she purposely said a sentence that made no sense whatsoever?

"Mrs. Benz," I tried to reply calmly, "I just think that if the teachers are looking into something that involves me, I should know."

"I promise that when it directly involves you, we will let you know," she said, and from the way Mrs. Benz was looking down at me I felt like she was trying to hypnotize me into agreeing. "So," she continued in a slightly cheerier voice, "who would you like to be paired with? We are willing to put you in any group."

Any group, wow! I thought. *They must really be trying to make up for something.*

"Just put me with the eighth grade boys," I said. "I'll be fine there."

"You will?" she asked, probably just to make sure. I nodded. "Okay. Now I want you to not worry about anything, Audrey, and just let us handle it."

Handle what? I desperately wanted to ask, but I just sighed and looked down, trying not to worry. "All right, Mrs. Benz. Sounds good."

She responded with "mhm" before swiftly walking away down the hall, leaving me with no choice but to return to the classroom.

The following day we divided into our groups during the last period and were asked to assign every member a role to play during the field trip preparations, such as *researcher* or *discussion leader*. Since I was with the boys, I had a feeling that I would be doing all the jobs in my group. Surprisingly, I found that I didn't mind that much.

After splitting up our tasks (each boy had a task, but I would have bet millions that only Danny would complete his), my group lounged around on the couch. We talked or laughed as we felt like it, and it was a comfortable atmosphere. That is, until I noticed that McKailey and McKenna were approaching our group with a look of purpose on their faces. I straightened up. I told myself to stay calm, that there was no way Miss Theresa had told the other teachers, and there was no way the M-C-Ks had gotten in trouble. After all, McKenna and McKailey would look *way* madder if they had.

"It's so unfair," McKailey said, pouting, as she approached us. It took me one second to realize that the reason they had come over here was simple and didn't involve me: they wanted to flirt with the boys. It had been a long time since I had been around while they did this. Now that I was so close to the boys, I was certain I would find it very amusing. "Why do you guys look like you're having so much fun?" she continued in a baby voice.

"'Cause it's our thing," Trey replied in a cool voice. "Wherever we are, we have fun." All the boys laughed and agreed. I leaned farther back against the sofa so that I was pushed deep into the plush fabric and my view of the action was obstructed by Cash's back.

"Sure," McKenna replied, rolling her eyes. She acted a bit less ditsy than the other two around the boys. "You know what else is not fair?" she asked, and I felt her brown eyes land on me in a bottomless fiery-pit-of-death stare. "Audrey!" she spit my name out. "Why are you in a group with the guys? It seems like you're having *so* much more fun because of it. Meanwhile McKailey, McKinley, and I are *suffering*." She spoke in a softer voice now, one that resonated with me as a cool grey tone. Was she trying to make me feel guilty?

"Yeah, why are you paired with the boys, Audrey?" McKailey asked. She looked genuinely curious, but that could be just an act. "Every other group is done by grade and gender. You should be with us." She sounded almost possessive. This was weird.

"I don't know," I said, looking down. "The teachers put me here." Okay, so that was a lie, a straight-out lie. I had asked to be with the boys, and if Mrs. Benz hadn't come to me I probably would have gone and *begged*. But the lie had flowed out of my mouth. This was weird. This whole conversation was making me feel uncomfortable. I was scared. Why was I so scared?

They aren't worth it, I repeated to myself. *They aren't worth it. Don't let them intimidate you.*

"Yes, the teachers did it," Trey said, grinning. I whipped my head in his direction, practically decapitating Cash with my ponytail. *Shut up, Trey.* But he continued, "They put you three in a separate group from everyone else on purpose." I sighed with relief. He had singled out the M-C-Ks, not me. He had made it seem like they had the problem.

Distracted by my racing thoughts, I didn't notice until too late that Trey was still talking.

"They're trying to make sure that you stay to yourselves," he said. "They think you're bullying a certain someone in this group."

Shut up, Trey! What part of shut up don't you understand? I glared at him ferociously, as though he should have been able to interpret the mental messages I had been sending him. My hands twitched with the urge to tape his mouth shut and then cover my face with my hands. My cheeks burned with frustration at his stupidity.

McKailey looked confused, her nose all wrinkled at the top, and she turned and gave an unreadable look to McKenna. "Well, that's…"

"McKenna! McKailey!" a voice yelled. All of our heads whipped around to see Mr. Joliah, the teacher in charge of organizing the field trip, stand up from his desk and stare in our direction. "Why aren't you over here working with McKinley?" he continued. "You girls are the smallest group and have extra work to do, so I suggest that you don't waste your time."

I silently thanked Mr. Joliah and tried to smile nicely as McKenna and McKailey said goodbye and left. I immediately turned back around and swapped my smile for a glare. "Trey!" I whispered harshly. "Are you stupid? How could you say something like that?"

Trey grinned like he was proud of himself. "What's wrong,

Audrey? I think it's hilarious how those girls act like you don't know that they spent months totally dissing you behind your back. It might as well be out in the open." Tyler was kicking his feet back and was totally relaxed. He didn't understand. For the first time in a while, I found myself wishing that my friends were girls.

Cash leaned forward and pushed Trey off the couch, making all the other boys laugh. "You're such an idiot, Trey," he said. "Can't you see that Audrey is worried this is only going to make things worse for her? To you that comment might just be funny, but to them it could be a declaration of war. You know the stupid ways that girls think."

Trey just frowned. "Stop being such a girl, Cash. You don't need to cover for Audrey. She can take care of herself."

I put my hand on Cash's shoulder and smiled. "Thanks, Cash. You're right." His warmth sank into my skin as I thought about how Cash had supported me, and then everything was all right. My worries slipped away into oblivion, and the air around me became oddly bright and warm. I had to blink because my feelings were so obvious to me all of a sudden, and I could not ignore it any longer. I smiled and he smiled as his eyes twinkled a green that I felt you could jump into.

I turned back to Trey, trying to keep myself from getting obviously flustered. The other boys had been sitting and watching the argument unfold. Why weren't any of them backing Cash up? "You shouldn't be so harsh on your friend," I said. "If someone doesn't like what you said then just accept it." Trey rolled his eyes at me and I was sure he was going to make another comment about my femininity when Ronnie interrupted him.

"It's all right, Audrey," he said. "We get that you're worried, but you don't need to get between Cash and Trey. We argue and make fun of each other because that's what we do. But we all know that when it comes right down to it we're each other's homeboys." He held his hands up in a uniting gesture and the other boys nodded. "Worrying is just not something that needs to be done."

"That's right," Trey said, staring at me intently and cutting off my reply. "And we're your homeboys too. So it's cool." His stare seemed threatening, but I understood that it was Trey's nature to stare like that. He was the closest to the stereotypical bad boy, and he had taken the other boys under his wing. I knew that the others just wanted the recognition that came with the bad boy image. I was getting reassuring vibes from the pools of satiny green that surrounded Trey's irises. My inner thoughts began to settle down, because I could tell he just wanted me to remember that they were all my friends. *You're too edgy*, I told myself. *Just calm down.*

But I couldn't help panicking. I'd worked so hard to bury everything that had come to pass in November, and now the past was being resurrected in front of my eyes because of the careless things people like my mom and Trey were saying.

"So this conversation is over," Ian said cheerily, clapping his hands together. He was obviously tired of all the seriousness.

"Yeah," I replied, unable to help the fact that my voice was somber. "I'm going to go to the bathroom, guys. I'll be right back." I turned around and started walking towards the door, trying to get rid of the stiff feeling in my joints. I felt a familiar pressure building up in my stomach, one that had been there almost constantly months ago. I hoped that a walk to the bathroom would loosen me up.

"Hey," I heard a voice say, and as I looked around for the speaker, a slender hand gripped my arm. It jolted me to the side and I found myself staring into McKenna's eyes, which were a swirl of chestnut and chocolate brown. The sight made me sick, and for the first time in as long as I could remember, I found myself trying to avoid the emotions flowing from her pupils and just concentrate on her entire face as she spoke.

I was sick and tired of brown eyes.

"Hey," she repeated, her grip on my arm loosening. "I was just wondering."

"Wondering what?" I asked, not sure at all where this was going. Out of the corner of my eye I saw the exit to the classroom, and I stared at it longingly before fearfully snapping my attention back to McKenna. It was in a person's best interest to make sure that if McKenna Marcum was speaking to them, they were listening.

"Do you need a map?" she asked, and I stared at her blankly, watching a mischievous smile break across her face. "Because it looks like you keep getting lost in Cash's eyes."

I felt myself blush intensely and I stepped back from McKenna, flashing back to when I had smiled at Cash after he had defended me. McKenna must have been watching, make that *spying*. She was trying to gain leverage. It was such a clichéd and classic mean girl quip, and it was obvious she was just trying to get to me. What horrified me was that it was working. This was so stupid – and yet everything was still spinning out of control because I couldn't get a grip on myself.

"I overheard something about how you all are homeboys?" McKenna continued, obviously pleased at how her comment had affected me. *Wait – she could see how her comment affected me? Why am I letting her see into me?* I thought, feeling the years of practice at protecting myself slip away. "Well," she continued. "*He* obviously doesn't want to be just your homeboy any more." I saw where this was going, and she was about to lean forward and whisper something else to me when I decided that listening to her was not worth my time. I just needed to escape. Before her mouth got close enough to my ear, I flinched away. Grace and Larken were sitting on a nearby couch, and I grabbed them by their arms and dragged them off the couch, forcing them to run with me out the classroom door and into the hallway.

"What is it?" Larken asked once we had safely reached the confines of the girls' bathroom.

I was out of breath from the escape and my words came out in a gasp. "Tell me – and be honest," I began. "Do you think Cash still likes me?" They didn't answer, but gave each other smug glances. I knew what that meant. "Do you think I like him?" I asked, knowing it was stupid, as I already knew the answer myself, but I couldn't resist asking. They still didn't answer, but their resulting smiles told me more than I needed to know.

I collapsed onto the bathroom floor and let out a large slow breath.

"What's wrong, Audrey?" Grace asked timidly.

"I'm sorry," I said. "You probably think I'm crazy."

Larken squatted down so that she was at my level. "It's obvious to us that you and Cash have some sort of," she paused, and I could tell she was trying to choose her words very delicately, "connection – that's all. It *seems* like more than friends, but–"

"Stop," I said, cutting her off. Larken was trying to console me, make things seem better than they were. I couldn't afford to do that right now. "People are getting suspicious," I said. "People are wondering why I've been paired with the boys. They're wondering if there's a reason that I'm not with the girls, and if they figure it out...."

I didn't want to finish my sentence.

"Wait, by *people* do you mean the M-C-Ks? Because everyone else pretty much already has a hunch something was–," Larken began, but was quickly cut off by Grace.

"What are you afraid that they'll figure out? That the other girls are bullying you? Er, psychologically, at least," she said, sidetracking. "I mean, you don't have any physical bruises on you, so that's probably the best technical term to classify it with," she said with a nod. I stared at Grace, not sure whether to laugh or be annoyed, as her logical analysis was completely wrong for the moment.

I eventually settled for being amused, but shook off the coming laughter. "I can't let everyone know," I said, trying to ward off the feeling that I was referring to something other than the bullying. "That will just make everything explode again and I can't deal with that. I didn't go through all this," I waved my hands in circles above my head, as if to represent all the changes I'd gone through in the first half of this year, "for nothing."

The room was silent for a second while I started to finalize my plan in my head. I looked up and saw that Larken and Grace were staring at the floor, nervously fiddling with their hands. "Audrey," Grace began, "you *do* know that everyone already–"

"I've got it!" I yelled, jumping up. I had a plan. Then I realized that I'd interrupted Grace, and I turned to her. "Whatever it is, it doesn't matter to me any more," I said. "All I can worry about right now is the real problem."

Larken tried again. "But you realize–,"

"Nothing else matters," I said almost desperately, cutting Larken off with my voice and stare.

There was silence for a moment as Grace and Larken looked at each other. Then Grace said softly, "We can help you." Larken just looked down nervously and bit her lip.

"That's all right," I said, resonance returning to my voice. "I'll deal with it." I smiled my thanks to both of them and started to exit the bathroom.

"But, Audrey," Larken began, speaking up for the third time just as I was leaving, "the teachers all know already and they've gotten Mrs. Darwin to–"

I didn't hear the rest of her sentence because the bathroom door swung shut. I decided not to let myself worry about it. I just continued walking forward – I was on a mission.

I walked into the classroom again, preparing myself for the question that I was about to ask Cash. I needed to know the truth about – *us* – so that at least something in my life wasn't beyond my control. However, as I approached the couch, I overheard part of their conversation and stopped in my tracks.

"Dude," Cash was whispering, leaning into the group, "I...I think I like Audrey."

"Our Audrey?" Danny replied, a shocked look on his face, as if he half-expected another Audrey to suddenly appear at Eastwood. "Dude, that's gay. She's like our brother!"

Cash reared back and I saw a blush creep up his face.

"Yeah," Ronnie began with a thoughtful look on his face, which was odd for him, "but she's a girl, so it's not technically gay."

"Exactly!" Cash said, looking relieved. "Thanks, man."

A Cheshire cat grin spread across Ronnie's face as he continued, "She's more like our sister, so that makes it incest."

Cash scowled and the boys laughed and patted Ronnie and Cash on the back, as if congratulating them for the great exchange. As their laughter became more joyous my ears began to roar, as if telling me to get out of there. I began to edge backwards, my feelings battling between happiness and horror. It was true – Cash liked me. Of course, I'd known it the whole time, deep down. But now I was going to have to deal with it. And *how* was I going to do that? If I'd proved anything, it was that I was awful at dealing with stuff the right way.

As soon as I'd safely reached the hallway and closed the door behind me, I let out a breath and closed my eyes.

"Excuse me," I heard a voice say and I whipped around to see a short girl, most likely a sixth grader, staring at me with a curious expression.

"Oh, hi, Clara," I said, rubbing my eyes and hoping that was actually the girl's name.

"I was wondering," she said, her voice suddenly excited, "is it true that you asked to be paired with the boys instead of the girls because you like the boys better than the girls? I mean, that's just what I heard. And I was wondering – what could possibly make you feel that way?" She was leaning toward me now, as though she was trying to get a juicy front page story for a newspaper. "You must have had one huge argument with McKenna, McKailey, and McKinley. I mean, not only are the boys annoying, but Cash and Trey are just–"

"I'm sorry," I said, interrupting her and trying with all my strength to resist hitting the side of her head to make her forget everything she had just said, "but I have to go."

I stepped around her and trudged down the hallway like a robot. I didn't know how the girl had heard what she did. I didn't know how

Cash had come to like me. I didn't know how Larken knew what my mom had said to Miss Theresa. I didn't know how I was going to solve all these problems. But there was one thing I did know – I knew the only way to make this stop.

I had to stop making people suspicious that I might like Cash – I just couldn't deal with that right now on top of everything else. My mind was racing so fast that it was hard for me to think of anything rational to do. I was so exhausted from everything that had happened, and the attention I was suddenly getting was suffocating – making me feel like I was pressed up against the wall. If I was going to make it stop, I was going to have to cut off my relationships.

This is rash, a part of me thought. Perhaps, but I couldn't think of anything else. I had to try something. *So as of now,* I thought as I breathed deeply, *I am no longer one of the boys*

As I continued walking I tried my best to try to ignore the sad feeling growing in my gut.

— BETWIXT —
chapter | twenty–three

I was arguing with myself internally. Or more precisely, my emotions were arguing with each other. Although I had made my decision, I didn't have the strength to completely get rid of everything that I had built up in the last month or so. I knew I would greatly miss the comfortable friendship I had developed with the boys.

I faked being stressed or mentally exhausted so that I could sit in a corner by myself during breaks and classes. Slowly, people stopped coming up to me and asking if the "rumors" (apparently there was more than one) about why I was paired with the boys instead of the girls for the field trip were true. It was agitating to have to repeat the same thing over and over. I had never realized what a big deal the mixing of genders was to some people.

I knew my decision had been rash, and possibly stupid. I could see that Grace and Larken thought so, in the nervous way their wide eyes met when we were together. But it was the only way I knew how to deal with the *feelings* aspects of the situation – how to deal with everything that was Cash. I was also afraid that I would feel too guilty if I asked Grace or Larken to help me decide what to do. Everything had become so complicated, and I felt bad for how I had been using Grace and Larken for their words of wisdom whenever I was overwhelmed, as though they played just cameo roles in my life. Especially Larken – now I realized that I saw a bit of the old, timid McKinley in her. I was afraid of what would happen if I dragged her into this too much more. Perhaps she would change, just like McKinley had changed under McKenna and McKailey's influence.

That left me alone, single-handedly fighting a battle with myself that I didn't really understand, and it bothered me. After everything that had happened this year, being alone again made me feel like a penny caught in the funnel-shaped coin drop in the school library, spiraling around and around in a deranged circle until gravity sucked me down into total emotional exhaustion.

The M-C-Ks obviously had a serious problem with me. They hated me, thought I was a loser, or something along those lines. And apparently everyone at the school had caught on and knew *something*. And *I* knew. And I was pretty sure that at this point the M-C-Ks knew that I knew... unless they thought I was a certified idiot, which was also a possibility. But when we were standing face to face, they either acted nice in a sugar-coated way or acted like nothing was wrong at all.

It drove me crazy.

Every time they opened their mouths I heard, *"Punch me, punch me, punch me."*

But I couldn't punch them, because I had chosen not to be a violent person. So I was forced to deal with it and learn to accept it. I chose to be the better person, because that was the only smart thing to do. But that also meant that I would absolutely never, ever have the one thing I found myself craving more and more: closure. As I sat on the rock outside Eastwood's front entrance, where I had sat so many times before, I was lost as to whether to stay on my current path – the one that had led me to being alone again – or change. I was betwixt and between.

I sat in a thinker's position, leaning forward and looking at nothing in particular as my mind whirred. When I got bored with the patch of grass that I was staring at, I slowly tipped my head to the left, and my heart almost beat right out of my chest when I realized that Cash was standing in front of me.

"Oh!" I exclaimed without realizing it, as I caught sight of his figure.

"Sorry," he said, grinning sheepishly. He moved so he was standing more squarely in front of me and his smile grew as he continued. "My, uh, friend told me to come over here and see if you were okay."

I stared at him suspiciously for a second before rolling my eyes and uncrossing my legs. "Cash," I said, looking at him seriously, "I saw you sitting over there on a bench by yourself less than five minutes ago."

"Yeah?" he said, looking insulted, "so what if he's imaginary?"

I stared at him again for a moment, confused, before bursting into laughter. He still looked slightly wounded. I shook my head as the laughter died down and gave him a familiar sheepish smile. "I'm sorry, but that was just so bad." He looked down at the grass and blushed.

I sighed, knowing that I shouldn't really be talking to him, but I couldn't help myself. "So, what's really up?"

"It seemed like something started to bother you all of a sudden, and none of the other guys had the courage to come and see what was up, so I figured I might as well take one for the group and do it. You know, be the good guy for once."

I smirked, strangely charmed that Cash was trying to do something for the better. "And how's that working out for you?"

"Well, I tried to make a joke, but it came out as a pick-up line." He shrugged as if in defeat and looked up at my amused face. "And then things got awkward."

My smile assumed blinding proportions and I tried to hold back a laugh. "How true."

Craning my neck to look up at him was uncomfortable, so I patted the rock next to me and told him to sit down. He moved slowly to the spot, as if thinking about his next move.

"So, as long as I'm here, you might as well tell me," he said. I looked at him, silently begging him not to continue. "What's the problem?"

I sighed, but couldn't stop my stupid mouth from continuing. "It has nothing to do with you, or Danny, or Eliot, or Ian..."

"Really? That's too bad." I looked at Cash, confused. "Because Ian was really hoping that you had a secret crush on him and were too embarrassed to be around him any more."

I laughed, relieved that Cash was making so many jokes to lighten up this conversation that was most likely not going to have a happy ending. "Yeah, not at all. You tell Ian that he's going to need a lot of luck if he's trying to get me to like him. He's about as charming as a broken toaster."

Cash laughed and then we fell into a comfortable silence, with the wind blowing my hair so that it intermingled with his spiky dark locks. We were gazing toward the soccer field, where McKailey was taking part in an extremely flirtatious game of tag with the rest of the boys.

"You know," I began, pointing at McKailey and feeling the words bubble out of my mouth, "her eyes have always been a centimeter too far apart for my liking."

Cash looked at me, amused. "Okay, not only was that random, but a bit OCD sounding." I half smiled, still looking in McKailey's direction. "What's this whole obsession about anyway?" he asked.

I was taken aback. "Obsession? What do you mean?"

"You know, your obsession with eyes. I've noticed how you always stare intently at someone's eyes when you talk to them, and you seem to know the color of every single person's eyes in this entire *town*." Even though his tone was light and joking, I looked down, embarrassed. "So, what's the deal? Why do you do it?"

"I don't know," I said almost instinctively. I had never really thought deeply about something that was so instinctive to me, but I could tell by the way he was looking at me that he wanted a direct answer. I searched desperately for the right words. "Aesthetic pleasure?"

"What is that?"

I smiled at his ignorance but then tried to wipe it away. I could feel people looking at us, noticing that we were sitting together on the rocks. On school grounds dotted with hyper middle schoolers in constant motion, the stationary once popular girl and assumed bad boy were beginning to stick out. This needed to stop; I needed a way out. "I'd explain it to you, but your brain would probably explode."

He rolled his eyes and bumped my shoulder with his. "Seriously," he said, begging me with his eyes.

I looked away. "Seriously," I repeated, "why do you want to know?"

He shrugged. "Maybe to get some insight into you?"

I gave him a look that said *Come on*. Cash might be sensitive at times, but he was still a fourteen year old boy.

He shrugged again. "It's just kind of creepy sometimes, like you're seeing straight into my soul or something."

His tone was joking, but I didn't smile and looked down, not wanting him to know that I felt like I could. He was sitting so close to me that I could feel his body heat through his arm and shoulder and I suddenly shivered, remembering the conversation I had overhead about him... liking me.

I suddenly realized that sitting here was a way to avoid going forward with my plan. I needed to keep going down the path that I had already chosen.

I stood up and turned to face him. "Break is going to end soon, and I need to go inside and check something for my next class." He nodded and smiled in response, and I tried to bury the happiness that was trying to make me smile back. Instead my mouth just twitched.

"Bye, Cash," I said, flicking my hand in a wave-like gesture.

He stayed seated. "See you tomorrow." My mouth twitched again, and I wondered why I was still standing in that spot. I tried to force my legs to move. "I would hug you goodbye," he continued, "but I already have one detention on my belt so it wouldn't really be smart of me to get in trouble for a public display of affection." I failed to keep a smile from cracking across my face.

I had managed to move inside the building and down to my locker when someone tapped me on the shoulder. I turned around, annoyed, sure it was another kid asking if the rumors were true, but instead I was met by Danny's azure eyes.

"Hey, Aud," he said, grinning. "Where've you been?"

"Um, I was outside talking to Cash," I said, gesturing in the general direction of the rocks where we had been sitting.

"Ooo," he said in a thick voice.

"Shut up," I replied automatically. He just looked more amused.

"So, what's got you down?" he asked. "Come on, I know it's

something."

I sighed and glared at Danny. He was lucky I knew I could trust him. "Three words," I said.

"Ah." He immediately understood. "McKenna, McKailey, and McKinley." I just grimaced. "Come on, you don't have to be bitter forever." He started to chuckle. "I mean, it was kind of funny, with them sneaking out the back door and running to hide in the prickly bushes, all to get away from you."

"Don't joke about that," I snapped. Danny looked taken aback.

"I'm sorry, Audrey, I was just–"

"I know," I said softly, trying to let him know that I wasn't really mad at him, and then I started to walk away into the girls' bathroom, where he couldn't follow me. *I'm sorry*, I wanted to say. *I'm sorry that I have to do this. But I can't let them win.*

I had my plan.

If only I'd known that the M-C-Ks had one too. If only I'd known about the rumor that was spreading through the school like wildfire.

— THE REDUX —
chapter | twenty–four

Just like with the M-C-Ks, I had decided that I needed to cut the boys out of my life. Only this time, the decision didn't bring a thrilling rush of excitement. Instead, I fell into a sullen mood where I never felt happy, let alone excited.

I started to spend my time with Grace and Larken and their friends. It was nice to be around sensible girls again and not to have to explain my every move and reasoning, but on the other hand I missed the blatant honesty of the boys.

It surprised me how much I missed the name-calling, and the joking, and the cheesy pick-up lines, and all the other idiotic things that the boys would say on a daily basis. I could remember every moment over the past two months where they had said something honestly funny, and I had laughed. Each time they had made me laugh, the smile on my face had gotten more and more real, until suddenly it was huge and honest for the first time since Jacklyn had moved away.

"Is everything all right?" Grace pulled me away to ask one break. We had been sitting on the rocks and playing rock-paper-scissors. Grace had been trying to make up a new version of the game involving a sea urchin, a piece of tape, and a sharpened pencil and was trying to decide what beat what. As the other girls laughed hysterically at her goofy reasoning, I had just sat there silently.

"Huh?" I said as I let myself be clumsily pulled across the grass, still in the process of waking up from the daydream I had been in. "Oh, yeah, everything's fine."

Grace half smiled. "You don't really mean that."

I sighed. "I'm just– I'm sorry, I'm being a jerk, aren't I?" I let out a sharp breath and looked down. "The boys and I used to play this game. They would come up with enchanted swords and evil flying squirrels and…" Grace smiled at me and I grimaced. "Oh my gosh, am I actually *missing* the boys? What is *wrong* with me?" Grace laughed, and Larken, who had followed behind us, joined in.

"They were your friends… are your friends," Larken said.

"But you guys are my friends too," I said. I felt awful. I had spent my time around Grace and Larken just beating down on myself for the fact that I wasn't with my other friends too.

Grace leaned down. "The best you can do is keep trying," she whispered.

"If this is really what you want," Larken added, looking at me expectantly. Grace smiled a smile as sweet as a swan's and stood there, waiting, as if she expected me to smile back.

I didn't – I was unable to force myself to. I just looked at them, plainly, until Grace's smile disappeared and they slowly turned around, walking back to where their friends were sitting among the rocks.

After they left, I slowly walked down the soccer field, staring at the blades of green grass as I crushed them with my feet. I beat each blade down swiftly, trying to work out my frustrations with myself. Breaths quickly left my mouth as I tried to figure out why I couldn't just be happy with this. I wanted to jump inside my own body and fine-tune my emotions so that they were on the same page as my brain.

I turned around and stared at the basketball court. The boys were all there, as usual. Trying to pretend that I didn't want to be there seemed pointless now. I used to be so good at tricking myself into believing things; I seemed to be failing now.

"Hi!"

The voice came from behind me and I jumped, breathing out sharply. I turned so quickly that at first all I saw was a blurry outline of a person. But after a moment my vision cleared and I saw who it was. My entire frame slumped. McKenna.

"Hey, McKenna," I said, acting surprised, and not bitter at all. She smiled falsely at me and I worked at solidifying my poker face.

"How are you?" she asked after a moment, slowly walking towards me.

"Why are you asking?" I said, not answering her question.

"It's just," and here her face twisted and she looked almost thoughtful, "you never hang out with us any more."

"Should I?" I asked. I couldn't help it.

"Well," and here she looked up in a way that could almost be interpreted as innocent – but I knew better. "*I* never wanted you not to," she said in a leading way, as if that fact was important, and I should remember it. On the contrary, I didn't believe her and I intended to forget her comment.

I let out an annoyed puff of air and watched with regret as it created a tiny cloud of smoke in the air. I was tired of the cold. "Well," I said as I adjusted my coat, "I'll think about it."

I was about to walk away when McKenna stopped me. "You seem so down lately, Audrey, never smiling. Is everything all right?" That was the second time someone had asked me if everything was all right today. I guessed it was time for me to start counting again.

"No, not really," I said, deciding to be truthful for once. "I just have some choices to make."

"Hmm," McKenna said, as if she found that amusing. Her eyes

were pools that had been locked with a key, holding their own secrets. Her voice dripped with amusement as it reverberated through the sunray-coated air around us. Today the sun was fighting to shine through the cold, reaching the earth in murky saffron beams. "Choices," she said simply. "How they must torture all of us at one point or another."

I was about to reply when a loud voice behind me called McKenna's name. She looked over my shoulder, alarmed, and I took that opportunity to slip away. Unfortunately, the memory of our conversation refused to go away, and her words echoed in my ears. What she had said was true; I was down, in the true sense of the word. I wasn't even smiling, not at Grace, not at Larken, not even at McKenna. And I had always intended to be nice to McKenna, to never show her that I was affected or bothered by her actions. I had failed at that so many times.

McKenna's comment about my disposition reminded me of an earlier time when I was friends with the M-C-Ks, a time when I was bothered by their views on life and their horrible dispositions and the fact that they wouldn't just *smile*.

Now here I was, unable to smile. How ironic.

It was a redux where I was reliving those moments, except now I was the bad guy. That couldn't happen. That's not what I had wanted to happen.

Suddenly I felt so tired, for I was tired of trying just to fail. I had once again gone back to letting these girls dance around me. Cutting off the boys hadn't helped at all – it hadn't stopped the rumors, or made the M-C-Ks leave me alone. All I wanted was for them to just leave me at peace once and for all, but instead I was letting them look down on me smugly once again. My attempts had done nothing but hurt *me*, and had not affected *them* at all – and the only reason I had done all of it was to keep my fears buried.

Perhaps if I kept those fears buried long enough, they would all disappear. Was it worth that? It wasn't worth that. It wasn't worth the burning and torment inside and feeling as if I would one day explode. It wasn't worth turning into something that I used to hate. I had made that mistake before, with McKenna and Jacklyn, when we were all trying to hide our weaknesses. Maybe weaknesses are in every corner of the world and you can't run from them. You have to face them.

"Danny," I yelled, still facing the opposite direction from where he was standing as I began to bellow his name. "Ronnie, Ian, Trey, Eliot!"

I turned and ran towards the basketball field. "Cash!" I yelled as I approached them. They were standing in a circle near the edge of the blacktop and they turned to face me as I ran.

"Audrey," Eliot replied, stretching his hands out over his head, "this is a surprise."

"Oh?" I asked, the glee already returning to my voice.

"Yeah," he said, stepping forward and holding his hands out, "I mean, I thought you weren't speaking to us. At least," and here he stuck his hands in his pockets, "that's what we heard through the grapevine."

"Through the grapevine?" I repeated. "Since when do you listen to 60s music?"

"Since never," Ronnie replied. I fell silent, my whole body suddenly tightening. That was the first time I had made a joke and Ronnie hadn't laughed. I looked around at the other boys' faces. They were either looking down or staring nervously at Danny. Danny – he was their leader, like always. Ronnie was a messenger of some sort.

"So, what's up, guys?" I suddenly felt small, like a mouse. I looked at Danny, and he looked back at me. His blue eyes were like the sky on a rainy day, but he gave me a half smile. I looked back at Ronnie – his face was stone cold. "What's up is that we don't want you around any more if you're just playing."

"What?" I breathed out, desperate. "I'm not playing – what?"

"You stopped hanging out with us," Cash interjected. He sounded almost hurt. "Look, we welcomed you into our group because we thought you were trying to get away from all that stupid drama. I mean, heck, it's not even really drama. It's just stupid things that you girls do to try to make a big deal out of things. It's idiotic and, frankly, I don't want any part in it. We thought you were done with that, but if you're just using us as toys in your game, then you're looking in the wrong place."

My intake of breath became sharper as his words hit me, wounding. I tried to look at him, to explain that there must be a huge misunderstanding of some sort, but he turned his head away. I concentrated on trying to breathe smoothly, as if nothing was off, but found that I wasn't able to concentrate without his gemstone eyes there. I ran my fingers over my palms nervously and wished that he would just get up the courage to approach me, stand with me, so I wouldn't feel like I was a fighter with no alliances. As unfamiliar burn started to form in my heart and I found myself wishing that he would just walk up and kiss me, maybe take away the pain.

"For like one and a half days!" I was screaming now. I didn't care who was staring. "I've realized it was a mistake. I was just trying to keep–"

"Keep what?" Trey interrupted me. He looked furious and I was scared, remembering Trey's history of anger management issues. I gazed into his eyes, trying to see if anger truly was the force behind this as he continued. "Keep it hidden? Make sure that no one would ever find out the truth?"

"T-the truth… what?" I felt the sky was spinning, like a whirlpool that would surely fall down on me. Or maybe just I was spinning, for soon I started to see colors that I'd never noticed before and felt as though I might faint.

"Audrey!" My panic was interrupted by someone calling my name from behind me. So many names had been called today – so many loud voices. I looked over my shoulder and saw Mrs. Darwin, anger etched on her face. My breathing slowed.

"Audrey," she repeated, more calmly. "I need to talk to you for a moment."

I stared at her from across the schoolyard. I knew that the question was written all over my face, and that Mrs. Darwin could see it too. But I was afraid to speak it, as something seemed to have taken over my lungs. "I need to talk to you and I need you to come with me," she said, "because I have McKenna, McKailey, and McKinley in my office."

Shock now made everything seem slow, as if underwater, and I tried to think about anything but the look of urgency on Mrs. Darwin's face as I made my way towards the door.

— FALLING —
chapter | twenty–five

Sitting next to McKenna, McKailey, and McKinley in Mrs. Darwin's office, I truly felt that I had hit rock bottom. In front of us stood Mrs. Darwin, Miss Theresa, and Mrs. Benz. Where Mrs. Benz came into this I had no idea. Maybe she was back up. If so, and if back up was truly needed, then this was bound to get messy.

Mrs. Darwin gave me a long look, as if to say *here we go*, before she turned to the other three girls. "Miss Marcum," she began, "We have sizable proof that you, with the assistance of Miss Harp and Miss Fitch, excluded and then mentally toyed with Miss Bass." I smirked. McKinley's last name was Fitch. How amusing that she would have such a harsh sounding last name.

"We got a complaint from a parent," Miss Theresa interjected. I looked down and clenched my arms against my chest, trying to keep myself from pointing out that my mom's side comment hardly counted as a complaint. I just wanted this to end, so I could get out of the room and run far, far away. "So I'd suggest that you tell the truth."

"We understand," McKenna said calmly in the sweet voice that made adults like her.

McKailey and McKinley remained silent. McKenna turned and stared at me. I stared at Mrs. Darwin.

We stayed in those positions as Mrs. Benz and Miss Theresa explained the M-C-Ks' punishment. In-school suspension. Lunch in Mrs. Darwin's office. Helping the teachers during after-school hours. A forced apology. It was nothing new to McKenna. Or me.

I walked out of there in a daze, my legs on fast forward. All I could think of were the M-C-Ks' odd facial expressions, especially McKenna's. They were all wrong, too subtle, too calm, too nice.

It was so weird that I almost wanted to say something to them, but they just walked away, down the hall and into their classroom, leaving me to walk into my own classroom, a different life. Break was over and I went on to my next class with a cloud of confusion over my head. Worse, it was Friday. I was going to have to deal with this hanging over my head for an entire 48 hours before there was any possible chance of it being cleared up.

My glum attitude that weekend made my parents worry, especially my mother. She was relieved, however, that I wasn't locking myself in my room or completely cutting myself out. I spent most of my time lying on the couch, switching between watching television and talking on the phone.

I spent most of my phone time talking to Jacklyn. It was wonderful – such a relief to feel as though I could truly share what was going on with something. It was the first time we had really talked in months. Jacklyn translated just as well over the phone as in person. It didn't matter how long it had been since you had last spoken with her; she would still sound like she was there for you one hundred percent.

"So let me get this straight, you like Cash now? And Danny is like, your best friend? I am so confused. Are we talking about the same Eastwood, or did you suddenly get transported to some parallel universe?"

"I don't *like* Cash," I said pointedly, stressing the defining word. "I never said that."

"Ahh, but you do!" Jacklyn squealed into the phone and I laughed, twirling a strand of hair. The pale lock made me think of Jacklyn and her identical hair. Was it still the same? Had it changed? Had *she* changed? There was really so little that you could find out over the phone.

"Well, maybe," I said, unable to keep away a grin. "But I wish I didn't. I mean, if I had to get all flustered over a boy, then why did it have to be him? And right when the boys start being my close friends! It's just made everything so much more complicated."

"Ah, well that's life," Jacklyn said. "You can't control who you fall for. That's why they call it *falling*." She laughed and I could imagine her eyes dancing like fairies. I groaned and put my forehead down on my hand.

"Could you stop saying that? It's embarrassing." I felt the heat creeping up my face, along with the fluttery butterflies that seemed to say *the feelings are there, and they're not going away.*

"No, I'm going to say it! Tell me more!" Jacklyn gushed.

"Ugh, why?"

"Because I want to know! It's exciting." Her voice was getting up into the squeaky range, meaning she was in full-on gossip mode. There was no getting her off the subject now except by hanging up the phone. "I've never experienced Audrey when she's had a crush on someone before," she continued.

"Yeah, it's not really me, is it?" I didn't know what to do with these sudden feelings, and that made me feel like a failure to myself – to what I could be.

"It's so hard for me to imagine!" I could almost see Jacklyn sitting on her bed, her legs curled up to her chest, deep in thought. "What color are his eyes?" she asked. The first true smile of the night lit up my face – she knew me so well.

I took a deep breath. "They're green most of the time."

"Most of the time?"

"Yeah, most of the time. They are the most magnificent shade of this jade color, but then it's swirled with a more pastel shade that's electric, like a lime green. But at moments there are these specks of purple and gold and sometimes when he speaks I see bubble gum pink–"

"Bubble gum pink? Whoa, where did that come from?"

"Ah, never mind," I said easily. Trying to explain the sudden flashes of glorious color that appeared in the air would be too confusing for Jacklyn at this moment.

She giggled. "All right then. So, how's school?"

Bad question. "Don't ask," I replied, stretching out across the couch. "I don't even want to think about it."

"About what?" The concern in Jacklyn's voice appeared suddenly.

"About what I'm going to have to deal with tomorrow."

"And what is that?" she asked.

"I don't even really know. I just know something happened, the M-C-Ks did something, and now everyone is mad at me or–"

"Whoa, whoa, whoa, slow down," Jacklyn interjected, and I realized she was probably very confused. So much had happened since the last time we'd spoken – it felt like ages. "First of all, who are the M-C-Ks?"

I giggled. "McKenna, McKailey, and McKinley. They named themselves that. It's actually a lot easier then saying their names, which sound really awkward when you put them together."

"They gave themselves a group name? Wow," and suddenly

Jacklyn's voice sounded just as sullen as mine had before, "that really brings back memories of when we were all together, like a group."

"I know," I whispered, even though there was no one else in the room. "I miss it."

"Me too," she said with a sigh. "So much has changed."

"It will never be the same." My reply was met with silence. Jacklyn knew it was true, but it went against her nature to agree to such a depressing fact.

"I wish I could say otherwise, but…"

"It's okay," I replied.

"Would it help if I said I was proud of you? Because I am," she said, and I believed her.

"Thank you, Jacklyn." I meant it.

"You're welcome, Audrey." She meant it too. "Good luck tomorrow."

"Thank you," I said again. "Good night."

Monday morning I felt numb as I walked out of the sheltering force field of my home and parents, into something that I couldn't see or understand. I felt as though I had been slowly losing my balance on a tightrope, and only now had I accepted the fact that I was going to fall.

I avoided everyone for the first part of the day, curling up into a ball on the white couch during homeroom. It wasn't too hard – a lot of people seemed distracted, chatting excitedly about some visitor. Maybe people from Oasis Academy were visiting today. Not that I cared. Miss Theresa looked at me worriedly, as if she had expected me to be bouncing off the walls with happiness now that the M-C-Ks had been dealt with. She knew nothing.

At break time I had to force my body through the door. The slate grey sky was a perfect accompaniment for my premonitions of doom.

The first person I saw was Grace. I walked up behind her and tapped her tentatively on the shoulder.

"Audrey," she whipped around and gasped. "Hi."

"Look," I said, skipping to the point, "do you think you can tell me what's going on here?" I gestured around the school yard and looked. There were already several people staring in my direction.

"I don't exactly know. I..." Her small features looked overwhelmed as she also noticed the people staring at me. "The M-C-Ks thought you didn't know, I guess. Even though that is absolutely ridiculous, because they were beyond obvious. But they thought you didn't know and now they know you did and they're taking it to a whole new level. And they have power – even over the boys."

I stared as her speech unfolded. Only part of it made sense. "Power? What do you mean?"

"They're coming this way," Grace said suddenly, looking down. "I need to find Larken," she said, and we both knew it was a lie. Grace just wanted to get away. She was afraid. So was I. Grace must have seen that in my face. "Just don't back down," she said as she started to walk away. "Don't accept a lie as the truth. Don't let McKenna fool you into thinking something different than what you *know*. She has a way of doing that."

I was left alone with her words flying around my head like the nervous butterflies whose wings were batting against my stomach.

Grace was telling me not to lie? How was *that* going to help? I guessed that I could, perhaps, promise to myself that I wouldn't lie.

But I had a nagging feeling deep down that that wouldn't do much. Because I found myself wondering if I *would* lie, if it meant preventing myself from being hurt even more.

— A PRISONER —
c h a p t e r | t w e n t y – s i x

"We need to talk," was the first thing McKailey said to me as she approached. Her voice rang in my ears. McKailey and I had never really been friends, and had never talked much at all. So I found it amusing that when she suddenly became so involved in my life, it was for such a negative reason. I held my head high as McKenna stepped forward.

"As I'm sure you've noticed," McKenna said, half smirking, "some rumor has spread and everyone at Eastwood has been eating it up. We thought, since you seemed so confused when the boys snipped you the other day, that we would do the honor of explaining it to you."

"Fine," I said, crossing my arms.

"All right," McKinley said and I looked at her, alarmed. It had been so long since I'd heard her make any noise that wasn't a laugh. Her deep voice was different, stronger, yet she still never spoke up during arguments. "McKenna will explain it to you." McKailey nodded in agreement and she and McKinley both stepped back so that they were standing at an equal distance from either side of McKenna, in a triangle formation. I thought how much they looked like a motorcycle gang, and suddenly flashed back to the conversation they had had right in front of me in homeroom about their plans to dress up as a motorcycle gang for Halloween. Without me. That had hurt at the time.

Let them, I thought now. I didn't want to be a part of whatever they had any more. It wasn't real.

McKenna was about to speak when I interrupted her. "Do you

think I'm an idiot, McKenna?"

She thought for a second and then replied cheerfully, "No, not in the least. Why?"

"Then tell me," I began, my face dark, "did you ever really like me? Were we ever really friends?"

She shrugged. "We've been friends on and off, Audrey. I'll always consider you a buddy of mine, in the back of my head. We want the same thing," she said as she absentmindedly played with a strand of her artificially streaked hair. "We want protection. I'll always remember how we helped each other last year."

"Fine," I said, feeling sick that her description of our past friendship made it sound like a business deal. I was sure she could see the hurt in my face, but I was unable to read any emotions from her. She looked too calm – I needed more. "So, tell me, when you, McKailey, and McKinley made plans to ditch me at lunch and then sneak out to break so that I couldn't find you, and ignore me and basically make me feel like I didn't exist, were you thinking in the back of your mind the whole time about how I was your *friend*?" My voice was incredulous but calm, trying to convince myself that I had this under control.

McKenna sighed. "Listen," she said as she stepped towards me, "I can honestly say that what happened was never my direct intention. But what's asking that question really going to do to help the situation? I mean – McKailey always disliked you. You knew that. You two argued like cats and dogs whenever you had the chance. McKailey and I were always going off separately from you and McKinley anyway, so it just grew from that."

"McKinley," I stated. "She was vulnerable. You used her to get what you wanted." *Whatever that was,* I continued in my head, but I was too afraid to dig any deeper. I had a feeling I still needed to stay a safe distance away from them and their actions, or I would regret it later.

"No," McKenna said, shaking her head smugly. "McKinley started to follow right along with us. She did it willingly." I stared at McKinley and tried to mask my face as I studied hers. Her eyes were sullen amber. I saw guilt – but was that only because that was what I wanted to see? McKenna scoffed at me, dragging my attention back to her dimensionless irises. "McKinley was never your friend." I tried to pretend that that jab didn't hurt. I could see by the satisfied look on McKenna's face that I had failed.

"I want you to listen carefully," she said to me, "as I'm not going to repeat this." I suddenly felt very afraid, and my vision zoned in on the triangle formation of McKinley, McKailey, and McKenna, and the colors of the grass and sky surrounding them. Was I still at Eastwood? It certainly felt like McKenna was sentencing me to a stony jail cell somewhere else. "We knew something was up when the teachers started to act like they hated us – I mean, more than they did before. So we started a little rumor. We planted a little seed in everyone's heads and kicked back as we watched it grow." I felt powerless to move my limbs, as though all I could do was stand there helplessly and listen as her words dug into my skin.

"You want to know what we said?" McKenna asked, not really wanting an answer. This was a monologue now. "We told everyone how you, being *so* jealous that you were different from the rest of us, made it seem like we were bullying you so that you would get the attention you craved and so that you could gather up a support team.

After all, everyone at this school knows how you like to be protected." McKenna's voice lilted as she said that, and memories connected to her words circled behind my eyes. "They all believed it. I mean, some people were a little resistant at first – it seems as though you managed to get some of the other people at this school to actually *like* you – but we were able to convince them with a little time," she said with a sweet smile, and I felt as though metal bars were slamming down in front of me.

Grace's words flashed back to me and I struggled to speak "I – I'm not going to let you lie," I said, swallowing hard. "I won't let them accept the lie."

"Too bad," McKenna said, "because we already have a plan to make sure you will." I just stared, my eyes locked on hers. I found myself speechless as she came even closer. "Here's where the listening becomes really important," she said, her voice almost a whisper. "You are not going to convince anyone that this is a lie. You're not even going to *try*. No one is going to know, and then we can just go on as we did in the beginning of November before you started to try to get new friends and all that crap." She spit the words out in my face, and the cruelty in her voice made me flinch. I was breathing hard, struggling to remain calm.

"Why are you so *mean*?" I yelled, unable to come to terms with what had happened here. McKenna used to be my friend and it made no sense. Nothing made sense.

My ex-friend smiled as my words vibrated around me. "That's just who I am," she said as she held her hands out in a *look-how-wonderful-the-world-is* gesture. "You used to be like that too, Audrey. Remember?" I closed my eyes and pushed back the emerging memories. I was trying very hard not to remember, had been trying hard for a while. "So," McKenna said, returning to the previous subject, "Here's the deal. You're not going to do any of those things that I listed before. And if you do, it will be bad. But you won't. And to make sure that you don't, I've prepared a little poetic threat for you. You ready?" McKenna was looking at me seriously and through my panic I couldn't help cocking an eyebrow. She licked her lips before she began. "You are *going* to comply with our instructions," she said persuasively. "This isn't a negotiation. It's a situation of do or die. Well," and here she tilted her head to the side and looked almost thoughtful, "obviously, you won't *really* die. But you'll be dead here." Her voice was so cheerful that I almost didn't understand what she was saying. But then her eyes met mine one last time and everything came crashing down on me.

McKenna was saying that if I didn't comply she would ruin me at school – at least, more than she already had. This prospect pressed down on me even harder and my limbs started to feel very heavy through a combination of exhaustion, unwanted knowledge, and fear. I closed my eyes, trying to concentrate and think if there was any way to get out of what had just been thrown at me. I couldn't find one. When I opened them again, McKenna, McKailey, and McKinley were walking away. It was obvious from their strut that they had accomplished their goal.

I teetered over to the basketball court. Then my fogged up mind remembered that the boys weren't talking to me. So instead, out of pure desperation and exhaustion, I stumbled over to the wall of the school that I used to sit against to watch the boys try to play basketball and collapsed against it, letting my back slowly slide down until I was sitting on the cold concrete. I felt lost, a stranger in my own house. I scanned the school yard and saw all the middle schoolers who were laughing and having fun. None of them would talk to me. They all thought I was a liar.

Anger suddenly flooded through my body. How dare these girls turn this school that used to feel like my home into a prison? Because of what they started that Monday in October, I was a prisoner in my own school, stuck behind bars sealed with threats and lies.

I felt so locked up inside my own body, having to deal with all of these problems by myself. I was stuck in my own mind – I was even having *conversations* with my own mind. Was this how all victims felt, everyone who was ever alone or lost or was ganged up against? Did they all dissect their problems in their own minds? I didn't know anything about it. I hadn't paid enough attention to those anti-bullying service announcements, and I suddenly wished that I hadn't found them so boring back then, because I might have absorbed something useful.

I desperately wanted to stand up and be the old confident, friendship-loving, sarcastic Audrey. That didn't seem to be possible, though. Too many things were holding me back – memories, guilt. In the past, I had forced people into the awful situation that I was in right now, because I was scared. I was scared of weakness, scared of bullies, scared of their Jekyll-and-Hyde nature that had lured me into their trap.

I saw now that my terror of bullies and my actions to protect myself had practically turned me into what I hated. I had become a person who was basically a bully. Now – sitting against this wall and fighting my stinging eyes – I wanted to go back and change every one of those actions. I wanted to apologize to every single one of those people. But I couldn't. I didn't have the opportunity. Most of them were gone now.

"Well, well, well," I heard a voice say. I jumped for what felt like the millionth time in the past two weeks and stared in a daze at the figure to my left. It was a girl my age, her short figure clad in jeans and a pastel top. But what really caught my eye was the fiery red hair that came down to the hem of her shirt, packed together in tight ringlet curls. Her emerald green eyes pierced mine in a familiar way. "It seems like I picked the right day to visit," she said in an amused voice.

I was overwhelmed with a fear and recognition as the girl smirked at me and memories swirled towards me like a typhoon. The girl's gaze did not falter and I knew that I could no longer hide. I knew that girl.

It was Emmaline Adams.

— MEAN —
chapter | twenty – seven

As my resolve collapsed and I gave in to the memories that were assaulting me, I was transported back to October two years ago, when McKenna, Jacklyn, and I were at the peak of our friendship. With such a strong bond, we knew that each of us would stand up for the others and get them out of trouble if needed. This made us feel more confident than ever. We became a tight group, one you wanted to avoid if possible. We were the closest thing to the popular clique at Eastwood.

I remembered that time with great happiness, and with great shame. I had never had more power than I did then, which meant that I didn't have to deal with people who annoyed me. I remembered it had been a sickeningly wonderful feeling – being able to control people like that.

That year, only three people really bothered me: Sarah Rathmann, Marisol Cruz, and Emmaline Adams. They were *best* friends. They were closer even than Jacklyn and me, and had been for as long as I could remember.

That bothered me. It bothered all of us. It made them a threat to our carefully built lives. Therefore, we made it our goal to make their lives as uncomfortable as possible.

P.E. class was one of our favorite times to mess with them.

"All right, boys and girls!" our P.E. teacher, Mr. Sassrick, called out one day as we spilled onto the playing field. We called him Mr. Sass for short, and constantly teased him about his name. "It's time to play a nice, fair game of lacrosse. Like always, we're going to start out by choosing team captains. So if you would like to volunteer, please raise your hand."

McKenna jabbed me in the side and winked, reminding me to raise my hand. We knew that if we both volunteered, there was a better chance of at least one of us getting picked, and we enjoyed having that amount of control over the game. Plus, McKenna and I were both very good at lacrosse, so we knew that gave us an even bigger chance of Mr. Sass picking us. Jacklyn, on the other hand, was not so coordinated, so she stayed back in the shadows. We'd learned to use this fact to our advantage.

"So let's see... captains – how about Audrey and Lana?"

McKenna looked at me and winked. I smiled back – I knew it would be easy to pick a winning team, especially with Lana LaMone on the other side. She was a very athletic girl and could run very fast, but she lacked any kind of killer instinct.

I stepped forward, and so did Lana. We were now standing on either side of Mr. Sass, facing the rest of the class.

"Audrey, would you like to make the first choice?"

"Yes," I replied, and with my mind whirring up a plan, my eyes wandered easily over the crowd. My vision zeroed in on Emmaline, Sarah, and Marisol. Marisol was strong, a good player. She always gave 110%, but she tried to avoid direct conflict with other players. Sarah was nothing to worry about. She was clumsy, even worse than Jacklyn. Those two would probably be the last ones picked. Emmaline was the biggest worry, if I had to worry at all. Not only was she a good player, she didn't back down. At least not without a war first. That meant that if I wanted to beat her, she needed to be on the other team. And I needed to make sure she was alone so I could zero in on her.

"I'll take Marisol," I said, nodding at McKenna to make sure she understood. Marisol walked up to me timidly, her dark hair shielding her eyes.

Lana picked her person and we continued to go back and forth. I couldn't tell if Lana had a strategy or not, or if she was just being nice. She had picked some pretty strong people. I could tell this bothered McKenna – she didn't just want to intimidate Emmaline, she wanted to win the entire game. I wasn't as vicious up front. I just liked the thrill of having the leisure to exercise some control.

The only things that really mattered to me were to have Marisol on my team and Emmaline on the opposite one. Sarah wasn't a real issue. As I'd guessed, the last two choices were between the clumsy Jacklyn and the even clumsier Sarah. I smirked as I watched Jacklyn chew Sarah out.

"Don't hold your breath, Sarah. No matter whose choice it is, Audrey or Lana, you'll still be picked last," Jacklyn said, smoothly leaning onto her lacrosse stick. Sarah gave Jacklyn a shaky look and breathed out slowly. It made me smile more; it was only October and we were already tiring them out.

"You know, Jacklyn, you aren't the brightest bulb in the bunch either," Sarah said with an annoyed look. The comeback actually would have been acceptable if it wasn't for the fact that the comparison had nothing to do with lacrosse at all.

"Yeah?" Jacklyn replied, a slightly hurt look splashed across her face. "Well, I'm blonde. What's your excuse?"

Sarah rolled her eyes and Jacklyn just smiled sweetly, turning back around to face the captains.

I picked Jacklyn to be on my team and Sarah was put on Lana's.

With the teams divided, Mr. Sass walked out to his watching seat on the side of the court and blew into his whistle. "Let the game begin!" he shouted in his booming voice.

"Correction," McKenna whispered to me, "let the games begin." McKenna's accompanying grin could have belonged on a wildcat's face. Its fierceness fueled my brain to concentrate solely on what McKenna had told me had to be done: get them out of the game, whatever it takes.

The boys were the first to charge, holding their lacrosse sticks out as if they were swords and running towards each other like this was tackle football. Jacklyn rolled her eyes in disgust and ran off in the opposite direction. We all knew the plan, and being in the midst of the game filled my veins with an excitement that clouded my judgment. Jacklyn was going after Sarah: weakest on weakest. Marisol wasn't an issue because she was on our team, and she bugged us the least because she never ever talked back. That left Emmaline. I zeroed in on her, watching her red curls bounce through the air as she ran. McKenna was right behind her. The look in her layered brown eyes was determined.

I faked being confused – it was all part of the plan. I stood in the middle of the action and looked from side to side, waiting until I saw McKenna charging in my direction, with Emmaline on her right side. That's when I darted into action, using my peripheral vision to find the ball and race after the person who possessed it. Luckily, she was on my team, so I hollered for her to pass it in my direction. Once the ball was mine, I dashed back around and pretended to stumble as I passed close to McKenna, who had been trying to keep Emmaline contained in a little patch of grass. My faked flail worked, and Emmaline's attention was soon drawn to me. She barged past McKenna, almost knocking her in the shoulder. Inside I winced. Poor Emmaline, she was no doubt irritated by our antics.

By this point Jacklyn had succeeded in getting Sarah out, and our team was winning. Emmaline was the only one on her team still trying with fervor to accomplish something. I stood still as she ran towards me, feigning shock from my stumble. Then, right as she was about to collide with me, I leaped to the left. This forced Emmaline to slam on the brakes and try to turn while she was still moving forward. While she was turning, McKenna, who was still at Emmaline's side, jutted out her lacrosse stick in front of Emmaline's feet, almost tripping her and making her lurch towards me. I leaned forward as though I was about to run at her, but then, just as her feet were about to meet mine, I groaned loudly and collapsed on the ground. I immediately grabbed my foot, faking a cramp. My sudden drop caused Emmaline to call out in alarm and throw her hands out to stop herself. I saw her left hand shoot over my head, and then her right, which was also still wielding her lacrosse stick. The stick was tilted up, as if to cruise right over my head, but then I straightened my neck a little bit so that it grazed the top of my skull.

"Ow!" I screamed, now faking a head wound and a foot cramp. I felt like a true actor, completely driven by the motive that McKenna had planted in my head like a movie director.

The sound of Mr. Sass's whistle vibrated through the air, signaling a timeout.

"Ladies, ladies!" he yelled, running out to our section of the field. "What is going on here?"

Emmaline slowly stood upright and brushed the grass off her

shorts. She frowned as she stared at my carefully constructed "hurt" face.

"Emmaline's stick hit me in the head," I whined, clutching my head to my knees.

"What? How?" Mr. Sass asked.

"I didn't hit her." Emmaline's voice interjected confidently between my whines. She looked down at me again and scowled. "It was an accidental collision." However, her eyebrow jutted up suspiciously during the last word. I looked down, concentrating now on my supposed cramp.

"Well, did your stick suddenly fly up in the direction of her head?" Mr. Sass asked, a bit sarcastically. His features were twisted in annoyance. I could tell that he was not in the mood to deal with us. That would make my victory all the more easy.

"No," I whimpered, bringing the attention back to me. "I collapsed on the ground because my foot cramped up. Emmaline was charging at me when it happened." I tried to hide my smile. Emmaline was in trouble now − Mr. Sass did not tolerate it when people viciously charged. He wanted us to be good sports with controlled attitudes the entire game through.

Mr. Sass straightened up. "Emmaline," he began, sighing, "I tolerate charging by the boys because they have a lot of pent up energy and this is their only way to get it out, other than rotting their eyes out on the couch playing video games. But you... I'm sorry, but I can't see any good reason to excuse you."

I concentrated on Emmaline's reactions as Mr. Sass said this. She was obviously reeling at the unfairness of it all. It was delicious. "I'm sorry," Mr. Sass said when she tried to speak, "but I am going to have to ask you to sit out for the rest of this game. Okay?" He walked over and patted Emmaline on the back before walking away, ignoring the fact that to her it was obviously not okay.

I stood up slowly as he left, still acting as though I had a slight cramp. McKenna, who had been watching smugly from the sidelines, walked up and joined me. Emmaline glared at us both.

"This is unfair and you know it!" she exclaimed, pointing in our faces.

"Calm down, Emmaline, it's only for one game," McKenna said. She gave Emmaline the same confident and amused look that I would recognize and remember two years later, when it was aimed at me. But back then I was on McKenna's side, staring and looking just as smug.

"You are faking," Emmaline accused.

I just shrugged my shoulders, knowing how to push her buttons. "That's not being a very good sport, Emmaline. But believe what you'd like."

"I don't believe, I *know*. You put Marisol on your side, you targeted Sarah, and then you faked this injury so that you could get me in trouble with Mr. Sass!"

"Look," McKenna said, annoyed that she was still standing there, "why can't you just accept your loss and move on?"

"Because this wasn't a loss. This was cheating. All I want is to be able to have a nice P.E. class without you targeting my friends and me." Emmaline's voice was softer now. She was obviously trying to calm herself.

McKenna gave me a look, as if to say *why is she being so stubborn?* I nodded, letting her know that I knew how to deal with it.

The situation suddenly seemed surreal as I straightened my shoulders and dug through my inner list of mean quips, preparing to say something radical. "Look," I began, "your lameness is cramping my style, and my foot. Now get off the field."

Emmaline's body began to twitch, which alarmed me, and I swore I saw a glistening teardrop slide down from her clear emerald eyes.

"Why are you so *mean*?" she yelled, before drawing in a shaky breath and running away to the sidelines.

My vision swirled again as Emmaline's last words repeated over and over until her voice transformed into mine, and suddenly I was the victim standing alone on the bright green field.

Slowly, both Audreys woke up from their dream. The Audrey dressed in a P.E. uniform realized what she had done and stood unmoving next to McKenna, who was cackling softly to herself. Emmaline had shouted her words and run away, leaving McKenna amused that Emmaline would even use the word *mean* as an insult. Audrey stood at McKenna's side, forced to pretend that the word – that evil word – didn't affect her at all.

"Audrey?"

The whirling memories vanished as Emmaline – the real-life Emmaline of today – walked towards me, repeating my name as she approached.

"Hi," I said simply. It came out as a harsh whisper.

She came even closer to me now and I felt some sort of understanding vibrate between us, which ironically I did not understand. "You're probably enjoying this, aren't you?" I said in the same tortured voice. I wasn't crying, but was on the verge so that I looked like I just had, and my legs were curled up with my hands framing my face.

"No," she said sincerely, shaking her head. "Why would I ever enjoy someone else's pain?"

It was meant as a reassuring comment, but instead it bit at my heart. It was a stab – *unlike you*, she was saying. That was what it really meant. She sat down beside me, sliding down the wall as I had. "Obviously," she said as she settled in, "a lot has changed."

I snorted. "Obviously. Look around you." I would not have sounded so angry if I had not already felt defeated. Emmaline must have felt this, because she looked over to me and let out a sharp laugh before sighing.

"You're just a fine mess, aren't you?" she asked.

I sighed as well. She was right. "I feel like my life is so fragmented. Like it's become this mess of bits and pieces of colors and people and feelings and I don't even know how to sort it out any more." After I said that I realized how ridiculously metaphorical that sounded – not at all an explanation one adolescent would give to another to explain the status of their life.

"Oh dear God," Emmaline said, leaning her head back.

"What?" I said, probably sounding more alarmed than the situation called for.

"You're starting to sound like me," she said, a dark humor evident in her voice.

"I'm sorry?"

"You're starting to sound all emotional and melodramatic and turning your life into metaphors." She paused and turned to stare straight at me. "That's what people do who've been locked up inside themselves and have just been re-thinking the same material over and over again and feel afraid to let it out in front of anyone."

Her words only partly registered with me, but I understood the essence of what she was saying. "I know," I said, slapping my hands down.

"So, this isn't like you. Even though you are less than my favorite person and I'll probably always feel a little bitter towards you, I think you need to get back up! I mean, you've obviously survived this long without getting absolutely obliterated by the MCKs' teenage anger. What's the use of giving up now?"

I looked at her plainly. As wonderful as her speech – or preaching, or whatever it was – was, it didn't hit home anywhere, didn't give me any new burst of energy or determination to continue.

"Don't you get it?" she said, obviously frustrated at my notable lack of reaction to her words. "Look, I know I haven't been here for the whole thing, but I asked around, and I found someone who told me all about it."

"Someone talked to you?" I whispered, suddenly breaking through my haze. "Someone talked to you about it?" I felt a bit incredulous, as I was unable to think of anyone who actually cared enough about me at this point to explain it all. My head swung suddenly to stare at Emmaline. "What did they say?"

Emmaline let out a breath through a half-smile. "They told me how you spent this entire time working to rise above the MCKs. You tore yourself apart from them," here she started to gesture wildly at our surroundings, which were quite empty since everyone seemed determined to stand the farthest possible distance away from me. "You got new friends, you built yourself a new environment, you made the school *yours* again, without bullying or bringing other people down." I stared hazily straight ahead. She let out a frustrated grunt and rotated herself so that she was in front of me before continuing. "I think that's amazing, Audrey! You could've just gone up to them and screamed. You could've just screamed all your accusations and pushed them and let all your anger out in one burst. But instead you stood up for yourself in a powerful way. I mean, you obviously made a statement to them by doing all this, or they wouldn't have gone through all this elaborate trouble to tear you down again. And now they're just walking tall on you again and you need to make it *stop*, just like you did before."

She breathed hard for a few moments, and my face began to unfreeze as I realized how true her words were. Was Emmaline actually congratulating me, in a way? She was making me sound like a *better person*, this girl who I used to be so cruel to.

"You've already found the road back up," she said softly. "That was the hardest part, and you found it. You've already started to lay the bricks for the pavement and now you just need to make sure you don't forget to seal all the cracks."

My face finally broke into a different expression; I was amused, and I almost laughed. "You know not everything has to be some deep metaphor, right?"

Emmaline laughed as she pulled her untamed hair back with her hand. She looked so vulnerable like that. She had nothing protecting her – someone could just walk up and puncture her skin, letting all her weaknesses flow out. I thought about how she might just be one of the bravest people that I had ever met.

"You know," she said as she moved back so that she was sitting beside me, "I know about all this stuff because Danny told me. He doesn't believe that stupid rumor that the girls came up with."

"Then why was he still not talking to me, just like all the others?" I asked. I wasn't able to keep the hurt, the feeling of betrayal out of my voice.

"They *all* stopped talking to you?" she asked. I nodded. Emmaline rolled her eyes, as if she was thinking about how ridiculous it was that they would do that, and sighed. "Well, you know how boys think. They don't want to be different from the rest of their friends because then they could be alienated from the group or something stupid like that." She paused for a second before speaking again. "Danny also told me the other boys didn't believe it at first, but then I guess McKenna found a way to convince them."

That made me sad. "I always thought that boys didn't get sucked up in stupid drama like this."

"They don't," Emmaline said, moving her eyebrows for emphasis, "usually. But this time they were threatened in more boyish ways." I looked at her, confused. "Danny alluded to the fact that McKenna threatened to kick them hard... where it would *really* hurt."

"Oh my God," I whispered, and laughed for the first time at the crude concept. My laughter turned stronger and Emmaline started to laugh with me. Our laughter filled the space around us, unfreezing it as well.

"But I think Danny and... Cash," she said slowly, as if she didn't understand why Cash would be in the group of people who believed in me more, "were more stubborn. They just pretended to go along with the rest of the group."

I nodded in disagreement and made a sort of noise between a grunt and a sniffle. "No, I think I scared Cash off with my obsession with his eyes," I said lightly as I moved to wipe my own eyes, even though I hadn't actually shed any tears. Emmaline laughed, and I watched as the sound erupted from her mouth. For the first time, I saw that in her green eyes there were darker pools that hinted at sadness.

"So, how is Thailand?" I asked, feeling that it was time to turn the conversation to her.

"It's all right." She was looking down.

"No," I said. "If it's *all right* then it's awful, or you're homesick." She gave me a weird look, so I continued, "I've been asked the question 'is everything all right?' enough times in the past few months to know that if you say it is, you're usually lying." Emmaline looked amused.

"Well, I'm dealing. It's just exhausting, sometimes. I tire of dealing with it all, of dealing with the changes and the constant questions." She looked down. "I feel like I'm in a different world when

I'm there, and that this one is frozen. Now that I've visited I see that that is *definitely* not true." I laughed again, but it was more like a bark.

"Do you ever feel yourself slipping?" I asked. "Like one day it's all just going to crack and you're going to get too fed up to stand it any more?"

Emmaline's lips pursed for a moment before she answered. "Yes. I think everyone feels that way about their life, no matter what they're going through."

"So, what do you do? How do these people deal?"

She looked at me smugly. "Those are very deep and somewhat broad questions."

"Sorry," I said, looking down, "this is kind of new to me."

Emmaline leaned in, as if she was telling a trade secret. "Well," she whispered, and I could feel her misty breath in my ear, "they just find something that helps them keep a grip until it gets better."

"It gets better?" I asked incredulously. At this point I felt like I'd be stuck here forever.

Emmaline's smile was melancholy. "That's the funny thing − situations are never as long or as permanent or as life-ending as we think they are. Humans naturally overreact. There are points when we realize that nothing is ever written in permanent marker."

"But until those points come…what do you do? What helps you keep your grip?"

Emmaline shrugged. I stared at her, urging her voicelessly to keep talking. She let out a sigh. "Do you *really* want to know what I do?" I nodded enthusiastically. She sighed more softly this time and continued, "Personally, I just try to keep myself calm, entertained." She looked almost embarrassed as she said the next part. "I listen to music."

"Yuck," I responded. "I hate music." Emmaline stared at me raptly, surprised by this outburst, so I quickly came up with an explanation. "A lot of it could've been made by robots." Despite being a viable opinion, that wasn't the real reason. But I didn't feel like trying to explain the fireworks in my brain to Emmaline, for I was already overwhelmed enough.

"True," Emmaline said, half insulted and half amused, "but you shouldn't be so quick to judge. There are some really true lyrics out there."

I suddenly felt a bit guilty that I had beaten down on her lifejacket so quickly, so I tried to think of a way to let her have her moment. "Well," I began awkwardly, "share some with me then. I need all the help I can get."

Emmaline cleared her throat and I sensed this was uncharted territory for her; she didn't normally share these things. "Well," she began, "there is one song that I like the most. The chorus is really powerful." She looked at me and I stared at her, waiting for her to continue. She cleared her throat again before glaring at me slightly. "I'm not going to *sing* it, but I'll tell you the title. It's called *Keep Holding On*."

"Well, just from the title I can already see why it's your favorite," I said, and I found myself smiling as I thought about the words some more. *Keep holding on, keep holding on, keep holding on....* It started to repeat in my head like a mantra.

"It's so uplifting," she said, her voice immediately happier. "It's a song that just makes you want to get up and make everything better. It's a celebration of life." She looked at me and smiled. "You should listen to it. I think that's something that could come in good use for you. After all, right now you look like you're singing a requiem." I laughed bitterly, amazed at how much she was helping, and how much I was feeling better deep down. Fueled by her words, something was starting to brew inside of me that was stronger than the hurt, the humiliation, the fear, everything.

"That's not even the best part," she said softly, pulling me back out of my thoughts. "There's a part, in the bridge, when the singer states, 'There's nothing you can say, there's nothing you can do, there's no other way when it comes to the truth'." She didn't sing the line, but her voice was lilting through the air as she spoke it. And I thought about how beautiful it was as her voice faded off into the atmosphere.

There's no other way. The phrase echoed in my head as Emmaline continued talking. "It's really inspiring, isn't it? Really uplifting."

"Sure," I replied, stuck in a daze. Those words had struck me just right, and it was an odd feeling, almost like I was stuck in a metaphor – and it was telling me that there's no other way out of this, other than the path that I'd already started on.

Emmaline could see that I was thinking. She tilted her head. "I think break is going to end soon." She continued to study me before saying, "Do you know what you want to do?"

"Yes," I replied, and my breathing was becoming excited.

"What if they try to fight back again?" she asked, smiling.

"They can do whatever they want," I said, my voice now defiant. "But that doesn't matter to me. All that matters is what I'm going to do."

"And what are you going to do?" I could hear the pride in Emmaline's voice; she knew she had made her mark.

I looked at her and smiled, almost giddily. The exhaustion that had been plaguing me drained from my limbs, and I actually felt that with a little support, I might be able to stand up and continue. "I'm going to stand up, and keep going. And I know, no matter what, it's all going to be okay," I said to her, smiling because I felt truly confident.

"Because…," she prompted me, expectation glowing in her eyes. I looked forward again and laughed as I breathed out, surprised that I hadn't had the will to do this before.

"Because," I continued, "I'm going to get by on the high road."

After I said this, I flashed one last smile at her before bracing my hands against the ground in preparation to get up. Emmaline placed her hand on my forearm and pushed to help me lift up. I looked down, surprised at her help, and her responding grin was blinding.

— CLEAR —
chapter | twenty – nine

It had no doubt been the longest Monday of my life. I spent the rest of the day talking with Emmaline, since no one else would talk to me, about much lighter topics and trying my best to keep a smile on my face.

That night I slept soundly, curled up around a pillow with my heart beating excitedly for the next day, feeling that it was time for me to wash all the stupid fears away and start anew. I also dreamed that night. I had one of those metaphorical dreams where you don't even remember what happened after you wake up, but suddenly everything is so much clearer. I woke up from my dream knowing that the first person I needed to talk to was Cash.

Classes were now incredibly awkward since the boys were all treating me like I was a traitor. It was so annoying, and I just wanted to walk right up and slap them all silly across the head until they came to their senses. Especially Danny, who apparently didn't even believe the whole thing, but was just acting otherwise. However, I told myself to stay calm and wait, because at first break I was going to start winning them back.

I realized, in the back of my head, that by doing this I was flat out defying the M-C-Ks. *Do or die.* McKenna's words still echoed in my head. *Obviously, you won't really die. But you'll be dead here.*

Well, too bad, McKenna, I thought. She might have seen herself as an all-powerful person, but even a bully didn't have the right to stop me from trying to be happy.

It was odd to see Cash acting hurt – his usually tough image seemed to have slipped off his frame and been forgotten. I approached him slowly on the basketball field at break, being careful not to slip on the patches of ice.

"Cash," I began as I approached him. He slowly raised his head to look at me and I suddenly felt sad. I had no idea in what direction this was going to go – it could very well be another failure.

"Audrey."

"Can we talk?"

"What, so you can stare into my eyes and figure out all my secrets?" he spit out.

It took me a minute to recover from being speechless. "I – I'm sorry? What?"

"You know."

"Well, obviously I don't," I said, now frustrated. "So can you tell me what I did wrong? Besides that fake rumor, which I know you know isn't true." I was looking at him desperately. I needed to get something, some kind of emotion or reaction. His words were coming to me as just that, words. There was nothing behind them.

He just looked annoyed so I sighed and walked away, going to sit on my rock. When I was about halfway there I realized he was following me. I spun around. "Do you want to just stalk me, or are you willing to hear me out?"

"Talk if you want to," he said in such a nonchalant tone that I felt foolish in ever believing that he liked me.

"I'm so stupid," I said, sitting down. He was still following behind, like a puppy.

"Not exactly."

"This whole thing is so stupid."

"Maybe we're all just stupid," he said, stuffing his hands into his pockets.

"I can't believe I ever thought I could make myself feel like I had an actual family at school again without Jacklyn. Everyone here just seems to hate me now."

"What?" Cash said. This seemed to surprise him. "Audrey," he started and then he looked around, as if to make sure we were alone. He had no need to worry; people were still avoiding me like the plague. "I like you," he said.

I beat the butterflies back. "No, you don't. You're just trying to make me feel better about myself."

"No, I really like you," he said again, and I inwardly chastised myself for starting to think that maybe he meant *like* like.

"No!" I said, wondering why I sounded so defiant. "Really, Cash, you can stop pretending."

"Really," he said, softer now. "I know you know."

Realization hit me and desperation floated away. "Wait, is that what you meant by 'figure out all my secrets'?" I knew it was true even before he nodded. "Cash, I overheard a conversation between you and the rest of the guys. That's how I knew."

Cash looked away, trying to hide the blush that crept up the side of his face. "Stalker," he said and I laughed.

"Cash," I said, but he continued to look away. "Cash," I rotated his shoulders with my hands so that he was forced to face me. "I like you too." The words came out of my mouth in a rush, and I was shocked as I found myself whispering them into the wind. His face looked shocked too. I had absolutely no idea what to do next, as this had never happened to me before, and I suddenly wished I had someone like Jacklyn, who was wise in the ways of boys, sitting next to me, whispering in my ear what to do or say next.

He smiled but then looked away. I smiled down, pride and happiness washing over me now that I had said it. The cold breeze blew around us as the words continued to register with him, but I felt immune to it now.

"Cash," I said slowly again, "tell me something."

"Yeah?" he asked, scratching his head. I saw the red on his cheeks and hid a grin.

"Did McKenna, McKailey, and McKinley ever actually hate me?" I asked. It was a prospect that had always bothered me. I had never really known if their actions were driven by hate or the fact that they had so much in common and I was an easy target.

"No, I don't think so," he responded. "Why?"

"It's just this whole thing with them… bullying me," I said the word awkwardly, but I knew I had to get it out, "is so confusing. I was wondering if you knew anything about it."

He chuckled. "Well, that's sort of vague."

"I mean, I'm always going to want to know how this all started."

He sighed. "I think maybe they didn't like you at the beginning of the year. But as it went on they became fine. Now," he shrugged and held up his hand almost in defense, "I guess they just feel like they need to finish what they started."

"Yeah," I said, looking down. "That's what I was always trying to prevent from happening."

Cash looked at me and grinned sheepishly, "I guess they got to everyone, didn't they?"

I nodded. "Everyone." I stared at him as I said this. *Even you.*

"I feel like I tried so hard to become friends with you this year, and then I just failed."

I was shocked by this. "You were trying? You mean, it wasn't just me being desperate for companionship that brought us all together?" He laughed.

"I mean, not that I was *trying* trying," he said, and I wanted to giggle at the alarmingly bright shade of red that splashed across his cheeks, "but I... you understand what I mean." He looked down and I smiled, knowing he didn't want to say the real word. "But I got distracted at the end and it unraveled in front of everyone," he said, gesturing to the group of guys who were rolling around in the snow.

"It's okay," I said, patting him on the arm. "Success always occurs in private, failure in full view." I looked down and muttered, "I should know."

Cash looked amused. "You need to not be so hard on yourself! One part of you needs to tell the other parts to lay off."

I laughed. "I'm just glad you're talking to me now, and actually listening. It's refreshing to be around you when you're not around your friends and acting like an idiot."

He scoffed. "Hey, I take offence at that!"

"Well, you know it's true! You pretend like you're such a godly person when you're around them. You always have to get everyone laughing at your stupid jokes."

"And I repeat, I take offence at that. I'll have you know that there are times that my friends don't laugh at my jokes, and that's when I just have to say 'you know what, eff you.'"

He stopped talking, as if he expected some kind of reaction – what kind, I had no idea – but I stayed silent.

"That was supposed to be funny," he said, obviously annoyed. "You're not laughing."

"I don't cuss."

Cash looked disgusted. "Well *that's* no fun."

"It's just who I am," I said, staring at him seriously.

He smiled. "See – there's the Audrey I want to see more often, the one who stands up for what she does."

I smiled back and realized that he believed in me. I liked the feeling, it was refreshing. We both smiled at each other for the longest time and I remembered when he first sat next to me in Science class. The same sparks of light were here as on that day. Except it didn't scare me any more as I felt them crowd around the edges of my vision. My eyes were sparkling too, I knew.

"Tell me something," I said, looking down as I felt a blush now creeping up *my* face.

"Again?" he asked, faking annoyance. I laughed and swatted his arm.

"Yes. And this is serious."

"Fine," he said, settling down. "What?"

I breathed deeply and turned to face him square on. "What color are my eyes?"

He frowned at me, confused. "Can't you just go look in a mirror?"

"Yeah, but," I struggled with how to explain it, "that's different. When I look in a mirror I can never really tell if I'm seeing the truth or just what I want to see. So, please, do me a favor and tell me." I scooted closer to him and was now sitting on the very edge of my rock. "What color are my eyes?"

We breathed slowly for a few seconds before he responded. His eyes were electrifying as they studied mine and became dotted with hints of a brighter shade. "They're blue," he said and I was almost disappointed at how normal that sounded. "Most of the time," he continued and I breathed in sharply. "Sometimes I think I see these flashes of other colors, or they become surrounded in rings of green, or when you're sad they darken so that they are almost hazel. But most of the time they are the clearest things that I have ever seen. They're almost like mirrors," he swallowed awkwardly, "the most gorgeous pair of mirrors that I have ever seen."

His words made it hard for me to breathe, and the fluttering in my stomach threatened to suffocate me. I found it so ironic that my one goal for so long was to keep my weaknesses locked up, and yet apparently you could see them all by just looking into my pathetically clear eyes.

But apparently they were also beautiful.

Cash grinned, but it was gentle. "Sometimes they're more indigo, but sometimes they spark magically, like the sea on a sunny day." His hand was an inch away from my face and I smiled.

"Thank you," I whispered.

He looked away again to hide another wave of shyness. It was endearing, the moment was over, and I smiled.

I stood up and straightened out my jacket, brushing off imaginary specks of dust. I wanted to clutch my stomach – the butterflies were attacking now.

"You keep looking away from me," I said to the air in front of me as I finished tidying my jacket. Cash stood up as well and joined me. His face had patches of coral red, and I was sure mine did too.

"Are you afraid?" I asked when he didn't answer. I knew it was stupid – you should never ask a boy that question – but it just slipped out. Expectedly, he didn't reply. "I won't tell anyone," I whispered, and I realized we were standing facing each other now.

"What would you do if I kissed you?" he asked, his voice a combination of fear, shyness, and a boyish smugness. Lights were flashing around me and a shocked part of me, the part of me that had thought this day would never come, realized that somewhere along the way I had succeeded. I wanted desperately to just give in, but I had to hold some ground.

"I might kiss you back," I said, feeling afraid but knowing there was a huge smile on my face, "and then punch you."

Cash shrugged. "I'll risk it."

And then he leaned forward and my stomach collapsed, taking in that last breath. I closed my eyes and watched in awe as all the butterflies flew up into the sky, free, mingling with the exploding lights.

— INNOCENT —
chapter | thirty

Once Cash and I had settled everything, he got the other boys to hear me out. It was easy to get them to stop acting like they were mad at me, since they had never really believed the rumor in the first place.

"They're gonna come after you," Eliot warned after school, as we were celebrating our reunion with donuts and hot chocolate. "They've got nasty tempers, especially McKailey. If I were you, I'd watch my back, Aud."

"I'm not going to worry about it," I said, shrugging. "It's not like I see them that often. We're only really in the same vicinity during break and all-school gatherings. And the next all-school gathering is the winter middle school dance. And I *know* they aren't going to show up for that."

The winter middle school dance was new this year. Usually there were only two dances each year, but our class decided to have another one as a fundraising opportunity. Not only would you have to pay to get in, you'd also have to pay for the delicious chocolate treats and other baked goods. I was looking forward to the dance, hoping it would come with a calm atmosphere and some humor.

I convinced Mrs. Darwin to let me bring Grace and Larken to help decorate, since the M-C-Ks refused to help and the boys popped at least as many balloons as they hung.

"Plus, I got someone else to do the music selection," I explained to Cash one day. "So this time neither the decorations *nor* the music are going to suck." He just laughed and told me that it was a good attempt to tease him, but he would still be the master at that art. I grimaced.

On the night of the dance, the gym was decorated beautifully, with streamers hanging down from the ceiling and a large hand painted welcome banner on the farthest wall. I took pride in my work, as I felt that setting the gym up right would be a testimony to the fact that I was back on my feet. I felt like I had everything under control.

The lights were dimmed and the music started, signaling the beginning of the dance. People started trickling in, and I was pleasantly surprised at how many more people were dressed up this time. It seemed like many students were more comfortable in the atmosphere, like we all knew what to expect from each other after half a year. I remembered that at the beginning of the year that had been my goal, for everyone to be more like a family. It was ironic that we were much closer now but in another way much more separate.

I was relieved to see that McKenna, McKailey, and McKinley were *not* among the people coming in through the door.

Even though so much had changed, I found that I still felt just as nervous about the first slow dance. The first few fast songs came and went and soon enough the first notes of a ballad floated through the air. No one moved. There was no Cash jumping out of the corner and demanding that I dance with him. No brave icebreakers stepped forward. Instead, boys and girls slowly trickled to the center of the dance floor naturally, on their own. I was able to slowly exhale.

Everything was calm as songs succeeded one another and echoed through the air. But then, about a half hour into the dance, I noticed a rift developing in the crowd as a few latecomers drifted to the main part of the gym.

I felt my heart rate increase as I realized who it had to be.

The M-C-Ks were not dressed up at all and made their entrance with a visible swagger that said *'that's right, I'm better than you. So leave me alone.'* And so people did.

I felt like all the gravity in the room was pushing towards me, pressing against my limbs and head. I had been naive to hope that all I needed to do was make up with my friends and that would be it. The M-C-Ks, especially McKenna, just had to get the last word in. It was who they were.

The girls never made eye contact with me, but they sat in the corner of the room and stared out at the dance floor, making everyone else feel uncomfortable. People continued to dance, on and off, but I noticed that the eighth grade boys were backing off now and were standing in a circle near the M-C-Ks, chatting with them. It made me angry that the boys could know everything that those girls had done, and be friends with me, and still talk to them. I guessed it was just part of who they were: people who, despite knowing every detail of the drama, refused to take sides. Most of the time I appreciated that about them, but at that moment a more selfish part of me was still peeved.

And as naive as my hope had been, I thought it was appropriate to let the conflict dwindle away, instead of confronting them and making a big scene. I would never do that, though I had fantasized about it many times. The M-C-Ks seemed to have other plans, though.

After brooding in the corner and making the people on the dance floor feel awkward, I saw McKenna get up and summon the other girls, packing up her stuff as if they were going to leave. McKailey looked unhappy, but after some back and forth she seemed willing to comply with McKenna's wishes. I didn't understand this change of plan, or what they had even wanted in the first place. McKailey was usually the vicious one; her anger drove the group forward. I wondered if, like me, they had planned a confrontation but then realized it would be better not to.

I watched curiously as the two girls left, noticing that McKinley had stayed behind, crouching against the wall. Had they left her as the one to do the talking? That didn't seem smart – she looked smaller than ever standing in the corner of the room. Of course, I realized now that a lot of things the M-C-Ks had done had not been smart.

My confusion at this new revelation was interrupted as Cash pulled me into a slow dance. He tugged on my arm repeatedly, trying to drag me out of my trance and out to the center of the floor. He liked the center, he liked the way that the light in that spot constantly changed from bright to dim as the artificial light from the ceiling fixture filtered through the miniature disco ball rotating above our heads.

"She's staring at you," Cash said as we shifted our weight to the beat of the song.

"Who, McKinley?" Cash nodded and I tried surreptitiously to turn my head and look in her direction. She was indeed, staring at me, and when I realized she had caught me staring back I quickly whipped back around.

"Smooth," Cash commented sarcastically, raising his eyebrow.

"Shut up," I muttered, feeling the girl's eyes boring into my back. "Make her stop staring," I whispered, clutching onto his shoulders.

"What? How? I'm not a magician."

"Just make her stop. It's making me nervous."

"Nervous how?" Cash was asking obvious questions, and I knew he was just doing it to spite me. He didn't see how close this situation was to teetering off into the danger zone.

"She might want to talk to me," I stated clearly, trying to make him understand with my eyes how nervous I was.

He didn't comply. Instead he argued back with, "So? Audrey, that isn't necessarily a bad thing."

"But I'll freeze up! I won't know what to say."

"Then don't say anything," he said, shrugging. Was everything this simple to a boy?

"You've got friends now, Audrey," he said, looking at me pointedly. "*Awesome* friends." I rolled my eyes at his self-compliment. "So, if you have to say something to her, you shouldn't worry about it. Because you *know* we've got your back. Whatever you say, you should do it for yourself, and no one else."

It made sense, but the prospect made me nervous. I felt safe, dancing on the floor. There was no way she'd push her way through throngs of people to come to talk to me, or embarrass me, or something worse. So when the slow song ended and Cash was pulled away by his friends, I just stood there. I tried to keep myself in the middle of all the action so that she wouldn't be able to find me, or at least would not have the nerve to come to me. After the slow song had faded away, one with a faster beat blasted through the speakers. The music was beating into my head and colored lights were spinning around me and all I could see was people dressed in glittery dresses and jumping up and down to a rock and roll tune. It wasn't my scene.

So a part of me was actually happy when I felt a pair of cold fingers tap me on the shoulder. I knew it was McKinley before I even turned around.

She clutched the sleeve of my dress and dragged me through the crowd – she was dragging me down with her.

"You looked like you were waiting for me," she said in a

suspicious questioning voice that you'd think only cops would use. I swallowed hard as the music continued to invade my senses. I thought of Emmaline, and how *she* would use this moment to her advantage. She'd turn her discomfort away and stare bravely in its face to try to extract some new information.

"You were staring at me," I answered coldly in defense. "It was obvious what was coming."

McKinley shied off at the bitterness in my voice, and I felt bad, because I had forgotten for a second that I wasn't talking to someone like McKenna, who was used to being treated like a mean person. I remembered what it was like to have to develop a thick skin and learn how to let people's insults run off your shoulders. I also had to develop a thick tongue in order to learn how to lash back.

"I just wanted to let you know," McKinley said as she straightened her shoulders, "that you can spend as much time as you'd like convincing yourself that we're *evil* bullies who *conspired* against you." She accompanied that phrase with the act of lifting up her arms and flittering her hands throughout the air like jazz hands, as if to point out how ridiculous it was that I'd ever think that. "But in reality what happened was just a situation that got out of hand."

"Oh, really," I said, my voice half shocked and half defiant, half weakened and half confident. This speech sounded very much like something that would come from McKenna or McKailey, certainly not McKinley. But what did I know. Obviously the McKinley I had known for a short period of time was not the McKinley standing in front of me.

"Yes. It was just us wanting some time alone, which you obviously weren't able to understand. So it became this huge deal when really it wasn't supposed to be. It wasn't supposed to turn into what it did. It was completely… innocent."

Innocent. The word echoed in my ears.

I almost wanted to apologize. I almost wanted to look ashamed and tell her I was sorry for interpreting her actions wrong. I almost wanted to believe that she was right. My mind rushed through replays of all the things that I had experienced during that time, all the things that had been done to me.

But then I remembered Grace's warning on the day that she left me standing alone in the schoolyard. *Don't accept a lie as the truth. Don't let McKenna fool you into thinking something different than what you know. She has a way of doing that.* This wasn't McKenna talking to me, but the words sounded like McKenna. I felt McKenna's influence in the air.

Maybe McKenna had actually had a good reason for leaving the dance instead of being here for this. She realized this was a good opportunity to give the new girl a chance to prove herself.

I looked into McKinley's eyes as she stood in front of me, waiting for some kind of reply. The longer I stayed silent the more uncomfortable she looked. Her pupils were twitching, her irises dark. I focused in on the intricate rings looping the edge of the colored circle, like age rings on a tree. As I reached further I saw someone who felt childish, seemed disordered. She was a just an ordinary girl whose name happened to start with three sacred letters, and who had been unlucky enough to be thrown into this school. I saw a younger version of myself inside the depths, one who hadn't been driven crazy yet by fear and stories of how I needed to fear the bullies who plagued the evil middle school years.

I felt a tiny pang zip through my heart as I couldn't help feeling a little sympathy for her. But McKinley still had a chance. *She* was still innocent.

"I'm sorry."

McKinley's entire figure seemed to perk up when she heard these two words. She didn't understand; she thought she was getting an apology for a different reason.

"I'm sorry you had to get dragged into all this," I continued, and she sank back down, her face returning to a headstrong expression that I now saw was forced.

"You were just unlucky," I said and I shook my head with a softened look. "You should've gone to a different school," I said with a sharp sad laugh, "or at least stayed at your Catholic one. I'm sure your preppy girlfriends would've been better than what you got here."

McKinley didn't answer – she just stared at my feet and I had a hunch her uncomfortable feelings had been increased by the way I was labeling her.

"I wasn't your friend," McKinley said, and although her voice was tough her face was apologetic.

"True," I replied immediately. McKinley was trying to hurt me – she was about to learn that I would talk back.

"It's not like you're being that nice to me right now anyway."

"I'm not being mean to you, I'm just being cold. There's a difference. And after all that's happened, can you blame me?"

McKinley's face flashed – distress, a weakness, covered in a second. I saw the old McKinley, a kinder McKinley in that second. She was mostly unrecognizable now. She had come in with such a blank personality that it had been easy for McKenna and McKailey to draw all over her like a whiteboard. "This crap is all past us now anyway," she said. It was obvious she was trying to cover something up.

I closed my eyes, trying to figure out what I wanted to say next, what I wanted to do next. McKinley was trying to downplay it, to make me doubt everything I had felt and experienced. It was easy, because of course it had just been another game to the M-C-Ks. For them the blow had been easily organized, just like a game of lacrosse. She was trying to make me feel crazy again. I refused to cooperate. History wasn't going to make a repeat appearance.

And as angry as I was, as hurt and bitter and frustrated as I was inside, as easy as it would be to just explode right then and there and yell all my thoughts at her, to scream, *"It was just innocent, huh? How about when you were crawling out of the school on your hands and knees to avoid me – was that innocent?"* I found that I didn't want to. It didn't seem worth it. If I yelled or screamed any of those things or even just got mad, it would restart all these things and McKinley – and the rest of the M-C-Ks, for that matter – would just fight back relentlessly. This was the only way to an end.

McKinley sighed. "Do you want to go over and talk with the boys?" she asked in a bitter tone. I had to stop myself from jumping at the offer of friendship she was giving me and dig deeper down.

"No," I said. "Sorry."

McKinley let out a long, frustrated breath. "We're never going to be able to act normal around each other again," she stated, for reasons that were unknown to me, since it seemed like a pretty obvious thing.

"No, probably not. I'm not mad though, any more."

"Why?" She seemed tired and confused. We were both being stubborn in arguing the points we believed in, or had been told to believe in.

"Because even though this was the worst year of my life," I said, firing the words off at her in a frustrated manner because I was trying to make her *understand*, "I see now that maybe it was worth something, because I have ended it with something priceless. And if I was given a chance to go back, I wouldn't change anything. Because now I know what it feels like to have *this*."

McKinley shook her head, like this strange and seemingly unlikely speech was too much for her.

"But you felt the pain," she said, swallowing hard, "I know you did. You just *told* me you did. And I know you think you're being the bigger person and everything – but don't you see? You've gotten *nowhere*. She gestured around to the crowd around us. The girl who used to be your best friend has moved away, and you don't have a replacement. You're right back to where you started."

And as her words penetrated my ears and sank into my consciousness, I took a moment to venture down the road I had taken, and look where it got me. She was right: externally it got me nowhere. But internally I was now miles away from where I had started.

McKinley looked stripped standing there, and I felt honestly sorry for her. She was just the messenger, sent to try to finish what McKenna had started years ago. When McKinley had first come to our school, she had been a shy girl with mysterious brown eyes that had a bit of a sparkle. Her hair had been long and wavy, a dark chestnut brown that was really quite close to black. Now, as she stood in front of me, her big eyes were flat, and a boring color at that; dead. Her hair had been burned by repeated attempts to straighten the waves, and its shade had lightened. It looked a lot more like mousy brown. It looked a lot more like McKenna's.

"I should go," I said, noticing out of the corner of my eye that Danny was motioning for me to come to the exit of the gym. I desperately wanted to run after him and have a good debriefing session to expunge the stress in the air. I didn't want any pointless stress. I just wanted to be happy.

"Bye, McKinley." My voice was as warm as I could make it. I put behind me for good all my years of slightly mean dismissals of unwanted people.

"Audrey." She answered in a single statement, just like she had when we I had first introduced myself to her. Now, as such a different person, I was saying goodbye. Her voice was no longer wispy.

We both stood there for a second, looking down. McKinley continued to stare, as if the layer of glitter that had been spread across the gym floor was extremely interesting. The quiet was refreshing, even cold, though it didn't make me uncomfortable. I could feel that it wasn't permanent. Yes, there was definitely still hope for her.

I smiled on the inside as we stood there in this silence.

Just like how it all began.

— A GIFT —
chapter | thirty-one

I've always found it hard to believe that something has really ended. And maybe that's because it doesn't. Maybe everything continues in the form of little sparks that reside in the back of our heads or hearts. Anything could resurface if the right moment comes up, but there's a point at which most people just choose to move on and take what they have learned with them with the faint hope that they'll be able to use it at some point in the future.

Whether I'd never have to worry about something like the M-C-Ks again, I wasn't sure. But I certainly appreciated some aspects of life that had always seemed like air to me before: you couldn't live without them. Now I knew you could, and having lived a period of my life without them, I never wanted to do without those things ever again.

One of those things was friends.

It didn't matter what differences you had with people – I'd learned that. They could still care about you and be there for you when you really needed them. A part of me, one that barely remembered the misery that I had gone through during those lonely months, was thankful for what had happened, because it had given me the boys. It had opened my eyes to the sarcastic, witty, annoying, hilarious, insensitive, yet joyful people they could be with their unique perspective on the world.

And looking back, another part of me wasn't even surprised it had happened. I had it coming, with the path that I'd been going down. My parents certainly weren't going to wake me up, so instead my social life did by changing drastically. Never mind that it was a horrible change at the time, and that now I knew what it felt like to have my entire world shatter when the last drop of hope that I'd used to fool myself into thinking I had a real friendship evaporated. I was left alone, and forced to learn that a friendship that is just a habit is no better in the long run than being by yourself. Sometimes we have to learn to be alone before we can be lucky enough to find the right people to be with. I now realized what a gift friendship really was.

On the morning following the winter dance, the sun rose like any other day. It was an odd feeling, waking up and realizing that everything was okay. Life was brilliant now, beautiful, coated with a new sense of innocence. People had moved on – most of the Eastwood students had forgotten about the psychotic ultra-drama that had constituted the showdown between Audrey Bass and the M-C-Ks. I wondered how McKenna felt about this. I could just imagine her flipping her hair behind her shoulder and saying with a well-practiced smile, "People move on."

And so they did.

When I got out of the car to go to school the following Monday, Mrs. Darwin smiled at me like she did to everyone else. But then she winked and I knew my smile was different than anyone else's – after all, we had gone through so much. We had an understanding.

I walked down the hallway and everyone seemed to move in slow motion around me. I had a new sense of excitement, I felt like I was being given another chance. I really did feel like I was reliving those first few days of school. Maybe now I could actually choose to be confident about them, unlike the choice I made back then. I wondered in passing if everything would have been different if I had just chosen to be happy, despite it all.

But most likely not. McKenna's, McKailey's, and McKinley's actions had been driven by something that was out of my control. I needed to accept that.

I was halfway down the hallway when Eliot and Ian jumped out suddenly from a classroom door and threw their hands out, booing like ghosts. I screamed, and they laughed. I groaned and clutched my head, extremely annoyed and yet almost bursting with happiness at the same time.

"*What* are you *doing?*" I asked in a reprimanding voice, laughing in a care-free manner as they continued to slap themselves on their backs for the good prank.

"Us?" Eliot snickered. "What are *you* doing, screaming like a girl every time we jump out from behind a door? What are you going to do when we amp up the pranks and start doing serious stuff?"

I looked up smiling – Eliot had already started his growth spurt and was on his way to becoming quite the giant compared to me – and sighed. "God only knows what I'm doing, hanging around with you guys."

Ian started to laugh hysterically as I rolled my eyes again and continued down the hallway. When I reached my locker I heard a loud squealing noise behind me and jumped up, causing my backpack to slide off my arm and land on the floor with a loud thud. The squealing grew still louder as I wheeled around and saw that the piggy shrieks were emanating from a huge hugfest between McKenna and McKailey in the middle of the hallway. I closed my eyes and rubbed my forehead, trying to shut it out. I realized that no matter how *over* everything was, I would still have to deal with the M-C-Ks for the remainder of the year.

"Here you go," I heard a voice say, and I opened my eyes again to see Danny holding out my backpack for me.

"Thanks," I said smiling, a tad embarrassed that I had dropped it in the first place.

"Caught off guard by the sudden burst of loud squealing?" he asked.

"Yeah," I said laughing softly and blinking a few times, trying to get the high pitched noise out of my head. McKenna and McKailey were still talking loudly behind Danny, in voices that persistently tried to catch my ear.

"Quite a loud bunch," Danny muttered, looking amused. He looked at my twisted face. "Making it hard to let go?" he asked, pointing back to the jumping girls.

"A bit." I shook my head, sighing. "They think that no matter what they do, everyone has to be drawn to them." I bit my lip and forced myself to look away, concentrating on Danny. "They have to learn that they're not always going to be the center of attention."

Danny half smiled at my reasoning and swung his own backpack over his shoulder again. "Well, I think I have something that will make you forget all about them. Mrs. Darwin is looking for you."

I tilted my head, confused as to why that would make a difference. "Oh? Why?"

He grinned. "Oh, I don't know… something about a new girl, I think." His grin widened as if he knew more than he was telling me. "She's down by Mrs. Benz's room," he said before turning around to go load his backpack into his own locker. I looked down the hallway and carefully wove my way around the still-excited girls. I soon caught sight of Mrs. Benz. Then I caught sight of the girl standing next to her.

Her eyes were brown. The sight of them made me groan. Here was another pair of brown eyes – a color that I already had enough of in my life. The previous new pair of brown eyes chose that moment to sneak a glance at me as their owner walked down the hallway. Despite our moment of understanding at the dance, her eyes were unfamiliar and cold. I looked again, and realized that in this new girl's eyes I could see only the sun. I decided to retire all judgment.

"Mrs. Darwin?" I said, stepping forward. The new girl smiled at me, as if instinctively. It caught me off guard, and I tentatively smiled back.

"Good morning, Audrey," Mrs. Darwin said, nodding her head. "We have a new student joining our school today. Her family just moved here from South Carolina. I thought you would appreciate the chance to show her around the school," she said as she looked down at me almost gleefully. I could tell that she intended more than her words let on; she wanted me to seize this as an opportunity to try to make up for McKinley, who was *supposed* to be my new friend at the beginning of the year. I smiled again, this time huge and real.

"All right," I said, almost giggling. "Well, hi," I said, half waving to her and she looked amused, waving back. I felt giddy and wasn't sure what to say to her. I had a feeling deep down that this girl was going to be my friend. Mrs. Darwin nodded at me one more time before walking off. I followed her retreating path with my eyes, and so did the new girl. She looked amused.

"Mrs. Darwin is nice," I said, smiling with my lips. "I don't know if you were scared off by her at all…"

"Oh, no," the girl broke in. Her voice was bouncy and sounded optimistic. "I mean, she seemed a bit uptight, but trust me, I've dealt with a lot meaner teachers," she said and looked at me almost like we were sharing a secret.

"I can hardly imagine," I said, shaking my head seriously. She laughed and I suddenly wished I could learn everything about her just from her eyes.

"I'm Audrey," I said, holding out my hand.

"Carson," she said, reaching her hand out as well and meeting mine firmly. Her face was serious as she shook my hand twice and then she broke into a grin again. "I always feel so serious when I do that."

I thought for a moment. "Me too. I've just always done it because it seems to come instinctively. I mean, you usually don't have to worry about making a fool of yourself if you offer to shake someone's hand."

Carson smiled up to the sky. "Oh, I'm sure I could still accomplish that, somehow."

"Don't think that, or you know it will *definitely* happen!" I said.

Carson shrugged, making her ash blonde hair flick up into the air and land behind her shoulders. It was stick straight, like mine, except hers was cut into straight front bangs. She radiated warmth, as if her presence was brightening up the world. I thought it would be appropriate for her to wear yellow.

Just then, Mrs. Benz stepped out from behind the door to her room and cleared her throat.

"Miss Bass," she began and pointed to the clock on the wall to my left, "you are late to homeroom. And so are you…"

"I'm her guide for the day," I filled in. "Mrs. Darwin said she was in your homeroom?"

"Oh, yes, I was told about a new girl." She took her clipboard out from where her elbow pressed it against her side, and scanned down what I assumed was a list of names.

"Ah yes," she said as her finger stopped moving and she smiled. "Just coming in from South Carolina... McKarson Saunders."

I almost choked on the air I was breathing.

"*McK*arson?" I practically squealed, stressing the three letters that were quickly causing my dream to spiral away. "McKarson with a K?" Brown eyes and that deadly name... I just thanked God that her hair wasn't brown too.

"Oh no," Karson – or McKarson – said, bringing her hands up in front of her chest. "My mom might have enrolled me under that name, but I prefer not to be called that."

Air started to flow more easily again. "What do you want to be called?" Mrs. Benz asked, obviously annoyed that she was going to have to change the attendance list.

"Karson. Just Karson, with a K. I don't like the M-C bit at the beginning."

She didn't like it – those three letters. She didn't like the one thing that would cause the M-C-Ks to try to take her in. Suddenly I was absolutely sure this girl was going to be my friend.

"I like you," I said, feeling that there was no use in hiding my feelings.

Karson smiled as if she liked the sound of those words just as much as I did. "I like you too. You have a lot to say."

"So I've been told."

She let out a surprised laugh at this, and then laughed harder. Soon I was laughing too – although I had no idea why – and as the sound rang out, I grinned, losing myself in those big brown eyes. We had no rational reason to be laughing, but soon we were smiling like two little children on Christmas morning who had been given the best gift in the world.

As we laughed, Mrs. Benz looked back and forth from me to Karson, a bit overwhelmed by our consuming laughter. "Miss Bass," she said, turning to me suspiciously, "is everything all right?"

"Yes," I said, watching in amusement as Karson tried to control her last burst of laughter. "Everything's fine."

– t h a n k | y o u –

I don't think it has ever been harder for me to write the acknowledgements for anything before. If I went into detail over every person and thing that has shaped the experience of writing this book ,it would take up too many pages for someone to be willing to read. So I will try to be simple.

– Thank you to Marc, Abby, and Hannah for always saying 'Hi'.
– Thank you Jordan, Ellie, Nolan, Morgan, Pierre, Ashley, Ryan, Liv, and Maya for being the best of the best.
– Thank you to Olivia for understanding.
– Thank you to Raj for letting me live at his Starbucks for a month.
– Thank you to Gloria Ha for always believing.
– Thank you to once again to Chris for being the best pep-talk giver ever.
– Thank you to my parents for everything you have done for me and this book.
– Thank you to all the people, some of whom may not even really know me, who have shaped this story in one way or another by just being in my life.

National Novel Writing Month is an amazing contest and opportunity. I suggest that everyone who loves to write, but just needs that extra push to get started, look into doing it at some point in their life. Go to NaNoWriMo.org for more details.

— n a t a l i e | b i n a —

has loved writing stories for pretty much as long as she can remember. This is Natalie's second book, following her first, entitled *World of Chances*. Although she is not the biggest reader, she loves books and is fascinated with the power of words. Natalie is attending high school in Singapore and lives with her mom and dad. She is currently plotting her next novel and counting down the days until the next National Novel Writing Month.